THE CLAIM

THE CLAIM

DAVID BRIGGS

Published by RedDoor
www.reddoorpublishing.com

ISBN 978-1-910453-73-5

A CIP catalogue record for this book is available from the British Library

Cover design: Clare Connie Shepherd
www.clareconnieshepherd.com

Typesetting: Westchester Publishing Services

Printed and bound in Denmark by Nørhaven

To Matt

One

'You guys must be born optimists,' the man in the store had said. 'All you prospectors. What else would make you do that sort of thing other than belief – blind hope?'

He meant more than the words implied: that people like Evan were loners who lived off their own company, didn't need the stimulus of a partner or a wife to keep them going, didn't need the earthly chances that normal people relied on. But he was right in his way. You had to defy probabilities; you had to have hope.

The storeman had recognised him as soon as he walked in: a regular customer, even though his visits were a year apart.

Evan had called there on the way in, as he did every year, for a last cup of real coffee, to fill up with fuel, buy a few provisions that he'd forgotten to pack. After the long drive across the Canterbury Plains, the Alps shimmering in the distance, refusing to draw near, then the slow haul over Arthur's Pass down to the coast, Silverstone was the last place that might claim the title of civilisation, and it only just merited that. A scatter of houses, a store that served as a café and fuel-stop as well, a tiny white church offering services the third Sunday of every month. Beyond that there was nothing. No internet or phones or radio. No duties or demands. Just the mountains, the river, the bush. His claim, solitude. Escape.

Then the man had said: 'Maybe that's the secret really. Maybe you have to believe to have luck. That's where I've gone wrong, perhaps, not believing.'

At the time, Evan had laughed. 'Luck's luck,' he'd said. 'I guess we all get our share.'

But whatever it was, belief or hope or just unseeing chance, his seemed to have run out. When he arrived, all seemed to bode well. The cottage had welcomed him, with a creak of the door, the familiar smell of winter mould and dust, two ten-dollar notes neatly folded on the mat. A few days later, when he'd set out to his claim the auguries had stayed good. On the drive up to the saddle the land looked fresh-spruced by the winter rains and spring snowmelt, the sky stretched, the air soft. On the walk from the car park, the fantails danced for him, bums out, tails splayed, while tuis sang and clucked and burped from the bush. At the claim, the stream wove between the gravel bars, beckoning him with its gentler song.

He'd tidied up his camp, stowed his gear, and the next day started panning. He began as he always did, at his favourite spots, exploring the riffles and pools and pockets of sediment that had formed since his previous visit. At first, no gold appeared, yet he did not worry. It was there somewhere; he just had to be patient. He was simply glad to be back, alone and free. In Christchurch, loneliness could be a torment; here it was a salve. And even now, two years after Juliette had left, he still needed that: the solace of solitude. So he had extended his search, remained content, and on the third day his patience and endeavour had borne fruit. His first finds. Bright flecks amidst the black iron and tourmaline sand.

Two days ago, he'd picked a target, a bed of grit and gravel, caught in the curve of the stream thirty metres below the camp. He'd set up the dredge, got to work. Soon, gold was coming out. Nothing dramatic, but a little more every time he paused the pump, checked the trays. Enough to justify the optimism that the storeman had talked about, to promise a good summer ahead. All he needed now was favourable weather and time.

Time, he had. Another eleven weeks before he'd have to leave, go back to work. The weather, though, seemed less accommodating. There was a storm brewing, and it was going to be a ripper. When it arrived, there'd be no more dredging for a while – not until the rain had eased and the river had forgotten it, subsided again. By then, the deposit he was working would have been swept away, the gold dispersed and lost.

He'd seen the storm approaching several hours ago. White wisps of stratus pulled out like combed wool. The change in the sun, losing its brightness, becoming pale and curdled. Later, the pillows of cumulus growing above the ridgeline away to the west. He might have called a halt then, scuttled back to the cottage while he could. He was due to do so in the morning, anyway; it was time for a rest, to replenish his supplies. But he wanted to grab what he could while he had the chance. So he'd kept going, even though he knew the cost. A wild night under tarpaulin, out here in the bush. All the discomfort: the last dregs of his food, damp clothes in the morning, a soggy trip back to his truck.

But now it was time to stop. In the last hour the sky had soured, turned grey and liverish. The birds were silent. Only the mosquitoes were left, riding the heavy air.

He felt for the fuel line, switched off the generator. The thrum and throb of the pump, the rattle of stones on the sluice, ceased. All became still.

He looked around, whistled for the dog. He'd last seen her half an hour ago. Then, she'd been sniffing around in the undergrowth, absorbed in some trace only she could detect. She wouldn't have gone far. She was a good dog, knew her legal limits, would be listening for his call. He whistled again.

She should have been a collie, or a huntaway, that's what friends who claimed to know had told him. They were the dogs you needed in the hills, they said: they had stamina, were fast, could track and catch rabbit or pig or deer – whatever you needed. They were quick to learn as well, could live outside. Instead, he'd chosen a spaniel. A springer, black and white, small, sinuous, with a coat like silk. A rescue dog, though what she needed rescuing from or why anyone would have failed to want her in their life he couldn't imagine, for she seemed to be everything a dog should be. Companion, friend, defender against unseen perils, source of constant amusement and affection. When he'd bought her from the SPCA, at fifteen months old, less than a week from being put down, she was called Molly. He didn't like the name; it was too girlish, too human. For days he tried out different names. Then, one evening, he told her: 'I'm giving you a life. You're going to help me with mine.' So he called her Viva – for life. And it was a private joke as well: Viva the Spaniel.

Once more he whistled, waited. Still she did not come.

In the distance, there was a flickering flash, lightning above the hills. In that same moment, he smelled the rain coming. A muskiness, an earthiness, fungal, hormonal, almost like the smell of sex. He'd misjudged; he had to be quick. Never mind the dog – the rain would bring her back. Right now, he needed to get the dredge and sluice to safety, his tarpaulin pegged down, everything under cover.

He worked feverishly. The water could rise almost as fast as you could move in a river like this. A half-hour respite while the canopy of the bush wetted, the trees soaked the rain up, and then the ground would start to darken, runnels would appear; they'd stretch, reach, join like fingers feeling for each other for comfort and strength. Runoff would drip, seep, surge into the channel. The stream would grow brown with silt; its whole tone would change. No longer a gurgle of laughter, a rippling song, but a thunder, a roar. The banks would sag and slump. Boulders would shift. Even twenty metres away you'd be able to feel the water's anger, its primaeval force.

He lifted the generator, heaved it up the bank on to the higher terrace, carried it across to his shelter and tucked it beneath his tarpaulin. He did the same with the dredge, hauling in the hose, coiling it up, stowing it in the hollow he'd dug under the trees. He broke up the header box and sluice, stacked the trays, tied up the struts and put them alongside. Then he paused, whistled again for the dog, listened.

For a moment, he thought he heard her – a quick yap – but though he strained his ears, it did not repeat. Just the sound of boughs creaking in the wind, or the wind in the boughs, or his own imagination.

Then the first drops of rain started, large, heavy. They beat on the ground, making craters in the silt, splashed on boulders and spat back at the air as if in spite. There was another lightning flash, a roll of thunder, only ten seconds apart. The storm closing in.

He looked around, checking that he hadn't missed anything, was leaving nothing to the elements. A spade stood, stuck into a sandy bar, in mid-stream. He cursed, waded out to it, grabbed it as the heavens opened.

He ran for the shelter. By the time he reached it, he was drenched.

He threw the spade down, pulled the flap of the tarpaulin behind him, tugged off his sodden shirt, slumped on to his bed.

Just the dog to come now. Where was she?

Half an hour later, and she'd still not returned. He started to worry about her. Had he credited her with too much intelligence, too much instinct? Might she be lost somewhere, out in the bush? Or trapped already by the stream? What if she was? Would she try to cross; would she manage it? Would she try to head home?

He crawled to the opening at the end of his shelter, peered out.

The world outside was dark. Not yet the darkness of night, but of something more threatening, more consuming – a world in turmoil. Pattern and shape had been destroyed. Mountains, sky, trees, stream were all as one, just a torn and torrid muddle. Colours had fused. What had been green, blue, white, ochre was all now grey and brown. The only relief from it all was when the lightning flashed. Then, for an instant, the old world would fizz and crackle again, and shape would emerge, a world in negative.

He called again, but his voice was lost to the blustering wind.

The rain came in another burst, clattering on the tarpaulin, drowning out his thoughts. He ducked back inside, lay on his bed.

The shelter was rudimentary, just a tarpaulin strung in the shape of a tent from two branches, in the lee of a mossy bank. In still weather, it served well enough. It gave some warmth, protection from the morning dews, and he'd made a bed of twigs and moss, covered with his sleeping bag, had a log to sit on, had brought a lantern and gas stove. But in weather like this, it was hardly adequate. The wind whistled beneath the edges of the tarpaulin, around the flap that served as a door. Water seeped in from the bank, soaking the ground, threatening his makeshift bed. The rain pounded on the canvas, dripped heavily from the trees.

He made some food, a simple meal: a handful of rice, a sachet of dried vegetables, some spices to give it all taste. He ate it, squatting on his bed, a bottle of beer to swill it down. When he'd finished, he put the pans by the entrance, donned his spare pullover to keep himself warm, called once more for the dog. She did not come, and he curled up inside his sleeping bag, fretful, trying not to imagine life without her.

*

When he woke, it was dark. The true darkness of night. He reached for his head torch, switched it on, checked his watch. Gone ten. Still, no dog.

He crawled to the entrance, looked out. The storm had retreated now, settled amongst the mountains where it grumbled and glimmered with evil intent. Here, there was just the rain. It came steadily. The wind moaned in the trees. The river rumbled and roiled.

He whistled, called the dog by name: 'Viva. Viva.'

The thunder growled back.

'Viva. Here girl.'

He got up, took a few steps into the clearing, stood, listening.

At first, there was nothing. Just the instruments of the storm, in irritable disharmony. But then, amidst it, he heard a yap – or thought he did. It was faint, strangely distorted, as though the wind had grabbed it, ripped it apart, reassembled it again. Then the wind billowed, and the bark was picked up by the other sections of the night – trees flailing, a distant thunder clap, the snap of a guy-rope beside him – and he knew that he had just imagined it. He was too good at that. Hearing what he wanted to hear. He turned back.

It came again. Not once but repeated this time. High pitched, short. It was the bark she gave when she'd found something that she could not deal with, something that didn't play by the rules – a hedgehog that refused to uncurl, an injured bird that wouldn't fly, a possum that sneered at her from the safety of a tree.

He went out into the clearing, whistled, though knowing that it was pointless, for the wind caught the sound and tossed it behind him.

Another yap.

She must have found something out there, he guessed, be guarding it. A pig carcass perhaps, or a deer. He'd leave her to it. She'd come back in the morning, reeking with its smell, belly full, repentant.

Or lay injured, was calling for him.

He sighed, went back into the shelter, pulled on his coat, put the head torch on.

'Bloody dog.'

He crossed the clearing, down to the stream, started to work his way along it, heading for where he thought the sound had come from.

It wasn't easy. The main path was on the other bank. On this side there was no real trail, thick bush. In the humid air, his torch fogged, so that he could hardly see. The ground was slippery with rain, boulder-strewn. There were fallen trees, logs, patches of gorse and broom, long vines of supplejack blocking and tangling his way. Bush lawyer tore at him from the undergrowth. Rain seeped into his coat, down his neck. His hands were scratched.

Again, he cursed the dog.

Once, he called, and thought he heard a brief, answering bark.

Slowly, stumblingly, he veered towards it. He splashed through a channel, knee deep. He squelched through mud. He ducked beneath a low branch, received a slap in the face. He found himself in a gully, called again.

The dog yapped. She was somewhere above him, up on the spur. He started to climb.

She barked again. Nearer now, the sound distinct, her tone urgent.

He reached a small clearing, paused for breath, moved his head slowly so that the beam made a sweep of the darkness.

Two pinpricks of light gleamed back. Just the reflection of raindrops? Or the dog's eyes?

They disappeared.

He shone the torch again, searching. All he could see was a tangle of shadows, shapeless and shifting in the relentless rain.

'Viva!'

As if in answer, the world was lit by another lightning flash, and in its aftermath he saw her, as if imprinted on to his eyes. She was standing next to a large boulder, head low, looking down.

'Viva,' he called again. 'Here girl.'

But instead of coming, she gave a whimper, then turned, disappeared. He ran in pursuit, still half-blinded by the lightning, felt the ground steepen beneath his feet. He slipped, tried to catch himself, and slithered, half fell down a dark and muddy defile. A rock jarred against his shoulder. He swore.

Then the ground levelled, and he came to an ungainly halt. He crouched there panting, scraping mud from his torch. As the light gathered itself again, the darkness shrank back to reveal a strange and ghostly scene. A wide slab of rock forming a flat bench, ridged and runnelled by weathering. Beyond, the pallid shapes of cliffs, looming above him. Black crevices, hunched trees.

In that instant he knew where he was: at the edge of the gorge, halfway down his claim. It was an area he rarely came to, for the stream here was deep and ran on bare rock, no place for fossicking. In the daylight, the area had a sense of portent and mystery; now, in the rain and the night, it seemed like the gateway to Hades itself.

He took off his torch, played it across the bench. Viva was standing ten metres away, her body rigid, nose extended, tail feathered. He shone the light past her, trying to see what might have drawn her to this place. What her game was, what prize she wanted to show him – what, in her canine view of the world, was worth all this disobedience and discomfort.

There was nothing. Just rock, boulders, the dark shape of flood debris piled against a low outcrop.

The dog wagged.

He got to his feet.

And the dark shape became a bundle of clothes. A human figure. A woman.

He stepped forward.

'Are you alright?'

The face stared back blankly, suddenly inhuman again. Just a mask, a scarecrow's turnip head. Or a hastily drawn charcoal hinting at what a woman might be: a small huddle of a body, a pale face, a hand; dark lines for cheeks and mouth, dark holes for eyes, long dark streaks of hair, the rest chalked in.

The dog nuzzled it, whimpered.

He leaned down, touched the woman's face. The skin was wet, doughy, cold.

'Who are you?'

He brushed the hair from her forehead, felt the roughness of a wound.

The head slumped.

He reached for her wrist, pushed back the sodden sleeve of her coat, tried to feel for a pulse. There was none.

He leaned closer, listening for the sound of her breath, for a muttered word, anything that might indicate life. Nothing.

He felt for the place at the top of the neck, just below the jaw. There was only the dull pulse of his own finger, pressed against her throat.

Again, Viva whimpered, pushed her nose against the woman's face, licked at it.

An eyelid flickered. Her lips moved.

Alive!

He pushed the dog away.

'Can you hear me? Are you hurt?'

There was no reaction.

He asked again: 'Can you hear me?' The body lay silent and slumped.

He hesitated, wondering what he should do. He couldn't leave her here; it would take him hours – maybe the whole night – to get back to his truck, drive the long and rough gravel road to somewhere with phone coverage, summon help. More hours to lead the rescuers here. Yet he knew the risks of moving anyone who might have fallen and have an injury to their spine.

He touched the woman again, tried to feel her limbs, seeking evidence of any damage: broken bones, a dislocation. They seemed to be intact.

He had no choice. He had to get her to somewhere dry, somewhere warm.

He put the torch back on to his head, bent down, slid his hands around the body, attempted to lift it. The woman stirred, then stilled. He pulled at her, trying to move her into a position from which he could pick her up. His actions felt rough and clumsy. The body slipped from his grasp.

He tried again. This time he got purchase on her clothes, managed to heave her up. He struggled to his feet, her body limp in his arms.

Could he make it? Could he carry her back to his shelter? What damage might he do to her in the process?

Slowly, he turned, made his way across the bench, started up the slope.

The journey back was a war against gravity and the night. Despite her smallness, she dragged him down: a dead weight. Every step sapped his energy. Every time he lifted a foot, felt the scree move, felt himself slip, he feared that he would drop her.

As they climbed out of the gorge, the wind strengthened, tugged at his coat; the rain came again more determinedly. Vegetation snagged at his legs. Once, he tripped, fell to his knees, felt the bump of the woman's body against his hip. She groaned.

'It's alright,' he said. 'I've got you.' He lifted her again, stumbled on.

When the ground at last levelled out, he paused for a while, resting. Viva stood a pace away, half-turned, as if anxious about the delay.

He shifted the body to balance it better, hauled himself upright.

'Home girl,' he said to Viva. 'Home.'

The dog trotted off. He followed.

The going was easier now, but the darkness seemed more enveloping. He hardly knew which way home was. At intervals, he found features he thought he could recognise from his outward journey – a fallen tree, a muddy bank – yet could not string them together as a route that made sense. But thankfully, the dog seemed to have no such doubts. She led him on, down a steep slope, through a patch of bush, across a small clearing. Sometimes, she went by ways that he could not take: squeezing beneath a log, snaking through low branches. When he faltered, or sought a way of his own, she waited.

They came to the stream. He turned up it, following its course. It was bloated and violent. It sucked at his legs.

He splashed through a channel, deeper than he'd expected, and the water reached his thighs. He held the woman higher, clutched against his chest.

Far away, the thunder growled.

He paused again. How much further?

They stumbled on. More water, more bush. Gravel beneath his feet.

Another muddy bank.

The dog stopped.

Something caught at his legs and he staggered, almost fell.

It was the guy-rope. They had reached the shelter. They were home.

He knelt down, gently now, as if here his handling of the woman suddenly mattered, and any roughness would leave a mark. Carefully, he fed the body through the entrance, then crawled in afterwards, manoeuvred it on to the bed.

He bent close, looking at the woman, trying to see life in the face, movement in the chest. In the light of his torch she had shrunk again to a blank and colourless corpse.

He touched her cheek. It felt icier than even before – no life in that, surely. He listened for her breathing. There was just the beat of the rain on the tarpaulin, the whine of the wind, the rustle of the forest.

But then, again, she moved, gave a tiny moan, the smallest whimper – life complaining.

'It's alright,' he said. 'You're safe now.'

Her lips shaped themselves, as if struggling to say a word, but no sound came.

He was no expert, but she had hypothermia, he was sure. Given the way she was dressed, the state of her clothes, that seemed almost inevitable. She must have been lying out there in the rain for hours.

'I need to get you undressed,' he said. 'Put you in something dry and warm.' Whether she'd heard him, he doubted, but he needed to tell her, to explain his actions. 'I won't hurt you.'

He found his lantern, strung it up, started to undress her. It seemed invasive, too intimate. The dog watched with a matronly stare.

Her anorak was sodden, heavy, torn. No tramper's coat, for sure. He dropped it at the back of the shelter. Beneath it, she wore just a cotton shirt. It smelled dank and soiled. He unbuttoned it, peeled it from her shoulders. The body it revealed was sparse, had no flesh on it. Her breasts were small, her ribs showed. Her arms were skinny, scratched and bruised; there was a gash across her belly. On her forehead, just below the hairline, was another wound, clotted dark with blood.

He turned to her feet. Her trainers were muddied, the laces broken, reknotted, her socks thin. Compared to her body, her feet seemed large. There were red blisters on her toes and heels.

And then to her jeans. They clung to her tightly, as he tried to peel them off, and he flinched at the way he had to handle her, the indecency of it all, the sense of abuse. There was a large bruise on one thigh, more scratches and wounds on her calves.

She was left in just bra and panties. They were wet, but he did not remove them. What he'd done already felt like assault enough. Quickly, he pulled his sleeping bag across her, warmth for her body, a shield for her nakedness.

For a moment, he sat observing her, seeking clues. Who she might be, what had happened to her, how she had come to this state.

And yet there seemed to be so little to tell about her in any way. No jewellery, not even a residue of make-up. No colouring or styling in her hair, which was dark, cut short and straight. Her face might have been chiselled in stone: deep cheeks, wide mouth, button nose, lifelike but lifeless. How old she was, he couldn't tell. Fifteen, maybe twenty?

She seemed – he reached for an analogy – not childlike, for she was too worldly worn and wasted for that. Not so much abused, as deprived. An ascetic, like an athlete, a long-distance runner, or a dancer, who deliberately denied her bodily needs for some other, supposedly, higher goal. Or one of those troubled young women who felt ill at ease with their bodies, and tended to anorexia or bulimia, perhaps.

He reached for his backpack, rummaged for his medical kit. Then, carefully, he uncovered her again, and using the pack of wet wipes cleaned her wounds as best he could, dressed them with antiseptic cream, added a plaster to the gash on her forehead, stemming the blood that was oozing again from the bared flesh. All the time she lay silent, limp, almost lifeless.

He burrowed in his backpack again, pulled out his few remaining dry clothes: socks, a pair of work trousers. He fed her feet into the socks, her legs into the trousers, looked around for something to use as a top. There was nothing. Everything was wet now, lay in a jumbled pile in the corner, muddied from work in the stream, or hung from the rope that he'd knotted to the branches to act as a simple clothes line. All he could see were the two hessian sacks that he used to carry his tools. He pulled one out, slit it, bottom and sides, with his knife, slipped it over her head. It made a simple smock, rough to her skin, hardly insulation, but better he hoped than nothing. At last, he lay her down, zipped up the sleeping bag, sat back on his haunches. He felt sordid, shamed, no Samaritan or saviour – just a man who had violated a defenceless woman.

Outside, the storm swept in again, voicing its own disgust. The tarpaulin flapped, wind whipped through the gap at the end. He crawled across, pulled the flaps together, pegged them as firmly as he could. Then, using his own body as a shield, he lit the stove, boiled some water, made sugary tea. He drank some, letting the rest cool. When it was ready, he tried to feed it to her, lifting her head, putting the cup to her lips. The tea dribbled down her chin. But then instinct seemed to work, and she swallowed; perhaps some went in.

The act soothed him. Crouching there, her head cradled on his knee, seemed more like an expression of friendship than abuse. 'Who are you?' he asked.

She made no reply.

'I'm Evan,' he told her. 'What's your name?'

Her lips moved again, as if she was trying to say something, and he leaned forward, in an effort to catch her words, failed.

*

He crawled across to the woman. She was shivering, moaning in her sleep.

He lay beside her.

Still she shivered.

She needed warmth.

He pulled off his damp clothes, unzipped the sleeping bag, slid in with her, zipped it up again, lay trying to share the meagre warmth of his own body.

Eventually the shivering stopped.

The dog curled against his feet, doughnut tight.

He slept himself.

And once in the night, when he woke, he thought that he was at home again, and someone was with him – Juliette, or a woman from long before, Lisha, perhaps, from all those years ago in Europe.

His hand was cupping her breast. So small, fitting easily into his palm. For a moment he let it rest there, soothed by the memory it brought, that sense of belonging.

When he withdrew it, the woman stirred slightly, groaned. He slept again.

Two

In the morning, he carried her back to his truck. The storm had abated now, and the rain had become no more than blustering showers, but the river was high, and in places uncrossable. It meant repeated detours, through tangled bush, and the track when he found it was slippery, every step a test of his strength and grip.

He carried her on his back, using the cradle he'd fashioned to haul in the pump for his dredge: a simple web structure, with a flat canvas base, strong broad straps. When he'd first woken her, she seemed to have no idea where she was, or what had happened. He offered her water and she tried to drink it, coughed, turned her head away. He asked questions – how did she feel, what was she doing here? – but she had no answer. As he put her trainers on to her feet, wrapped her in the sleeping bag, her efforts of help were dull and confused. When he tried to get her into the cradle she struggled weakly against him, as if afraid of his intentions. But somehow they managed it and he lifted her on to his back. She dangled there, her legs straddling the web, her arms around his neck, head against him like a child as he picked his way down the slope. Occasionally she muttered something, words he couldn't make out, or gave a groan of pain. Sometimes, her head lolled, her body slumped, her arms slipped, and he had to stop, adjust her position and heave her up again before he could continue. For a while, when she became too weak to support herself at all, he carried her in his arms.

It took over two hours to cover the four kilometres back to the end of the road. By the time he got there, he was exhausted, and she seemed to have lapsed into sleep or unconsciousness again. He laid her on the passenger seat of the truck, strapped her in, stood regarding her. Her breathing was shallow. Her pulse when he felt for it was feeble and irregular. Would she survive?

He started the engine, reversed the truck, turned it round. He wanted to hurry: she needed to be warm, dry; to take some water and food. She needed to be in hospital. But he knew how dangerous this stretch of the road was, even at the best of times. In these conditions, the slightest moment of inattention could cause disaster. For the first kilometre, it was hardly a road at all. Just a rocky track cut into a narrow bench a century ago, for miners and pack mules. Three metres wide at best, sheer-sided, rutted and littered with stones. In the rain there had been slips and washouts. At one of the slips he had to get out, shovel the debris away, ease the truck past.

Then, as they reached the saddle, the land opened out. A wide expanse of reedy pools, bare mud, hummocky pakihi and sedge. Through it all, the road seemed to roam blindly, veering off one way or another around a boggy slack, separating, rejoining, losing itself. Often, it was no more than a vague network of ruts in the peat that wandered, wavered, gave up hope.

When he'd driven up in bright sunshine, he'd been able to read the terrain, feel his route, though even then it had tricked him and he'd made more than one false move. Now, the rain and runoff had turned the land into a featureless desert of mud and mire. The cloud level was down. Mist wreathed and billowed, taking any sense of distance or direction away. The world was grey. He strained forward, seeking any clue that might exist. A smudge that might be his own tyre-marks from his journey in, the places where the vegetation had been flattened, a line of puddles that might indicate a track. He tried to head north, following the compass on the dashboard. Yet time and time again he was misled, baulked. A pond or a stream blocked his route, or the track looped, came back on itself. Or he found himself in a maze of hummocks and pools, heading nowhere. He stopped, reversed, tried again.

Then, suddenly, the road seemed to gather itself, dipped. The surface grew hard again, the mist shrank. He was heading downslope. In another twenty minutes he was driving through bush, the river swollen but familiar to his left. The trees thinned, opened out and he was in a broad clearing, thick forest below him where the river ran, gorse and broom scrub upslope. His cottage sat, backed by the scrub, waiting for him. He pulled up outside.

The woman lifted her head. 'Where are we?' she asked.

'Home,' he said.

He ran up the steps, opened the door. It jammed, as it always did, against the rug, and he forced it with his knee. He had closed the curtains when he left, and the room was dark. He pulled them back and the light filtered in, waking the dust motes.

He returned to the truck, lifted the woman in his arms, carried her up the steps. It might have been a bridal ceremony, he thought, bearing his new wife across the threshold, except that she was just this pale and fragile wretch. He took her into the bedroom, laid her down.

*

Gently, slowly, he moved his hand across her back, over her shoulder, down her arm. She lifted the arm slightly to help. He washed her wrist, her hand. Then the other side, back and shoulder and arm the same. He rinsed the flannel, washed her neck, up beneath her hair.

After he'd lain her in the bed, he'd fetched her food. Warm soup – thin but nourishing – a slice of toast, a hot drink. He'd supported her with a hand as she drank the soup, sipped at the tea as if it were nectar – too good to waste – nibbled at the toast.

When she'd finished, he'd told her: 'I want to wash you, clean your wounds. Do you mind?'

She'd given a shake of her head, which he took to be consent. Hardly informed, he knew, but it was all he was going to get, for her eyes had closed and she was dozing again. He fetched a bowl of water, face-cloth, towel. By the time he'd returned, she was fast asleep, her chest rising and falling with each heavy breath. It seemed a pity to wake her, and for a moment he'd wondered whether to wait, almost welcomed the excuse to do so. It would be, he knew, that same ambiguity repeated. Abuse and care in equal measure, the division between them vague and personal. Yet she looked so muddied and bloodied. Her body was scratched, scarred, bruised, her hair matted. Gently, he'd raised her, begun the task. And in truth, it had hardly seemed to disturb her. She remained in a state of semi-stupor, responding to his movements more by instinct than any conscious effort.

He shifted down the bed, turned back to her, washed her face, her throat, carefully cleaned around the clotted wound on her forehead.

It felt so strange, so indulgent, handling a woman like this. It felt so long since he'd touched one this way.

Her eyes flickered open and alarm seemed to grip her, as if she were seeing him for the first time.

'Who are you?' she asked.

'I'm Evan,' he said. 'Evan Cadwallader. Don't worry, you're safe here.'

Her lips moved, as if struggling to frame the word, then she said: 'Evan.'

'What's your name?' he asked.

She muttered something, a name he didn't quite catch – Annie or Abbie – and he asked her to repeat it. But she seemed to have slipped into sleep again and did not reply.

He continued with the cleaning of her wound.

'Addie,' she whispered. 'They call me Addie.'

And then she lapsed into sleep once more.

Quickly, as discreetly as he could, he completed his task of washing her, covered her again. Then he turned back to her forehead. The wound there was the worst of all. A hard lump, a ragged cut, clotted with dark blood. She must have fallen, he guessed, struck a rock; he wondered if she'd been concussed. Carefully, he cleaned the wound, wiping the blood away, exposing the cut. He dabbed it dry, reached for the antiseptic cream, smeared it generously.

Finally, he sat her upright again, tilted her head forward, and slowly yet firmly, combed out her hair.

At last, satisfied with what he'd done, relieved to be finished, he lay her back in the bed.

Her eyes flickered open again, and she smiled.

'Thank you,' she said. And then, belatedly seeming to remember his name: 'Evan.'

Afterwards, he sat with her for a while, watching her. The wash had done her good, he thought, removing the streaks on her face that had added to her gauntness, smoothing the scratches and grazes away. She looked whole, more human.

He tried to read her, to see in her features something of her character and history. A darkness in her skin – a sallowness – that might have been Maori or Asian blood, when she had any blood in her at all. The wideness of her mouth; the way it ended in deep creases, so that it seemed to be slightly downturned; it gave her an air of quiet acceptance, almost superciliousness, as if what she'd been thinking all along had been proved right. A faint birthmark on her neck, behind her ear.

Who was she, he wondered; where had she come from? What had happened in those hours or days before he'd found her?

She must have been walking in the hills, become lost – that much seemed clear. It happened often enough in these western ranges, where the tracks were narrow and winding, badly marked, the slopes precipitous, the bush an impenetrable cloak. The majority of cases ended happily. Most of the victims were rescued, survived. But some died; and some were never found. Often it was tourists from overseas. Solitary walkers, not realising how unforgiving the land was; or a member of a party, straying from the others, panicking when they found themselves alone.

Yet sometimes, it was people who should have known better, who just made a mistake in a moment of inattention, or overreached themselves. The storeman at Silverstone had told him a tale of one. A prospector like Evan, from only a few years before

The man had called in on his way into the valley, as everyone did, promised to call again on his way out. That year, he never reappeared. Months later, a pair of trampers had discovered his body in a cleft in the rocks. An autopsy had been performed. It showed strange cut marks on the bones of one leg. The prospector had fallen, it seemed, trapped his foot between the boulders, been unable to pull it out. He must have tried to cut himself free – self-amputation – hadn't succeeded.

'Bloody awful way to go,' the storeman had said. 'Me? I'd have done the easy thing – just slit my wrists.' Then, later, coming back to the topic: 'I sometimes wonder, though, whether it was my fault. Whether I should have called the police or something, when he didn't turn up. Maybe they'd have found him in time.' A shrug. 'But I just thought he'd forgotten – or maybe didn't like my coffee.'

'I can't believe that,' Evan had said as he finished his cup, put it down. 'And anyway, I'm sure he'd have been long gone by then. You shouldn't blame yourself.'

'No, probably not.' Then, drily: 'Still, there's not much else to do around here.'

At the time, the story had seemed allegorical, and Evan had smiled as he left the store. Now, it seemed to have a crude realism about it, and he gave a shudder at the thought.

Compared to that, he reflected, this woman had been lucky. Luckier than she knew.

He wondered what he should do about her, what he should do next. From the way he'd found her, from her wounds, he suspected that she'd had hypothermia, might well have been concussed. Both were serious issues, far beyond his limited medical expertise. She needed proper attention. Yet even to phone for advice meant an hour's drive to reach somewhere with cell phone coverage, and the nearest hospital was in Hokitika or Greymouth, another two hours away.

And in this weather, could he do it? Would the roads be passable? Would she survive the trip?

Another night, he thought. Let her rest until the morning. He would take her then.

He bundled up the clothes he had dressed her in, took them into the kitchen and piled them by the sink. Then, suddenly, his own needs engulfed him. He realised how hungry he was, how much he ached. He hadn't eaten since his hurried meal the evening before. He was bruised, sweaty, caked with mud. At some point, he must have twisted his knee for he was walking with a limp.

He took a shower. In a small cottage like this, out in the wilds, forty kilometres from the nearest power line, showering was a simple affair: stream water fed through a coil of black hose on the roof. The water ran slowly, was icy cold in the winter, hot on summer days, lukewarm at other times. Right now, he didn't care. It both scoured and soothed him, washed the sting of his cuts away, the grit from his hair. He towelled himself, dressed in clean clothes, went into the living room.

The dog, too, was tired. She lay by the hearth, head low, eyes raised, watching him, her tail wagging slowly. He fed her, and she wolfed the food, then went back to her place, dropped to the floor with a sigh.

Finally, food for himself. He made porridge, ate it with the last of his bread, baked a week ago and stale now, but anything tasted good. He found the peanut butter, spooned it out, eating it straight from the jar.

At last, replenished, he checked in on the woman. She was still asleep. She did not stir as he opened the door, stepped across, looked down at her. Her face was still thin and drawn, like that first glimpse of her he'd had – as if sketched in charcoal, all shadows and lines and blankness. But she seemed peaceful now, her features more relaxed, and she slept deeply, her breath coming in a slow and even pace. The sleep of the saved, he thought, and told himself: don't worry, she'll be alright. She'll live.

Back in the kitchen, he sorted out the clothes, washed them in the sink, rolled them in a towel and wrung them as dry as he could, then hung them on the line on the veranda. He was left with the sack that had served as a top: no use now. He took it to the brazier that he used to burn the rubbish, stuffed it in. The act felt strangely dishonest, almost criminal, as though he were destroying evidence of some kind – proof of all his clumsy handling of her, all the tawdriness. Yet it brought, too, a flood of relief.

He went to the old armchair that stood on the veranda beside the door, settled himself into it with a sigh. Viva came and leaned against him, inviting a safer intimacy: man and dog. He stroked her, letting the rhythm of the action soothe him, drain the day away.

And it was going now, the day and all its tumult. The storm had abated. The sky was clearing, the last clouds streaming eastwards as if from the scene of their crime. The sun was lowering, throwing long shadows across the clearing, casting the land in pewter and bronze and gold.

It was a scene he loved, a place. He loved its depth and durability and the way it changed, ever ancient yet always new. Land and sky rewriting themselves, night after night. Somehow what had happened, the woman there in his room, added to that notion. A place of sanctuary. Refuge for the world-weary and torn.

The cottage had been his father's. He hadn't known that at the time, had known very little about his father in those years while he was working overseas. He'd discovered the fact only later, after his father had died, when he'd been summoned back from Europe by the news of the event. He'd found out so much about his father then – things he should have known. The dismal state he was living in, his failed business, the debts. The house in Christchurch – the place that had once been Evan's childhood home – remortgaged and falling apart around him as he'd drunk himself into his grave.

Amidst all that – the drawers full of tax claims and rates demands and unpaid bills, the boxes full of bottles in the cupboard beneath the stairs, in the loft, in the garden shed – the discovery of the deeds for a small and unnamed cottage somewhere out in the bush seemed of no real consequence. According to the purchase agreement, it had been worth only a few hundred dollars when his father had bought it a dozen years before; it would be worth next to nothing now. He'd ignored it, hadn't even bothered to try to find it. But later, when he'd sold off the house, the beat-up old estate wagon that sat in the drive, had auctioned off the remnants of his father's printing machinery – relics now – to a collector in Dunedin and still found himself faced with a pile of his father's loans and debts, he'd wondered whether the cottage might be worth some small price. Eventually, expecting the worst, hoping for something better, he'd driven out into the mountains to check.

When he got to the clearing, it seemed that even his most meagre expectations had been too optimistic. The cottage sat low and hunched in a tangle of grass and young gorse, its presence indicated merely by the stub of metal chimney poking from a rusty tin roof. He'd almost turned around on the spot.

Yet he'd come all this way, he decided; he might as well take a look. He got out of his car, pushed his way through the undergrowth, went up the rickety stairway on to the veranda.

Proximity didn't improve the place. The steps were uneven, the veranda crusted with lichen and moss. Cobwebs meshed every crook and crevice; the windows were opaque with dust. The woodwork was flaking.

He tried the latch on the door. It was unlocked, but the door stuck as he pushed at it, and he'd had to lean against it with all his weight to make it yield.

Inside, the prospect was no better. As he roamed around, the rooms felt shabby and dark, smelled dank. Dust lay on every surface; there were rat droppings in the corners, mould and damp.

The layout was simple. An open plan living area and kitchenette; a narrow corridor leading to a bedroom, just large enough to take a double bed and dressing table; opposite it, a smaller room that might have been a box room or a second bedroom. At the end of the corridor, a simple bathroom that had been inexpertly added on the back.

The furnishings were the same: basic, unlovely, ill-matched. A few wooden chairs, a worn leather sofa, an armchair in greasy red moquette. Grey carpets, stained with use. Moth-eaten curtains in drab brown. The light bulbs were bare and scabbed by flies.

More squalor, Evan had thought; more failure and defeat.

Yet on a whim, he decided to stay there for the night, and that evening sat with a beer on the veranda, listening to the birdsong from the bush, the sigh of the wind in the trees, and realised that in some way he felt touched by the place. It seemed to reach to him from across the years, from the father he'd once known. It felt like a memory, a legacy. One that he could not simply sell or scrap.

He'd tried to imagine why his father had bought it, what use it had been. An escape from all the worries of life at home in those years when his business had started to fail, he surmised, for that would have been typical of the man: spending what money he didn't have on a place like this to take his mind off his debts. And if so, he'd no doubt used it for fishing, because that had always been one of his father's few interests, his only real escape and passion.

Once, when Evan had been young – perhaps seven or eight – his father had tried to inculcate him into the art. It ended as most of his father's random acts of parenthood did, with frustration, resentment. Evan had no interest in the sport, disliked the idea of killing living creatures, and made no effort to hide his indifference. Facing it, his father had responded as he always did, with yet more insistence, more assertiveness. So the two of them had battled, and neither had won. Just another grudge to come between them.

Yet then, sitting on the veranda, Evan had realised that, had things been different, he once might have sat there with his father just like that. Sharing the evening, talking of the day just gone. The catches, and the fish that got away. And the notion had felt like an apology, both offered and accepted. A reconciliation, wiping all their past disagreements and disappointments away. Father and son together.

So a few months later, he'd returned, spent several weeks camping in the cottage as he cleaned it up. He'd fixed up the water supply, scrubbing out the tank, replacing the feeder pipe from the stream, unblocked the sediment trap and taps. He cleared the bird-nests and twigs from the flue by the simple act of dropping pebbles down it, listening to them rattle as they fell, then hosing it out. He piled the furniture out in the sun to air and bleach; he tore out all the carpets and curtains and replaced them with second-hand furnishings he'd bought in a charity shop. He scrubbed the windows, wire-brushed the veranda, repaired the steps. He refurbished the generator, cut back the vegetation.

And the next year he came back again and stayed there for a while. And soon the cottage seemed to adopt him as it had perhaps adopted his father. Offering a place of solitude and peace. A still oasis away from the loose and shifting life he led in the world outside; his life in Christchurch, doing whatever work he could get, living in cramped rented rooms, making do.

When he started to pick up regular work with the lines companies – harder work, but well paid and at a peak in the winter – his visits had become more regular and prolonged. A few weeks every summer, living out there alone. He spent his time doing more repairs, or out walking, or just sitting on the veranda reading.

He was there, unknowing, in 2011 when the first Christchurch earthquake happened, and the remnants of his childhood home were shaken to the ground. No sad loss. He was there equally unaware when larger rumblings shook the wider world. When terrorists attacked Paris, when Typhoon Haiyan hit the Philippines, when Trump was elected in the USA. And each time, afterwards, he was thankful for his extended interval of ignorance.

And he was there the day an old man drove up and asked if he could stay.

Something about the man had instantly appealed to him. His runnelled features, the take-it-or-leave-it look in his eye. The contradictions in his manner.

So he had obliged and had offered the man the spare room.

That evening, they sat on the steps together, sharing a few cans of beer, putting the world to rights.

'My name's Jeb,' the man said, long into the first beer, holding out a hand. 'Jeb Baird.'

'Pleased to meet you Jeb. I'm Evan Cadwallader.'

'Fancy name,' Jeb said. 'Welsh?'

'My father was.' He indicated the cottage. 'This used to be his.'

Jeb had nodded. 'Yup. I think I remember him. I met him a couple of times as I passed through – years back, before it got like this. I can see the likeness.'

Evan had grimaced. 'The son's curse,' he said. 'Like father like son.'

'It's not all a curse. It doesn't have to be.'

They were silent. Then Evan had asked Jeb where he was heading for, what he was doing up here.

'Prospecting,' Jeb had said. 'I've been doing it for years.'

He talked about it. The way prospecting gripped you, became an obsession. Not so much because of the reward, but for the process itself – the perpetual pursuit.

'It's like love,' Jeb had said. 'It's like life. Better to travel than to arrive.'

'I do too much of that,' Evan had said 'travelling. I come here for stillness and peace.'

'There's that, too,' Jeb had assured him. 'There always is with a river.' Then he had tapped his temple. 'You get to know the river, panning for gold, like you would a lover, too. You learn to read it, know how it thinks. That's how you find it, you see – the gold. It's all alluvial up here, river gold. So you find it by sluicing or panning. That means it's mainly fine stuff, flakes, small nuggets – not the sort of big finds you can make with a lode. But it's there if you search, if you think.'

He'd told Evan about his claim, over in the next valley, on Tokatoka Creek. A good claim, he'd said, he should know. 'I mined here once. After the war, they reopened some of the mines. Government subsidies, to try to get something happening in the area. Companies came in, grabbed the money, hoping for a quick killing. It lasted a few years, then they realised the truth. No one makes a fortune out of gold any more, not here, not in New Zealand. So they sold off the land. There were claims going cheap. I bought one.' He grinned. 'Silly buggers didn't know what they were selling. To them it was all just the same. But if you'd worked here, you knew where to look, where the panning would be good. I bagged the best claim in the valley.'

But a few weeks later, when Jeb called on his way out, he was less sanguine.

'How'd it go?' Evan asked.

Jeb shook his head. 'Bugger all.'

Evan commiserated. 'Well, I guess you get lean years.'

'No. It's not the year, it's me.' Jeb spat. 'I'm too old for this lark. My eyes are gone. I imagine more than I can find, and miss more than that. It needs someone younger. Someone who can see and think straight.'

'You'll do better next year,' Evan said.

'Nope. There'll be no next year.'

'What do you mean?'

Jeb grimaced, patted his chest. 'I shan't be coming back. Six months, that's what the doctor gives me. He didn't want me to come on this trip. I told him to bugger off.' He grinned. 'So it's time someone else had a go. Time that you did.'

'You mean, prospect in your claim. I can't do that.'

'Of course you can. It's no use to me. But it might be to you: I've left you all there is. It's yours if you want it.'

Evan tried to argue against it, telling Jeb that you never knew, that doctors got it wrong, that a pig-headed old guy such as he was could deny all probabilities. Insisting, too, that he had no clue how to prospect, wouldn't know what to do.

'You'll learn,' Jeb said. Then: 'Tell you what. Just to help you along, I'll leave you my pans. Try them out up there, see if you like it. Look after it for me, until I come back.' He laughed. 'Man or ghost, whichever.'

For a while they argued about it. A strange, seemingly hypothetical debate about something that could never be. The gift of a claim, a man's death. Words laden with pathos and irony.

'If I did, I'd have to pay you' Evan said. 'Rent. And anything I find we split fifty-fifty. How's that?'

'How, indeed.'

'It's a condition. There's no deal otherwise.'

Jeb shrugged. 'You can make what conditions you like. You can't hold a dead man to those.'

'Well, relatives. They might expect it, even if you don't.'

'Relatives? You won't find many of those. And if you do, they'll definitely be here to haunt you. Last of the line, that's me. And I don't reckon the world will grieve much about that.' He leaned across. 'So, deal?'

They shook hands, and Jeb went to his ute, took out three pans, put them on the steps. 'Yours,' he said. 'Good luck.' Then, as he got back into the ute, he asked: 'Where do you live? I need your address.'

Evan told him.

Jeb nodded, started the ute.

'You come back,' Evan said.

'And you, bugger off,' Jeb called as he drew away. 'Bugger off to that claim and find something.'

That first year, Evan had tried and failed. Panning by hand, with no idea where to search, what the technique was, he'd found nothing, and felt relieved at the lack of success. Perhaps Jeb had been unfair on himself: not his eyesight or judgement after all, just the river keeping what it had to itself. Maybe the whole thing had been a fiction, a joke.

But back in Christchurch, there was a package waiting. It was addressed in a shaky hand, with his surname misspelt. Inside were the deeds to the claim, the concession form. Attached to it was a single sheet, written in the same hand: 'I hereby bequeath my claim, number K4375 to Evan Cadwallander. Jeb Baird, 16 February 2007.'

There was an address on the concession. He wrote to it, thanking Jeb, asking if he could pay something for the claim. No answer came. A few months later he drove to Blenheim, found the address. It was a small, simple house at the edge of town. He knocked, was greeted by a young woman, a child in her arms. She looked at him blankly when he asked about Jeb. She'd only lived there for six months, she told him, didn't know who the previous tenant was.

Since then, Evan had prospected every year. At first, he still looked out for Jeb, expecting to see him, to catch some sign that he'd been there, had visited. In moments of wilder imagining he convinced himself that he'd glimpsed him coming down the trail or out of the bush – the man, or his ghost. A figure at the window of his cottage, a shadow in the trees by the claim, a voice on the wind. But as he learned the claim and how to pan, he became more successful in his prospecting. One year, he found three ounces of gold – over 4000 dollars at the assay house. He invested it in a pump and a sluice, to pan mechanically; the next year earned enough to add more. Strangely, success brought not memories of Jeb, not acceptance of the gift he'd been bestowed, but guilt at his good fortune. He felt unworthy, as though he'd earned it through a trick.

Cottage and claim, he thought; both, it seemed, unfairly won. Neither of them really his.

Three

'Hello.'

He had awoken the next day as if after a wild party. Body worn, head aching, his mind a jumble of disconnected pictures and sounds, no immediate memory of why he was on the sofa rather than in his bed. In the night, the storm had returned. He'd been dimly aware of it – a backdrop to his turbulent dreams. It meant trouble, but for a moment he could not remember why.

Then realisation returned. The woman, Addie. Discovering her, bringing her back. The need to get her to hospital. The state she was in.

He should have taken her yesterday, he thought, while he had a chance.

He got to his feet, stiffly, went to the door, shooed Viva out.

Across the clearing, the trees tossed and swayed like a wild sea. Water rilled the soil, yellow with mud. Over it all, the clouds churned heavy and low and grey.

The dog returned, shook herself on the veranda, slunk past him with a surly look, giving him the same message: your fault.

He went to the bedroom, stood at the door, listening. There was no sound. Should he leave her, or should he go in? He hesitated, then knocked, received no reply, peeped in. She was as he had left her the previous evening, lying on her back, her dark hair splayed on the pillow. One hand rested against her chin, knuckles to her mouth, as if she had been sucking it for comfort. A child's face, he thought, vulnerable and innocent. But she was breathing evenly, looked calm. He left her, went back to the living room, feeling relieved. Let her rest.

He set up his lamp and hand lens on the table, took out the small box-safe he used to store his finds, began to sort them. Soon he was engrossed.

Now, when she did at last emerge, she caught him unawares. He looked around at the sound of her voice, startled.

'Hello,' she said, again.

She was standing in the corridor into the living room, one hand on the wall, steadying herself. She was wearing the shirt he'd left out for her, loose like a smock. Her feet were bare. She looked tiny, overwhelmed – a child in grown-up's clothes. Her face was like ash.

He rose, stepped towards her, then stopped, unsure what protocol might apply.

'How are you?'

She shook her head. 'I'm – I don't know.' She looked around, blinking. 'Where am I?'

'You're in my cottage. You're safe now.'

She swayed slightly, and he went to her, took her arm, guided her to a chair. She lowered herself into it gingerly, as if every bone in her body hurt.

'Who are you?' she asked.

'I'm Evan. I found you. I brought you back here.'

'Evan,' she repeated.

'Evan Cadwallader,' he said. 'And you're Addie. Is that right?'

She regarded him emptily, as though even her own name had been ripped from her memory by the events of the night.

'Addie,' she said. 'Yes, Addie.'

'Addie what?' he asked.

Another hesitation. 'Yes, Addie. Addie Watson.'

'I'm glad to meet you, Addie,' he said. He held out a hand and, after a moment's indecision she gave him her own, let him shake it, limply.

Again, he asked her how she felt, whether anything was broken, whether she was in pain.

'Just tired,' she replied.

'I ought to take you to hospital,' he said. 'Will you let me?'

She shook her head. 'No. Thank you. It's not necessary. I'm just tired, that's all.'

'You should,' he insisted. 'You've had hypothermia. You may be concussed. You need to be checked out.'

'No,' she said again. 'No. Please. Just let me rest.'

He was about to argue, and yet he knew what the journey would be like. The rivers swollen, straining at their banks, slips and floods on the road. The bridges dangerous, the fords impassable. Discomfort and delay. Should he subject her to all that?

Outside, the rain lashed at the window in a sudden burst, the timbers of the building creaked.

Better to delay if he could.

'OK. But if you feel ill – if you get worse, we go. No arguments. Understood?'

He asked her whether she was hungry, what he could get her to eat, but once more she seemed not to be listening, looked past him, her brow creased.

'There – there was a dog,' she said, the words hesitant, drawn out of some deep void in her mind. 'I remember.'

Evan glanced back. Viva was lying on the rug in front of the stove, watching, as if waiting to be summoned.

He smiled. 'Yes. That's Viva. It was she who found you.'

Addie nodded, frowning. 'Yes. Yes – she came to me. She stood there and looked at me and just wagged. But when I looked again, she'd gone, and I thought it must have been a dream.' Her frown deepened. 'It was all like a dream by then.'

He called Viva. The dog rose immediately, trotted across, lifted her nose. Addie fondled her. 'Thank you, Viva. You're a clever dog.' Then she turned, looked up, gave a fleeting smile. 'And thank you – Evan.'

Her eyes slipped past him again, towards the table. 'What were you doing?'

'Just checking my finds.'

'Finds?'

'Gold,' he said. 'I'm a prospector.'

The word seemed to mean nothing to her, and she made no response.

He went to the table, stowed the finds in the box-safe, switched off the lamp. 'I'll get you some breakfast.' He spoke, gruffly, like a father to an errant daughter. 'You can eat what you want. But you must eat.'

She did as instructed. Her hunger suddenly discovered, she ate greedily, asked for more. He sat opposite her, watched. She ate as though she had not eaten like this for months, one hand curled around the bowl protectively, eyes restless as if she were afraid that someone might intervene and snatch the food away.

'When did you last eat?' he asked.

She shook head. 'I don't know. I can't remember.'

'How long were you there, out in the bush?'

The same answer, then: 'Days. Two, maybe three.'

He made her coffee. She cradled the cup in her hands, seemed to savour every sip.

'What happened?'

Once more, her reply was hesitant, abstracted. Her days on the mountains were a blur, it seemed, with no sequence or shape. Before that, there was just an abyss. The effects of concussion, he guessed, and worried again: should he get her to hospital?

'Where were you? What were you doing up there?'

She shook her head, but seemed to regret the act, for a hand went to her brow, and she grimaced.

'It's alright,' he said. 'We can talk later, if you want.'

'I was walking,' she said. 'I'd just gone walking.' Then she was silent, and he thought that she would say no more. But after a while she began to talk again, her words stumbling, the phrases short. She had got lost, tried to find her way back. She had walked for hours, more than a day. She had been hungry, thirsty, afraid.

'Were you with anyone?'

A small shake of her head. 'No. Just me.'

'Is there anyone who knows that you're missing? Someone who's worrying about you – maybe looking for you even now?'

'No. No one.'

'No one you told?'

'No.' Another grimace, rueful, bitter. 'I should have done, I know. I should have told someone where I was going. But I didn't have a chance. I was just – I just wanted to be alone.' Then her face crumpled, her head dropped. 'I'm sorry. I can't think now. I'm just tired. I need to sleep.'

She slept on and off most of that day. In the bedroom, or on the sofa, wherever she chose to lie, sometimes in the armchair by the hearth. She seemed to lapse into slumber at the merest thought, as though that was her natural state. All else were effort and artifice.

In-between, she would sit by the window, gazing out into the grey and diffuse world. It seemed to draw her, magnetise her, and once he asked her: 'Do you want to go home?'

She turned to him quickly, dismay on her face. 'No! I like it here. It's – it's what I need.'

He stood for a while beside her, wondering what it was that she could see, why this strange attraction. Then she extended a hand, touched the pane and, as if hearing his thought, said: 'I like watching the raindrops, the way they wriggle down the window, the tracks they make. And I like the colours and the shapes outside. The way everything is merged, so that nothing is itself, nothing is clear.'

She felt, he guessed, at one with the scene, strangely fragmented and undefined. She seemed to be reaching back into herself tentatively, into whatever memories she could find, patching things together as she discovered them, making herself again.

And perhaps it worked, for as the day wore on, he saw a change in her. Colour of a sort returning to her face. A wry acceptance to her voice: it has happened, and is done now, and I am safe.

She began to ask him questions, each one delivered with a sudden abruptness as though the information was vital – a peg on which she could rebuild her world. She asked what day it was, how long she had been there, where he had found her, how.

Everything he told her seemed like a revelation, and she clung to his words with what felt like desperate intent. Another piece of the jigsaw. Another fixed point in her world.

Sometimes, his answers jogged memories, ones she did not know she had.

She asked him how he had managed to bring her here, and he explained.

'You carried me?' she said. 'Yes, I remember. I thought I'd imagined it.'

He mentioned the tent.

'Yes. I heard it flapping, and the rain on it, like a soldier-boy on a drum. I thought that was a dream, too.'

But of the rest, she seemed wholly unaware, and given the way he had had to handle her, undress her, lie beside her in the night, he was relieved.

But where were they, now, she asked, where was his cottage? He tried to describe it: in one of the tributaries of the Arahura River, forty-five kilometres inland from Hokitika, fifty-five from Greymouth, deep in the heart of the ranges.

She shook her head in puzzlement, as if all the names he mentioned meant nothing to her, and she had no picture of the area in her mind.

Only its remoteness seemed real.

'It's so far,' she said. 'No one would ever come here.' Then she gave a small grin. 'Except you. And Viva. If you hadn't found me. . .' Her voice trailed away.

'I come here every year,' he said.

'Why?'

He told her again: 'I'm a prospector. I come looking for gold.'

'Gold? You find it?'

He nodded. 'It's just a hobby. Nothing serious.'

'You find gold out here?' He expected her to ask the usual question – had he made his fortune, was he rich? Instead, she said: 'But all you found was me. Sorry.'

About her own life, however, how she had come to be lost, he could discover little. When he tried, she sidestepped the question, or answered with a shake of her head, a shrug. And because the questions seemed to disturb her, he ceased to ask.

But then, suddenly, she said: 'I lost my pack.'

'How? Where?'

'Up on the track. Before – while I was walking. I put it down and it fell. Down a scree, into a river. It had everything in it. My clothes. My wallet. My maps. My boots.'

'What did you do?'

'I tried to get it. I climbed down. But the scree was too slippery, too steep. I only had trainers on. I was afraid of falling.'

He tried to pursue the story: 'What happened next?'

She did not answer, but sat, her brow creased, fingers clenched, so that he wondered what she was thinking, what images she could see in her mind. 'I tried another way,' she said at last. 'Further along the track, to see if I could get back to it. It was grassy there, looked easier. But the slope ended in a cliff. I – I almost fell. I was terrified.'

Again, he waited, wondering if she would continue. This time, however, there was no sequel, and he left her to her thoughts.

But later, after they had eaten, as they sat together in the living room in the fading light, she asked: 'Did I say anything?'

There was a strange urgency in her voice, as though the question had an importance far beyond the words, and he looked up, puzzled. 'When?'

'When you found me – when you first brought me here.'

'What sort of things?'

'Anything. Crazy things.'

'No. Not that I remember. Why?'

'I used to,' she said. 'As a child. I used to talk in my sleep, especially when I was ill. Apparently, I used to say all sorts of weird things.'

He laughed. 'No. Don't worry. You didn't swear, you didn't shout. You gave no secrets away. Not even your name.'

She gave a small nod, a wry smile. 'OK. That's good, anyway.'

There was silence again. Just the sounds the fire made in the stove, fizzing on the rain-damp wood, and outside the restless groan and moan of the wind, as if it was roaming the land, searching for her, soulless without her company.

*

The next day, the weather was the same. Grey clouds filling the valley, fogging the hills. The rain less heavy now, but just as unremitting.

The cottage felt dark and cribbed, and again he wondered whether Addie was yearning to escape, but as before she batted his question away, insisting that she was content there, that she was getting all she needed – a chance to recover, rest.

As if in proof, a memory occasionally flared, sometimes a spark of humour or mischief, too.

'Do you think it will be the next fashion?' she asked suddenly from the sofa, where she sat, her legs curled under her.

'What?'

'The checked shirt.'

He laughed, apologised. 'I'm not sure they were ever in fashion. Not even for men.'

She grinned, looked down at herself. 'Still, better than a sack, perhaps.'

'You remember that, then?'

'I was wearing it when you brought me here – when you washed me. I couldn't work out why.'

'It was all I had,' he said. 'I'm sorry.'

'No. You mustn't apologise.' She sat for a moment, reflecting, then gave a wide, beaming smile. 'It was appropriate, really. Much more than you probably realise.'

'What do you mean?'

'I used to wear something like that.' She regarded him levelly, seeing his puzzlement, perhaps, and letting it build. 'I was in a revival band,' she said. 'Punk. Sack Cloth and Flashes we called ourselves. The joke was: what were we wearing underneath?'

He was amused, yet embarrassed too, and suddenly aware of the direction of his eyes. He asked what she played.

'Guitar,' she said. 'And I sang. Pretty badly, but that doesn't matter much with punk.'

'Should I have heard of you?'

'Not unless you frequented the seedier dives in New Plymouth.' She paused again, looked out of the window, but after several seconds added, as if to the world outside: 'And the answer, by the way, was not much. I'm sure you'd remember if you had.'

Later, as the afternoon wore on, Evan worked at the table in the living room, trying to repair the mantel-clock. It was a job he'd been promising to do for years, was always on his list of tasks for rainy days, yet somehow the days were never rainy enough. Now, it seemed appropriate. A companionable yet unintrusive task, while Addie dozed, or sat gazing out of the window, watching the day slowly billow and fade.

Then, he felt her at his shoulder, standing close.

'What are you doing?' she asked.

He indicated the scatter of cogs on the table. 'It's a clock,' he said. 'Correction. It was a clock, until I took it apart. It was my father's. It was here when I came. But it's never kept proper time. I thought I'd try to repair it.'

'Can I help?'

'I don't know. You can sit and tell me when I do it wrong if you like – and help me not lose bits.'

She pulled out a chair, sat beside him. He felt her eyes on him as he pored over the skeleton of the clock, searched amongst the scatter of parts for the one he needed, tried it, fumbled it, searched again.

After a while, she said: 'It would be easier if the pieces were in some kind of order, wouldn't it? I'll sort them for you.' And when he agreed – or gave a grunt that was not exactly disagreement – she rearranged them in neat squares and rows: cogs and springs and brackets and screws and nuts, all laid out by shape and size. His tools, too: the assortment of suitably small screwdrivers and pliers he'd managed to assemble from his own toolkit and the various items that still lay around in the outhouse – inheritances from his father.

She asked him what was wrong with the clock, how it worked. He answered both questions vaguely. It didn't keep time, he explained, though why he didn't know, nor what he needed to do to mend it. So he was just taking it apart, cleaning everything, putting it back together again: the last resort of every amateur engineer.

He cursed as he dropped a screw, and it spun on to the floor. She knelt down with him, searching for it on the rug.

She handed him parts, tools.

She took on the task of washing the pieces in the watch-glass of methylated spirit that he usually used to clean the best of his gold, dabbing them with three-in-one oil, letting them drain.

She was as absorbed as he was, and he found himself enjoying the experience. Two minds focused on the same delicate task, heads close.

And as she watched, as she helped, memories seemed to filter back, muddled and incomplete, and she began to talk again. He listened, yet did not look at her, and prompted her only with simple questions, knowing that interrogation would put her off and make her memories clog.

'It was the storm,' she said. 'That's what freaked me. I thought I'd be alright until then. But it came so suddenly. I didn't see it. I didn't know which way to go.'

She paused for a moment, rolling one of the cogs between her fingers, her brow furrowed.

'It was awful,' she went on. 'Not just the rain, the lightning – in fact, I almost welcomed that. At least I could see. But the noise. And the trees, all the branches creaking and crashing as if they were alive, stuff coming down all the time – twigs, ferns, leaves, everything. I never thought the bush could be like that, so angry, so – so personal. It was as though it hated me. I just wanted to get out.'

Later, she said: 'The nights seemed so long. There were no stars, no moon. It felt like being in a cave. It was so dark in there.'

'Where had you been walking?' he asked.

'Up on the hills.'

'Where? On a track?'

'Yes. I was following a track.'

'Which one?'

'I'm not sure. I can't remember now. It was high up.'

'Where had you come from?'

But she seemed not to hear, or misunderstood the question, for she said: 'I was just following the track. I'd been to a hut, the night before. I slept there. Then I set out the next day. That's when I lost my pack.' She told him the story, again: how she'd put it down on the grass, how it had slipped down the slope, how she'd tried to retrieve it, had become confused, couldn't find her way back. It seemed to be the one fixed thing in her memory – that brief scene, when normality fled, and she was suddenly alone, directionless.

As she talked, he tried to picture the ranges above his claim. The wide expanse of tussock grass beyond the bushline, the rock and scree; the tracks and mountain huts, the gullies and valleys where she might have dropped her pack. He didn't know the area well, had walked it only two or three times over the years, never explored it in full. But there was only one stretch of track that seemed to fit.

'Was it Old Man Hut?' he asked. 'The one that you slept in?'

'I don't know. It might have been.'

'Or Persimmon's, perhaps?'

She shrugged.

'Were you going to Dolly Top?'

But she shook her head, said she couldn't remember, and he knew not to persist. Instead, he said: 'You were concussed, I'm sure. That's why. Give it time. Your memory will come back.' Then he added: 'Either way, I'm taking you to see a doctor as soon as this weather clears.'

'No,' she said. 'There's no need. You've already been too good. I've caused enough trouble.' But, as if from instinct, she reached up to her forehead, touched the wound.

'How did that happen?' he asked. 'Did you fall?'

'Yes. On the slope. When I tried to get my pack.'

But anything more about the event eluded her.

He continued with the clock, slowly rebuilding it, checking the movement each time he added a cog, blowing the dust and Viva's stray hairs away. Now and then, he glanced up and caught

Addie's eye, received a smile; at other times, she was just sitting there, staring at the pieces, biting at her lip.

'Can you pass me the face?'

She picked it up, handed it across, watched as he fitted it.

'Will it work?' she asked.

He grinned. 'Do you doubt my skills?'

She shook her head, said seriously: 'No. Of course not.'

She passed him the hands, then the glass. He held the movement up, checked it for any misalignment, slipped it into the case.

'Here,' he said. 'You can have the honour of winding it up, making it go.'

She shook her head. 'No. You do it.'

He picked up the key, wound it slowly, easing against the resistance of the spring. When he'd finished, he put it to his ear, listened, then held it out so that Addie could do the same.

The tick was as uneven as before.

He grimaced. 'Ah well. I did my best. But I guess it's just what it is. It's a clock with a limp. We can't all be perfect.'

*

'There was a big crag,' she said. 'With really steep sides.'

It was dark now. A light glowed in the kitchen, but he'd not bothered to switch the lamp on in the living room, so they sat in the gloom. He'd found a disc to put in his old CD player – late Van Morrison, the only music in his meagre collection that he thought she might be able to tolerate: gravel voice, Irish rhythms with clipped chords. She sat on the sofa, legs curled, the smooth skin on her knees shining in the reflected light. Viva lay beside her, stretched along the rest of the seat, her head on Addie's lap. Evan sat opposite in his armchair.

She'd begun to talk again, unprompted, just memories and thoughts spilling out. Once more, she was going over her days in the hills, searching, it seemed, for details that she'd missed in earlier retellings. They appeared to matter to her – those details – as though without them, her story could not be complete.

'I kept trying,' she told him. 'I tried for hours to get down, to get to my pack. But I just couldn't find a way. And by the time I gave up, it was nearly dark, and I was lost.'

She was in the valley by then, she explained, and really beginning to panic. 'I shouted for help, blundered around, just got myself more lost,' she said. She paused, as if trying to find a reason, something that felt like an explanation for what she'd done.

Was there one, at moments like that, Evan had wondered: when terror gripped you, when your world went awry?

'I found somewhere to sleep,' she continued at last, her voice quieter, more restrained. 'Well, to spend the night anyway. A hollow, beneath a rock. It had some moss in it, which made a bed. And there was a little dribble of water down the rocks. It gave me something to drink.'

The next morning, she told him, she tried to find her way back.

'I couldn't. I just got more and more lost. Then I did what I thought you were meant to do. I tried to follow the river. It had to go somewhere. I thought I'd be alright. I spent all day at it, but it was so overgrown, so steep. In the end, it went into a deep gorge and I couldn't get down. So I tried to get into the next valley. It meant lots of climbing. The bush was really thick. Horrible stuff.' She looked down, chewing at her lip, arms huddled around her. 'I didn't know where I was. I was hungry, filthy, cold. All I'd eaten since I lost my pack was some chocolate I had in my pocket. I had another night out there. This time, just on the ground. I was terrified. I hardly slept. Sometime in the night I heard someone – or something. I thought it might be a hunter or a tramper, and I called out. I yelled and I yelled, but no one came.'

'It was probably a deer,' he said, 'or a pig. They're all through this area.'

She nodded. 'The next day, I tried to go on. Then the storm came.'

She fell silent, closed her eyes, shook her head again, slowly, as if in despair.

'I thought I was going to die.'

'It's alright now,' he said. 'You're safe here.'

'Yes.' She seemed to consider the matter, as if it needed weighing up. Then she smiled, her face pale in the dim light. 'Yes, I feel safe. Thank you.'

For a long time afterwards, she said nothing. The CD clunked to a stop. Evan made no move to replace it, just sat, watching her, allowing her the solitude of her thoughts. But eventually, when she still did not speak, he asked: 'What were you doing up there in the mountains, all alone? You still haven't told me.'

'I was being stupid,' she said.

'In what way?'

'Every way. I was stupid.'

He waited for her to go on, but she remained silent and it was too dark now to see the expression on her face.

'Why?' he asked. 'What happened?'

'Everything. That's what happened. Everything.' She drew in her breath, a long, slow inhalation, as if struggling against sorrow or fear. 'I split with my boyfriend. We had a row. He was – well, doing what all men do, don't they? He was cheating me, two-timing me. I told him to fuck off.' She gave a short, hard laugh. 'We'd been together for five years. Since university. I thought I could trust him. It hurt.'

He nodded, thinking: that much at least, he could understand.

Perhaps she realised, for she said. 'OK. I'm not the only one it's happened to. It just felt like that. Personal. Unfair. I felt rotten. Really, really mad, sick, bitter. I've never cried so much. Like I say, I was stupid. Then – well, then I got stupider. I decided I wanted time out. I took myself off into the hills. I just wanted to walk and walk and be alone. I don't know, maybe I wanted him to follow me, or worry about me and come and find me. Or just miss me. I don't know.' She reached down, stroked Viva, running her hand along the length of the dog's back. 'I didn't plan, didn't pack properly, just threw stuff in. I mean – I should have known. I've been tramping before. Hill running even. I used to do a lot of it when I was at uni. Like I say, I was stupid.'

'We all make mistakes,' he said. 'The important thing is to survive – come out the other side.'

She made no reply, and he imagined her picking again over the entrails of the events, trying to see some moral in them, some balance of justice. In the kitchen, the light flickered as the generator kicked in, and for a moment her face became that same ghostly mask he'd seen when he first found her. That gaunt sketch in black and white.

He waited for her to continue.

Instead, she blurted out, almost as if in terror: 'What's that noise? What is it?'

'It's just the generator,' he said. 'That's all. It's what gives us the electricity.'

'Are you sure?'

'Yes, of course.'

She nodded, but he could see her still straining to listen. Then she relaxed, laughed. 'I'm sorry. I'm –' She touched her head where the scar was. 'I'm still a bit confused. When I was out there, I thought – you know, maybe they'd send out a helicopter. That somehow someone would realise I was missing and come and find me. I was listening for one all the time. I still am.'

'But no one knew you were there,' he said.

'No. I know. But I hoped all the same. You can hope for anything, believe in anything, when you're desperate. I even prayed.'

'You're still confused,' he said. 'You ought to see a doctor. I wish you'd let me take you.'

'No. I've told you. There's no need.' Her voice hardened, became vehement: 'I do know. I was a nurse once. I just need rest.'

'Is that what you want?' he asked. 'To stay here?'

She nodded. 'Yes. But it's alright, I know I can't. I know you want me to leave.'

'Why do you say that?'

'You do, don't you. You come here to escape, to hunt for gold. I've invaded your space, I'm keeping you from your prospecting. You don't need me here.'

'Do you want to stay?'

Another nod.

'Why?'

'Because –' She looked down at Viva, stroking the dog's neck, gave a sigh. 'Because it's beautiful. And it's quiet. And you're kind. And I can sleep here and just be myself and forget everything. What happened, my boyfriend. Everything.'

He looked away, battling with his conscience. She was right: he wanted her to leave; he wanted to be alone again, able to go back to his claim. But he'd been there himself – that lonely and muddled place when love had fled. He knew what she felt, what she needed. An impossible combination: companionship, distraction, solitude, escape. If she was finding it here, who was he to deny her?

'OK,' he said. 'You can stay. Stay as long as you want.'

Four

Before he set out, Evan counted back the days, marked his calendar. One of the problems of living out here, with no phone, no radio, no communications of any sort, was that it was easy to lose track of time. In the short term, that didn't matter, but life outside was not so forgiving. He needed to be back at work on the ordained date. So each morning, he crossed the day off his calendar when he woke, dotted the ones ahead before he left for the claim, completed the task when he returned. Addie's arrival had disrupted the routine. He'd lost all track of time. Five days since he'd found her, he decided; this was the sixth. That made it the twenty-fourth of January. He put a line through the date, a dot above the next three days.

He was hesitant to leave, though eager to go. He felt guilty about abandoning Addie. He still didn't know if she was ready to look after herself, whether tiredness or confusion would engulf her again, and she'd need help. Whether sadness would overwhelm her, and she'd yearn for his company. Yet he longed to get back to the deposits he'd been working on when the storm struck, to see what damage it had done. He was worried, as he always was when he had interruptions like this, that nature and fate would conspire to cheat him, whisking the gold away again, before he'd had his chance.

Addie, though, had had no doubts. 'You have to go,' she said. 'You can't stay here with me. How would I feel? I can only stay if you do what you want to do, live your life like you did before. That has to be the deal; that has to be the arrangement.'

When he still prevaricated, she said: 'Anyway, you can do me a favour. You can rescue my clothes. I've had enough of wearing yours.'

So he agreed, though he'd keep the trip short, he promised. Three nights, no more. She scolded him gently in return. He didn't have to do this, she told him, pander to her like a child. She'd be fine. Just staying there was enough.

As he drove up to the saddle, his doubts about leaving faded. The world seemed bright in anticipation of his return. The air was clear and freshly washed, the cloud tassels spotless white. The ground had been recoloured in brilliant greens and browns. In the ponds and mires on the saddle the water was stretched flat as a mirror, reflecting the wide skies. Further away, to the south, the jagged peaks of Mount Murchison and the Shaler Range: pale rock, white pockets of snow, the silvery threads of streams glistening in the sun.

Yet on the other side of the saddle, the landscape told a different story. The forest was dark, still steaming. Beside him, the headwaters of the river ran fast and deep. There were slips and washouts to negotiate; the road was potted, runnelled, making the truck slur and buck and splash.

At the end of the road, the parking area was empty, its surface skimmed smooth with mud. It clagged his boots as he moved around the truck, collecting his gear. Viva stood forlornly by the cab, as if knowing what it meant: grumbles and warnings and an enforced wash before she'd be allowed in the tent, no cuddles tonight.

The trek to the campsite was slow. He had to wind his way beneath bent branches, around fallen trees, over logs. When he reached it, the campsite was no better. Branches and twigs littered the clearing, covered the tarpaulin, were massed into piles of flood debris along the stream-bank. The grass was flattened, puddled with water, rank.

He went across to the tarpaulin, pulled back the flap, peered in. It sagged in the middle, looked heavy and dark from its weight of unasked for thatch. It smelled of wetness. Damp soil, damp vegetation, damp clothes. In the far corner, water had seeped in, soaking the end of his bed. In the doorway was a collection of worms, bloated and bleached by the rain. He scooped them up, threw them into the bush.

He spent the rest of the day putting the camp right. He wiped down the tarpaulin, washed it with water from the stream, restrung it to make it tight. He dragged out his bedding and looped it over the bushes to dry. Then he collected Addie's clothes from the rough pile where he'd dropped them, shook them out, scuffed away the wrinkles, spread the anorak on the tarpaulin, hung her shirt and jeans on a branch. They were torn, muddy, but they would give her something to wear other than his shirts when he got back.

On an impulse, he went to the anorak, felt for pockets, searched them. They were empty. He did the same with the jeans. Just a handkerchief, screwed tight, sodden, and in the back pocket a scrap of paper which disintegrated as he tried to unfold it, whatever words it might have carried long ago lost. There was a pocket in the shirt. He tried that. A small tube of lip-salve. That was all.

For a moment, he stood regarding the line of clothes. They hung there like some strange semaphore. Other than Addie herself, they were all that existed of that night; the only things marking her existence in his world. Shouldn't they tell him something? And yet they were blank, impersonal. They might belong to anyone, or no one at all. Just unwanted tramping gear, that had served its purpose, been abandoned in the bush.

With what felt like a sense of righteous zeal, he turned to the clearing, and attacked the scattered playthings of the storm. He pulled out the branches, stacked them by the edge of the bush, where they might dry and one day become useful firewood. He pushed and kicked the flood debris into the stream, watched it wash away. He found his spade and dug shallow trenches to drain the water from the puddles around his tent. Finally, he brewed up coffee, sat on a log by the stream, and surveyed what he could see of his claim.

It had changed. It always did after storms. It was different every summer when he returned. He could never predict the way it would be, for under winter's hand, the river went to its task angrily, or with cold and insatiable intent; sometimes it seemed to blunder blindly, with no real plan at all. It moved boulders, swept islands away. Made pools, obliterated them. It gnawed at the bank, meanly undermined trees, grabbed them, dragged them away, then left them as if they were nothing but a nuisance. It scoured out channels, reshaped old ones, shifted the bars one way or another, plastered its creation with gravel and sand, silt and mud.

Yet it revived the place, too. It brought in new gold, buried it; it uncovered deposits that had lain hidden, scattered them along the stream.

The game was to work out where.

Over the years, he'd talked to dozens of prospectors about that question: where to look. Each one had a theory, some had several. It's the pools that attract it, a few said. The gravel catches it, others claimed; it stands to reason, it lodges between the stones. It's on the inside of the bends, where the water slows, several had told him, as a matter of simple fact. Others proclaimed the opposite: gold's heavy; it collects where other things don't – in the faster flows, on the outside of the bends. In the lee of the rocks where the flow comes together; upstream of boulders where the flow divides. In the black sand, in the red, where the iron is. If you put all the theories together, gold was everywhere. Except, in Evan's experience, it wasn't.

His own theory was more subtle; so subtle, he told himself at times, that it hardly amounted to a theory at all. It was based on what Jeb had told him when he'd given him the claim, and on the books he'd read since. But mainly it was based on doing what he always did when faced with a problem: observing, thinking, trying to work the logic out.

So he tried to read the stream, and to see the world as the gold would. To imagine himself in the flow, being swept along, feet dragging on the bed, bumping and tumbling against the rocks, sifted by the gravel, spun in vortices, tossed in cascades. And sometimes it seemed to work, and he found what he was looking for, and at other times he didn't, and was left believing that there was nothing there to find. Selection bias, he'd been told once, by a professor of statistics or mathematics or something like that, with whom he'd spent a long night in a bar, holed up in snowstorm. You only know what you know, and what you know biases what you expect to happen and what you therefore do, so helps shape what happens next. Whether he understood what the professor had said, he wasn't sure, but it had the ring of truth in it, he thought; not just in terms of gold but life itself.

But today, standing on the bank, coffee mug in hand, looking at the scene, he was not sure what he knew, nor what to expect. The stream seemed to have reinvented itself totally. Whatever story he'd been reading when he was here a week ago had been torn up and thrown away. In its place was a new plot, all jumbled and complex. The pool where he'd been working when the storm broke had gone, wiped smooth by gravel. The riffle above it, where the water had rippled and chuckled as it flowed, was just a mass of boulders, piled higgledy-piggledy together. The maze of bifurcating channels that had criss-crossed the wide bar in front of him had coalesced into a single current, fierce and determined.

There was hardly anything left that he recognised. No fixed point. He had no choice but to start again. To work through the claim, once more, sampling, panning, trying to decipher the pattern. It would take days. There'd be no dredging on this trip. There'd be no dramatic finds.

He sighed, drained his coffee, emptied the dregs into the water at his feet. The dark grains settled into the pool, were lost amidst the sand.

*

By the end of the next day, he knew that even that plan would not work. His mind was just not in it.

The fault was not his alone. Despite the promise of the world when he'd set out, the river wasn't really ready for him yet. It was too deep, too full, the flow too fast. There were too many places he could not reach, or where the gravel had not yet settled. His panning seemed irrelevant. Whatever he found today might not be there tomorrow, and would almost certainly be changed before he'd be able to come back and dredge.

But it was Addie, as well. The way she had ruffled his life, disturbed him.

In many ways, the reason for that was obvious enough, and he would have predicted it. He was not used to a woman's presence in his life these days, especially one so young. She was a distraction. She drew his eyes as she moved around the cottage, and when she sat on the sofa wearing his shirt like a smock, neck open, legs bare. She drew his thoughts with her snatches of biography and tiny, disjointed revelations, the hinted at gaps in her life.

Where she lived. Dunedin, she'd said, but then shrugged and added: 'Well, I did. I'm sort of between places now.'

Her age: twenty-five. And when he expressed surprise, she'd laughed and said: 'I was the runt of the litter. That's what people tell me. An afterthought. Well, no thought at all, really. Just an accident.'

Her brothers and sisters: 'We're not close. We never really were. I've not seen them for years.'

Her childhood. On a farm in the Waikato. She'd been brought up with the cows, she said, when she was a toddler must have spent half her time with them, as if she were just another calf.

About that – her childhood – she had, at least, been more forthcoming. She'd been taught, she told him, just like any farmer's daughter was – preparing her for life ahead. She'd learned to milk, she'd learned about mastitis and brucellosis and bovine TB, how to tell the signs, what to do when she saw them. She'd watched the cows be inseminated, strained with her father to birth the calves, fed the ones that lived, dragged those that didn't to the dump round the back. She'd run out fence-lines, driven quad-bikes and tractors, mucked out cow-sheds, dug drains. In-between, she'd picked up some of the more basic life skills: how to trap possum, shoot rabbits, skin them; how to tickle a trout. She seemed proud of what she could do.

But school had been different. She'd been the tomboy, she told him, as if he couldn't have guessed. Always fooling with the lads, always in trouble. Sitting in class had bored her and she'd been labelled dim. Her parents had been summoned to see the head teacher more than once. Each time, her father had given her a beating like he would have done the dogs when they misbehaved, full of rage and bitterness, made all the stronger by his self-disgust – by the fact that he hated punishment of any sort, but corporal punishment the most, so that he flayed her even more wildly. She always took it without a murmur, though she knew that it made the beating worse. Yet to flinch would have given him the excuse his regret required – and she refused to do that: she wanted him to suffer for his cruel love.

'I wasn't very bright,' she said, with a rueful smile.

Yet everything she told him seemed to beg more questions. Every glimpse he got of her left him wondering what more he might see. Whether it was deliberate or just an accident of the way she thought, the way her mind worked, he could not say. But he felt himself enticed, hooked.

In response, he'd already begun to change. On his own, in the cottage, he lived modestly, with few pretensions. His meals were humble affairs, quickly cooked, and eaten as they happened, standing at the stove or from a plate on his lap as he sat on the veranda, with a mug of water to follow or beer straight from the can. In the days since Addie had arrived, he'd felt obliged to adorn them with some sort of formality, however ready-made the food might be. Eaten at the table, with cutlery and glasses and a torn-off sheet of kitchen roll to serve as a napkin, salt and pepper to hand. He'd adapted his own hygiene in the same way. He washed more often, shaved more thoroughly, combed his hair when he got up. He tucked in his shirt, rinsed the toothpaste out of the wash-basin, tried to remember to put the toilet seat down. It all felt strange, intrusive, an enforced ritual, yet it gave him a curious satisfaction, a new purpose to his humdrum life.

As he panned, therefore, as he tried to read the stream, he found his thoughts drifting, his concentration refusing to hold to the point. His mind kept slipping away, back to Addie, back to the questions he wanted to ask, the gaps he wanted to fill. What had happened to her in the years since her childhood on the farm? How she'd got to university, what she'd done there. Her time in New Plymouth playing in a band; somewhere amidst it all, training as a nurse. How it all fitted together. How she'd become the seemingly troubled young woman she now was. What waited for her back in the life she'd fled.

It wasn't unusual, this constant churning of his mind as he worked. The very task seemed to beg it, with its slow rhythms and the background chorus of the stream and the birdsong from the bush. But normally, his thoughts were introspective, and angled at the past. Previous trips out here to the claim, the way that they had rewarded him or failed him, the promises they'd made and sometimes kept. Other prospectors he'd met, talked to, the stories they'd told him. Other life events and lessons, bubbling up from his memory. Successes and failures. Victories and losses. Truths and deceits.

Amongst them all, inevitably, the women in his life, and the places they were connected with, the work, the times of life.

Rana in Kenya, Yasmine in Canada. Juliette, here in New Zealand, the most recent, and her simple choice at the end: a career or love; to leave rather than stay.

Lisha – the one he'd loved the most, perhaps the only one really, but too briefly – years ago in Greece. Dark, vibrant, laughing. Careless and carefree. What had happened to her, he would wonder; what life had she chosen instead?

Now, though, his thoughts had a newer and more acute concern. A woman in the present tense. One who lives and eats in his cottage – sleeps in his bed, albeit without him; occupies his thoughts and his time. One who somehow leaves him always guessing, for everything she says and does seems to hide more than it reveals.

The thoughts tantalised him, tugged at him, wove themselves into a tangle.

He dragged his mind back, looked at the contents of his pan. There was nothing there. No gold. Just quartz, feldspar, iron, worn crystals of tourmaline. Silvery flecks of chrome. He threw the residue away, dipped the pan in the stream, washed it clean. As he did so, the sun arrowed low through the branches, making bright starbursts between the fern fronds. A whole day, and nothing to show for it other than pans full of rubbish, a mind the same. Time to stop.

He waded to the nearest bank, hauled himself out, stood, indecisive.

He was fifty metres from the top of the gorge, where he'd first found her. He must have come this way in the dark as he searched for Viva, perhaps came back this way, Addie in his arms. He looked up, towards the bluff, trying to make out the route he'd taken. In the daylight it did not seem so bad. The slope was gentler than he'd imagined, the bush thinner.

He smiled to himself: not such a heroic feat of endurance after all.

'Come on.' He called Viva and she bounded across the stream from the opposite bank, shook herself as she reached him. 'Let's find Addie,' he said, and started up the slope. Viva followed, hesitant at first, then seemed to catch his intent and pushed past him, ran ahead. He clambered after her, laughing at her enthusiasm. 'Good girl.'

Within a few minutes she had led him to the path – or the faint deer-trail or dried-up channel through the bush that he assumed he'd taken that night. He climbed in her wake, picking a way up the rocks, slipping on scree, forcing his way through tea-tree scrub. They came to a boulder, worked their way round it, scrambled up a bank. The land levelled. Then a gully that he thought might be familiar, a gap in the bush, and the path began to dip. Viva wagged, leapt down between the rocks. He slid after her, down a short muddy cleft. He was on the bench.

Standing there again, in the place he must have stood then, felt both a reward and an incursion, as though he'd entered some sacred space. It might almost have been that, for it had the simple grandeur of a shrine. The pale, lichen-crusted columns of the cliff. The smooth contours of the bench, where the water had worn it long millennia ago. A low ridge of paler rock, glowing copper in the setting sun, seeming to divide the ledge in two. At the edge of the gorge, a ragged line of crenulations where the rainwater ran off. Ferns and gorse making gargoyles in the wall.

But of Addie, he could see no sign.

He encouraged Viva to seek her: 'Where's Addie?' and received a look of canine bafflement in reply.

He went to the ridge of rock, crouched beside it. Is this where he had found her, is this where she had lain? He felt along the surface as if seeking some indication of her in the rock. There was nothing. No mark, no tag of cloth, nor footprint, nor even a bloodstain on the stone.

He stood up, tried to picture her there. In the darkness. In the swirling rain and wind. In those moments when he first saw her. Before that, when she must have waited here alone, strength and hope fading.

No image came. It was as if she'd never been.

*

What would she have felt? What would she have done? How would she have seen the land?

As he walked, striding out, the questions teased him, and he tried to imagine himself as she must have been then. The argument, the fight behind her. Just anger now, seething in her mind. Bitterness, contempt. All those he could imagine, had known himself. The loyal lover, wronged.

The echoes, too, of whatever words had been traded, repeating in her mind. Words said better now, with more force, sharper scorn, perfect timing. Different words, landing a harder blow against the man who had betrayed her, providing a more telling Parthian shot. Regrets, too, for all the chances missed: to see the betrayal coming, catch the first signs when it happened, finish it all then. And older regrets. For not knowing what sort of man he was, or knowing and not admitting the fact, for ignoring what she knew.

Yes – he could imagine all that. He'd known it, too.

But the hills: what did she make of them? How did she read the land, how did she respond? That he could not grasp, for to him the hills were friends. He knew them, understood them, shared their thoughts.

It mattered, he knew. If he was going to find her pack, retrieve it, that was the only way. He had to imagine her there, be her, and know what she would do. Just as he did with the gold.

Did she stop here and rest? Did she march along this path, storming in her mind? Wander here, distracted, into the grass; stand here, reproachful; sit here and cry?

His decision to search for the pack had been made the previous evening, as he'd stood on the bench above the gorge. It was more impulse than plan. An acknowledgement, in part, of the futility of his endeavours to find any gold when the stream was not yet ready, and all was unruly and unsettled. But it was a reaction, also, to the muddle of his thoughts. The emptiness of the place where he'd found her – no sign, no sense of her ever having been. As though she was a figment of his imagination. Yet the presence of her, tugging all the time in his mind. Pictures of her, echoes of her voice. The questions she posed. Where she had been, how she had got there, which route she'd taken. How she had suddenly appeared in his life.

Before he'd left the cottage, he'd asked her again about her journey, though gently so as not to reopen the wounds in her mind. To help her, he'd fed her suggestions, hoping to stir memories. The hut she'd slept in: was it the one with a big water tank, next to the door? The track: could she remember a large rock, shaped like a frog? Toad Rock, people called it – and just for once, the name was deserved. Another place, high on the ridge, where the track ran along a narrow arête, scree on either side. Did she remember that?

As before, she'd struggled to respond, or at least to do so with anything like confidence. Perhaps, she'd said; maybe. Yes, she could vaguely recall something like that. And yes, perhaps that, too.

He'd tried, therefore, to construct some sort of image of her, there on the hillside, some sort of map of where she might have gone. Persimmon's Hut to Dolly Top, along the Lewisham Ridge. It made sense. He'd walked it himself a couple of times, and he could think of places that matched her meagre memories, others that might have tricked her into getting lost. Two sections, at least, where she might have rested, eased her pack off and sat; watched in horror as it slipped and bounced down the slope.

That morning, he'd packed his sleeping bag, his food, his stove and set out early, Viva bounding eagerly at his side. He'd made his way up the stream, along the bank to the end of his claim; then on, where the path ran out, following the channel to the headwaters, climbing out of the valley on to the ridge above, working his way up that, through thick bush, to the divide. There, he'd picked up the line of an old miners' track, overgrown, zigzagging up the slope until it suddenly, almost dramatically, broke out into the open terrain of the hills. An hour and a half later and he had reached Persimmon's Hut.

It was as he remembered it, as he'd described it to her; as she herself had thought the place she'd stayed might have looked. A simple square edifice, made of macrocarpa and marine ply. A roof of iron. A large plastic water tank on a plinth beside the door. On the western side, a low hump of greywacke, giving shelter from the wind.

He went inside, looked around, searching to see if her pack had been left there: discovered, perhaps, by a passing tramper, returned there in case the owner came back. If not that, then a note. 'Backpack, found on Lewisham Ridge. Will deliver it to Greymouth Police Station. Call there to collect.' It was the sort of thing that trampers would do, part of the mountain code.

There was nothing. Just a string of names in the visitor book, notes of the routes they were taking, their expected arrival times. Addie's wasn't amongst them.

He wasn't surprised. It had always been a long shot. Far more likely that the pack was still there, down in the bush where it had tumbled, out of sight.

Now he was following the trail, north towards Dolly Top, scanning the land as he went. Asking himself all the time: might it be here? Or here? Or there? How would she have acted? What might she have done?

So far, there'd been nothing, but still he was unsurprised. From what she had said, she must have walked for several hours from Persimmon's Hut before she lost her pack. There were plenty of possible places yet.

Even so, doubts had begun to grow. The landscape out here was so big, so unconstrained. There were so many screes, bluffs, rocky defiles. And how could he tell where she had really gone? Had she kept to the track or wandered off? Down one of the minor side-paths, along one of the sheep trails that laced the hillslope, perhaps seeking shelter from the wind, or to answer the call of nature, or perhaps just to sit and weep?

Was she even on this track at all?

He walked on. Viva ran ahead of him or ranged in wide arcs across the grassland on either side. Hunting for a scent of Addie, perhaps, or just for carrion, rabbits.

Where the track climbed over a spur, he slowed, looked more assiduously. This section of the path was rougher, rocky, boulder-strewn. It was flanked by outcrops, patches of scree, here and there by steep bluffs ending in cliffs. He searched them as best he could, climbing on to boulders for a better view, picking his way between the rocks, peering into clefts and over crags. He worked his way down the screes, scoured the bushes and grass beyond.

But still there was nothing. No pack, nor any sign of where it might have been lost.

As he climbed back on to the track, he found himself screwing his eyes against the low sun. Time, he realised, was running out. It was taking longer than he expected. At the rate he was going, it would be dark by the time he got to Dolly Top.

'What a lovely dog.'

The woman had appeared out of the sun, materialising like a mirage. Then another beside her. Evan shaded his eyes to see. They were in their thirties, he guessed, regular trampers from their gear and their air of fitness. One had fair hair, cut short, the other was a redhead, with a long pony tail.

'And a lovely evening as well,' the redheaded woman said.

They exchanged greetings. Viva snuffled at the women's legs.

'She's after trail tucker,' Evan said. 'Best ignore her.'

The blonde woman laughed, apologised to Viva that she had none.

They stood for a moment, enjoying the view, sharing it in silence.

Evan asked where they were going, where'd they come from. They were walking the western ranges, they told him, from north to south – from Arthur's Pass to Franz Joseph. They'd set out two days ago and were enjoying every moment. Their accents sounded American, or Canadian perhaps, and he asked where they were from.

'The US,' the blonde woman said: 'From Seattle. But we live in New Zealand now. In Wellington. What about you? Going far?'

'Not on this occasion,' Evan said. 'I'm camping down on the East Branch, near the end of the trail.' He pointed downslope, into the valley. 'I'm just out for a couple of days. I head back that way tomorrow.'

'Are you a hunter, then?'

'No. Well – sort of, I suppose. But not for game. I'm prospecting for gold. I've a claim down there.'

The women were intrigued, quizzed him about the claim, how he did his prospecting.

'You seem to know more than I do,' he said.

'It's all those old movies we watch, westerns. *Pale Rider*, *Paint Your Wagon*.' The redhead began to sing: 'I was born under a wandering star . . .'

He grinned. 'You've even got the voice.'

'Gee, thanks.' Then she asked: 'Did you feel the earthquake the other day?'

'No. But I've been up here for a week or more – where was it?'

She told him about it: in Wellington, she said; three days ago, just before they'd left. It hadn't been large, had caused no serious damage, but had been enough to cause a scare.

'I'm a real Kiwi now,' she said, with a grin. 'I just dove under the table like we were meant to and hung on tight. I just wish someone had told the table what it was meant to do. It seemed to be making a bolt for the door.'

He laughed, asked about other news; anything else important that he'd missed.

'Nothing but death and destruction,' the woman said. 'That's if you believe the guy in the hut with us last night. A disaster freak I think. He made it sound like NYPD out there. A tramper killed in the Paparoa Range. A manhunt of some sort for an escaped convict. A missing toddler in Westport.' She grimaced. 'We thought that the US was bad, but it's a breeze compared to here.'

He thought of Addie – another drama, though one they did not know about, and on this occasion with a happy ending. It brought a stab of satisfaction, almost pride, his role in it all. Find her pack now, he told himself, and his success would be complete.

'Which hut were you in?' he asked. 'Dolly Top?'

'Yep.' The redheaded woman nudged her companion. 'She chose it specially. It meant an extra five miles, but she insisted. Her name's Dolly. I'm Josie, by the way.'

'Evan.' He held out a hand and they each shook it with an air of formality. 'Was the hut busy?'

'No. Just us and the harbinger of doom. He'll have moved on by now. You should be safe.'

'You haven't seen a backpack, have you?'

Dolly shrugged. 'Quite a few. Any one in particular?'

Evan suddenly realised that he didn't know what shape or size or colour it was. 'It was a friend's,' he said. 'She lost it up here a week or two ago, just before the storm.'

'How'd she manage that?'

'She was with a group. She thought someone else was carrying it.' Why he was inventing this fiction he wasn't sure. If it was to keep the story simple, it was failing. Was it in some way to protect Addie, cover up for her foolishness?

Josie shook her head. 'We've not seen anything. But there'll have been other people through since then. Wouldn't they have picked it up, checked it for ID, taken it to one of the huts, or put a note there at least.'

'I'd take it to the police,' Dolly said. 'It could mean anything – someone lost, someone hurt. She'd have heard by now, if anyone had found it, I'm sure.' She picked up her pack, slipped it on. 'I'm sorry we can't help.'

Evan thanked them, wished them good walking.

'Good luck to you, too. I hope you find it.' She gave Viva a last, quick stroke: 'And I hope you find some trail tucker before long.'

He watched them as they walked away. Josie led, half a pace in front. After a few paces, Dolly raised a hand to Josie's shoulder, straightened the strap of the pack. It was a gesture of subtle intimacy – unasked for, instinctive.

Sisters, he thought, or lovers perhaps. A minute or two later he looked back again. They had disappeared over the brow.

*

The hut was dark as he approached it. He breathed a sigh of relief: at least, he'd have it to himself. But as he opened the door and went in, there was a gasp of surprise from the far end of the room. In the shadows, he could make out two figures coiled together on the lower bunk. There was little doubt what he'd interrupted. He pretended not to notice, called a cheery greeting, dropped his bag and went outside again, closing the door in his wake.

It had been a disappointing day. Although he'd continued searching, spent three more hours scrabbling in rocky ravines, overgrown gullies, wading through streams, trying to see some sign of Addie's pack, he'd found nothing. He was tired, dispirited. He just wanted to eat, go to bed.

Half an hour later, he tried the hut again. The lamp was lit now, and the couple who'd been on the bed sat at the table, eating. They looked up briefly, nodded their welcome, said something in a language that Evan didn't understand, and the woman laughed. She was young, brunette, wild in what he thought of as an East European way, with that don't-mess-with-me demeanour of women he'd encountered in Slovakia and Serbia. She stirred in him instincts he thought he'd forgotten. Something animal, pure lust. Perhaps she did that in most men, and knew it. For whatever reason, his eyes rested on her longer than they needed.

He cooked a meal, trying not to look at her, several times failing. Each time, she returned his glance with a knowing stare. When his meal was ready, he took it outside again, glad to escape. He ate it on the bench at the back of the hut, dropping morsels to Viva, and at the end letting her lick the plate clean. Then he sat back, his head against the wall, his legs stretched out, and watched the slow passage of the world from day to night. The sky losing its colour. Land darkening to a scissor-cut silhouette, until, when only blackness seemed possible, the moon suddenly silvered the horizon, and emerged as a pale face above the mountains.

When he went inside the hut was silent, and he quietly laid out his sleeping bag, undressed, slipped in. Viva curled up against the wall, at his feet. Within minutes he was asleep.

He was woken, though, sometime in the deepness of the night. Movements, murmuring, muffled giggles from the far bunk, then a rhythmic thud. He waited for it to finish, the last sigh to fade, but afterwards could not get back to sleep. Instead, he lay staring into the darkness, remembering.

Long, long ago, in Germany. Lisha beside him, in almost the same manner. Tight against him, loin to loin, hardly daring to breathe. Around them, in the men's dormitory of the hostel, the snuffles and snores and farts of other hikers, like a comic symphony for flugelhorn and bassoon. She had waited until they were asleep, sneaked in from the women's quarters. Now, they made love in slow motion, and without a sound. When all was done, she slipped out of his bunk, padded softly to the door. From one of the other bunks, someone called, in German, 'Die nächsten Werden auf zwei Uhr,' and a ripple of laughter went around the room. Lisha had translated for him the following morning: 'The next performance will be at 2 a.m.'.

'Bugger, I slept through it,' he'd said, earning a punch to his ribs.

Lying there, in the darkness a quarter of a century later, he thought how it had been a precious moment, and yet how odd it was that he should remember that. Not the act of their love-making, the specifics of what they did, but just the moment of absurdity in its epilogue.

Perhaps laughter, mockery, bathos lasted longer than any physical sensation, he thought; longer than love itself.

And he remembered lying beside Addie that night he'd found her. His hand on her breast. The tiny movement in her, hardly breath at all, making a faint pressure against his palm. Meaning so much more than love or lust or sex. Just proof that she was still alive, hope that she might last the night.

Five

When he'd set out on his search, he imagined himself coming back in triumph, with her pack in his hands, presenting it to Addie ceremoniously: a gift from her past. Instead, it was she who greeted him – with a fish.

She was waiting for him on the steps of the veranda when he arrived.

'I was afraid you'd got delayed,' she said.

'How did you know I was coming?'

'I've been watching out for you up on the saddle. There's a place over there where you get a good view.' She pointed up the bank, behind the cottage. 'I've cooked you something. I hope you're hungry.'

He could smell the fish already, but could not believe his own nose.

'What is it?'

'Trout,' she said. 'I caught it especially.'

'Caught it?'

'In the river. You can see them in the pools. I assumed you knew.'

He did know. He'd seen them often when he went down to the stream, would watch them in the mornings as he sat there, while the light played on the mist, made patterns on the water. If he'd been his father's true son he would have caught them himself, baked them on an open fire for breakfast, for he'd have inherited the fly-fishing gene. Instead, he'd grown up with a purely functional attitude to food: to take it as it came, and not ask too many questions.

'So – do you want some or not?'

Meekly, he followed Addie into the kitchen, sat at the table, while she served him with the fish and a flourish of professional pride.

The trout was baked, presented elegantly on a plate with a garnish of herbs, gratin potatoes.

'How did you catch it?' he asked. 'We've no rods.'

She smiled. 'With my hands. I told you, I learned to tickle fish as a kid. It's easy enough.'

She had told him, though at the time he had not really believed it. Her lack of preparation for her trip in the hills, the mistakes she'd made in getting lost, had caused him to think of her as naïve, not practical or resourceful. Now, he realised, there was more to her than he'd allowed.

'It's illegal,' he said. 'Do you know that? You're meant to have a licence.'

She laughed. 'I promise not to tell. And, anyway, that always makes it taste better, I find.' She regarded him a moment, her fork half-raised to her mouth, mockery playing in her eyes. 'So is that why you've never done it; why you don't catch them? Because it's not allowed.'

'Not really.' He told her about his experiences with his father, the legacy it had left. 'I just don't much like the idea of killing them. I'm a bit squeamish I suppose.'

She shrugged. 'You shouldn't be. Just don't think about it too much. A quick tap. Done.'

But then she looked away, as if having second thoughts herself, and was silent.

He asked about the herbs: where had they come from?

'Behind the cottage. There's an old bed of them there. Didn't you know?' He shook his head and she regarded him, lips pursed, as if in mild reprimand. 'I expect your father planted them, don't you? They were overgrown. I've tidied them up for you. If you weed and trim them now and then, they'll be there whenever you want them.'

Another revelation, he realised: not just about her, but his father, too.

After the meal, they sat together on the veranda. The night was calm, warm. The sky was clear. Stars were beginning to appear, pricking into existence wherever he looked. From across the clearing came the sound of a morepork, calling its name.

Viva wandered across and sat between them, seemed to consider which lap to lay her nose on, chose Addie's. Evan smiled at the tableau they made. It seemed strangely familiar, as if it might always have been like that – woman and dog.

Addie asked how his prospecting had gone, what he'd found.

'So-so,' he said. Then: 'Well, no. A failure, really.' He told her about his panning and how the river had changed, yet had still not settled. 'I was too impatient,' he said. 'It needs a few more days yet.'

'So what did you do?'

'I looked for your pack.'

'You what?'

'Looked for your backpack.'

'How did you know where to go?'

He explained: from what she'd told him about her journey, his memory of the huts and the trails.

'You silly man,' she said. 'Why did you do that? You had no chance – there was no need.'

He was surprised by her vehemence, almost disdain, as though the whole search had been futile from the start.

She seemed to sense it, for she apologised. 'It really wasn't worth all that trouble. It was old and battered and had nothing in it of value.'

'Your wallet?' he asked. 'Wasn't there anything in that? Money? Credit cards?'

'I've told you. There was nothing. A few dollars. No credit cards. I didn't really think I'd need one out here.' She shot him a glance. 'You're not expecting me to pay by EFTPOS, I hope?'

He laughed but spoke seriously. 'No. No payment necessary. Not of any kind.'

Again, she glanced at him, reading in his words perhaps a meaning that he hadn't intended, yet which now rang in his ears.

Then she got up, came across to him and laid her hand on his shoulder. 'Dear Evan. You're so good, so generous. I'm sorry you did all that for me for nothing. I'm grateful. But please, please stop fretting about it. The pack doesn't matter. I'm safe. I'm here. That's all that matters to me.' And she bent down and quickly, lightly, touched his head with her lips, then turned and went indoors.

*

He watched her as she sewed. She was repairing her jeans that he'd brought back from the claim. Her head was bent, her brow furrowed, her lips tight. It was the way his mother used to sit when she sewed; all her concentration trained on the task. A pose as timeless, he thought, as Rodin's *The Thinker*, and just as evocative.

They were sitting on the veranda. They spent a lot of their time there now. The weather had turned hot, still, sultry. During the day, they tried to blank out the humid air with drawn curtains; at night they slept with the windows and doors wide open, welcoming every breath of air.

Evan was back in his own bedroom now, and he was relieved. Addie had arranged it before his return from the claim. She'd tidied the spare room, moved in the few things that she might call hers, restored his to where they belonged. She'd made herself a sleeping mat with an old quilt from the outhouse, washed and aired. She'd made other small changes, too. A simple vase – an old coffee jar – filled with wild flowers collected from the clearing, on the table in the living room, another in his bedroom, one in what was now hers. A blanket thrown over the armchair on the veranda to hide the cigarette burns and stains that its various users had left. The rug beaten and aired, the windows washed. It was part of the deal, she insisted; her contribution in return for being allowed to stay. That, and the herb garden, and the cooking; the wild fruits – raspberries, strawberries, cherries.

'There must have been an orchard here, once,' she'd told him. 'Behind the cottage. You'd hardly know it now for the weeds, but there are apples and plums, too. You could have fruit every day if you wanted.'

He'd wondered again about his father: had he done that, planted it? If so, it was another glimpse of the man, of a part of him he'd never known. Another hint about what this place had been: an alternative world, an alternative life. An escape, just as it was to him.

Now, he asked her how she'd torn her jeans. Had she slipped?

She paused in her sewing, pulled back the hem of the shirt she was wearing so that he could see her knee. There was the shadow of a wound there. She pointed to it: 'Yes, it's how I got that.'

He remembered treating the wound that first day, when he brought her back to the cottage. Then, it had been muddy, raw. He'd picked pieces of grit out of it, felt her flinch as he did so. Now it was nearly healed.

She healed quickly, he thought, as only the young do.

'I was trying to climb up a gully, to get out of the valley I'd got trapped in. I lost my footing and slipped.' She grimaced: 'I swore a lot. It hurt like hell. But I was past crying by then. I just hated everything. My boyfriend, the tarty woman he'd taken up with. And the world and what it was doing to me. Swearing seemed appropriate.'

He grinned. 'The barbaric yawp,' he said. 'It's good therapy.'

'Barbaric yawp?' she asked.

'"I too am not a bit tamed – I too am untranslatable; I sound my barbaric yawp over the roofs of the world,"' he quoted. 'Walt Whitman. If he thought it worked, I'm sure it does.'

'A poet, too,' she said.

'An idle reader, that's all. Poetry is – well, companionable. Therapeutic.'

'And you need that do you?'

'Sometimes.'

She nodded, said nothing.

'Does he have a name?' he asked.

'Who?'

'Your boyfriend.'

'My ex, you mean.' She went on with her sewing, did not look up. 'Why do you want to know?'

'No reason really. Other than that I wouldn't have to think of him just as your boyfriend any more – especially when it seems he isn't.'

She scowled. 'You don't have to think of him at all. I don't.' But quickly she seemed to reconsider, for she said: 'Still, fair point.' And after a pause: 'Mark. He's called Mark. Mark Brown. And for the record, he was a prat. He probably still is. Just a fucking, deceiving prat. And that's what he did. Deceive people, fuck them around. That's all you need know.'

In the wake of the exchange they were both silent. Addie continued to sew, huddled even more closely over her jeans, as though she were shutting Evan out. He felt rebuked. She was still hurting, he thought, and he should have realised. His question had been tactless.

But then Addie put the needle between her lips, stretched the cloth to ensure that the stitches were even, and gave a small nod of satisfaction.

'One done,' she said. 'One to go.' She grimaced. 'And sorry. I didn't mean to take it out on you.'

'It's alright. I understand.'

'No. It's not alright. I've no right to be bitchy with you, after all you've done for me. I guess I'm still a bit sore. I'm sorry.' Her face softened; she grinned. 'But, if you want to do me a favour, if you ever meet him, you can kick him in the balls, just from me. Preferably with your work boots on.'

'I'll see what I can do.'

She nodded. 'Now, change of subject. Tell me about Viva. How did you get her?'

He explained, glad to be on safer ground.

She showed her surprise as he told her that she was a rescue dog: 'Who on earth would want to give her away?'

When he'd finished, she asked: 'Have you always had dogs?'

'No. She's my first.' Then he laughed. 'Well, second really.'

'What's so funny?'

He told her about the other dog, the first, when he was a child. He'd found it on the way home from school. It came out of the hedgerow, head down, tail slowly wagging, the epitome of obeisance and servility. It might have been waiting for him.

The dog was big. Almost as tall as he was then, aged seven or eight. It was shaggy, too: a Newfoundland, perhaps, or a Saint Bernard. It was other things as well, lurcher or wolfhound, leaner and hungrier, maybe all of those combined. He'd liked it immediately for that miscellany. He could relate to it, imagine it in himself: nothing and everything, someone who didn't quite fit because he fitted everywhere and had no place that was his own. He put out a hand, called it to him: 'Good dog. Come here, boy.'

The dog came. It nuzzled at his hand. It cocked its head on one side, inviting further fondling. He took it home and it followed him docilely, as if already it had become attached.

The house was empty. His father was away on some business matter, his mother was out at work. He fed the dog milk from the fridge, gave it some leftovers from the previous evening's dinner as titbits. It drank, ate greedily, its sides heaving, its tail wagging with the pleasure.

Belatedly, he knelt by it and looked for some form of identification. There was no collar, nothing to restrain or define it. Yet that very anonymity seemed to specify it nonetheless. It didn't need a name, he decided. It would do without one. It could stay there, nameless, and be his.

He sat on the carpet in front of the open fire, and the dog stretched beside him. It was still there when his mother returned. She heaved her shopping bag on to the kitchen table, began to unpack, saw the dog. 'You can get that thing out,' she said. Then, turning to the dog: 'D'you hear? Out.'

The dog eyed her, seemed to weigh its chances and decided that they weren't good. It padded to the door, slumped on the veranda with a sigh, head on its paws.

'It's a stray,' Evan said. 'I think it's lost.'

'That's what it can get,' his mother said. 'Lost. It's not staying. Your father would never agree.'

'I want it,' he insisted. 'I want to keep it.'

'It goes,' his mother replied. 'Either back where you found it, or to the SPCA. Take your pick.'

He lay awake that night, hoping that in the morning she'd relent. He imagined the dog outside by the door, the loyal companion and guardian, waiting for him to appear. He thought messages to it, projecting them with all his will: you'll be alright; you'll be my dog; you can stay here with me.

In the morning, though, it had gone. He never saw it again.

Another moral for life, he thought.

Opposite him, Addie continued sewing, saying nothing, and he wondered if she'd listened, or whether she'd got bored and her mind had wandered off. But as she tied off the thread, she said: 'You like taking in strays, don't you?' She looked up, gave him a smile. It was warm, affectionate. 'Luckily for Viva. Luckily for me.'

Then she asked: 'Are they still alive?'

It took him a moment to realise that she meant his parents. He shook his head. 'No. They both died some years ago.'

'I'm sorry.'

'No. It's alright.'

'What happened?'

Her questions were asked incidentally, he realised, yet always felt direct and undeniable. He had no choice but to tell her.

He told her how his mother had died, fifteen years ago, while he'd been working in Kenya. Ovarian cancer. His parents must have known about it for a year or more before they revealed the news to him. Even then, he delayed returning. He was working on a critical contract, in the remote north, battling against delays and troubles with supplies. There seemed to be no ideal time at which to leave. She died before he returned.

'Did you feel guilty about that?' Addie asked.

He nodded. 'Yes. I did. I still do a bit.'

She shrugged. 'We can't be everywhere. We're not free agents, are we?'

There was more, though, which he didn't tell her. That it hadn't been only his work that had kept him, but Rana, too. She was an official from the Ministry of Works, who'd been assigned to the project he was working on, to ensure that nothing went wrong – that the bribes and handouts and the off-site deals which inevitably happened involved the right people and weren't too indiscreet. At work, she was a mistress of her trade, inscrutable, blank. At night, in his room, she was open and generous, and he could imagine her as a wife. When he'd at last returned for the funeral, she'd promised to wait for him. Yet by the time he got back to Kenya, she'd moved on. Another project, another engineer. Ever the professional, he thought.

'What about your father?' Addie asked.

'He died a couple of years later. He drank himself to death.' A bald statement, and true to the limit that one could translate a death into anything so pithy and simple.

'A broken heart? Did he love her so much?'

The question shocked him. In his own mind, his parents' marriage had been practical, largely loveless. Whatever affection they might have felt at the beginning seemed to have gone by the times he could remember. To his father, the family business seemed to be all that counted – more than any wife or son. It was the failure of that, Evan had assumed, that had killed him, not widowhood, not love.

'I don't think so.'

'What then?'

'His business.' He tried to explain. How his father had run the family printing firm, inherited from his own father. A business that could never fail, he'd professed, for the world couldn't function without books and luggage tickets and account slips. How he'd resisted modernisation, sticking to the old ways, to letterpress, even as the world was moving on to offset litho and digital techniques. How he'd devoted every hour to it, almost his whole life.

'The eternal paradox,' he said. 'Too much work, too little.'

'And you didn't know? Never guessed?'

'No. He kept it to himself. It was his way. I only found out after he died, when I cleared out the house. All the bills, all the debts. I'm not sure that even my mother knew how bad it all was. At the end, I think that he had no answer to it all, except oblivion. Drink, death.'

*

Another evening, she asked him: 'Do you have bad times? I do. Do you?'

He nodded. 'Sometimes. I guess most people do.'

'Really dark? So that you want to – well, hurt yourself, or someone.'

He looked at her sharply, seeking meaning in her face.

She met his gaze, returned it evenly. 'I do,' she said.

'What? Hurt yourself?'

'I used to. Not any more.'

'Why? When?'

'When I was a kid. Life was difficult then.' She rolled up a sleeve, showed him the arm. He could see faint scars in the crease of the elbow. Were they the legacy?

'I'm alright now, though. I don't do it any more.' She pulled the sleeve down. 'So what brings it on for you?'

'The same, I suppose. Life. But I've got different ways of coping with it.'

'Like running away to here?'

He was silent and she gave a short laugh.

'I would. It's nothing to be ashamed of. It's better than cutting yourself, I'm sure.'

He shrugged. 'You're young,' he said. 'It's not a matter of simple choices: light or dark, of running away or staying, of being ashamed of what you do, or not. Sometimes, it's more complicated than that. Maybe you'll find that out one day. Life can be all of those at once.'

'Tell me,' she said, ironically, but then corrected herself. 'No, I mean it. Tell me. What works for you?'

He didn't respond at first, and she challenged him: 'Poetry? Is that what saves you?'

'It helps,' he said.

'And what else? Stony silence, bottling it up, like your father? Is that what you do?'

'Perhaps. But I didn't mean that. I meant staying above it all. Detachment. Maybe what the Greeks would have called stoicism.'

Again, she regarded him, her lips pursed. 'OK. Not running away. Just keeping your distance. Is that it?'

He hesitated. 'No, not really.' But then he grimaced. 'Well, maybe. Maybe that's what I do.'

*

In-between, he went to the claim. He was less worried now about Addie. She'd clearly recovered from the trauma of her days in the mountains; perhaps, had started to come to terms, too, with what had happened before – her boyfriend, splitting up. But the more he got to know her, the more she revealed, the more he saw how complex and hurt she was. Her joking, her laughter, her moments of sudden philosophy or wit couldn't erase that. So he kept his trips short. Three days the first, then four. And it was for his sake, also, of course. He enjoyed coming back, the surprises with which she'd welcome him.

'Rabbit pie,' she said, holding up the ingredients. Caught with a snare, she told him, and promised to show him later how it was done – a simple loop of wire, hidden in the grass along one of the runs from a burrow. Afterwards, a quick twist of its neck. He'd flinched as she told him.

'All meat's the same,' she said, seeing his response. 'Someone killed it. Mostly, nowhere near as kindly or painlessly as that.' She handed him the rabbit. It was limp, warm in his hands, a strangely comforting feel, as if even now there was life there, and all might be well – as though killing it had, indeed, been a kindness.

'And you'll forget all your qualms when you taste the pie,' she told him, and with only the smallest effort, he did.

The veranda, sparkling in the sun. Addie on the steps, face daubed with splashes of white: on her nose, in her hair, on his shirt that she still chose to wear like a dress, rather than her patched-up jeans and top.

'I found some paint in the outhouse,' she said, 'and some old brushes. They're not very good. But they're better than nothing. What do you think?'

'I think it's wonderful,' he said.

She'd stood back, admiring her own handiwork. 'I'm quite good at it, aren't I?'

'A true artist,' he agreed. 'I can tell.'

'A true helper, that's all. I used to paint our house. No one else would bother. Not my parents, definitely not my brothers, so it was either that or live in a slum. I used to scrounge paint from anywhere. Any colour, any amount. The house ended up like a kaleidoscope, all different colours.' She laughed at a memory, continued with the railings of the steps, the smile lingering on her lips, then said: 'I painted a mural once. Well, more graffiti than anything. Not quite Banksy. It was on the end wall, the one everyone could see from the road. Flowers and fields, and cows drinking from the river, and the sea. And birds – pukekos I think they were meant to be – strutting in the grass. Not representational stuff, but abstract – or as abstract as I could make anything at that age. My mum hit the roof. She wanted it all scrubbed off, repainted. She threatened me with everything she could think of. No tea. No pocket money. A beating from my dad when he got home. But I got really cross and defiant; I refused.'

'What happened?'

Again, she painted on, then shrugged. 'What always happens. What happened with you and your dog. The voice of authority wins. I had to paint it all over. It took me days. I hated them for that. I hated both of them.'

'What about you?' she would ask. 'How did you get on?' And he would tell her about the claim, and what he had found or what he hadn't, and try to describe for her the beauty of the place – so unlike the experience she had had of the rough mountains, the devouring bush.

Each time he told her, she was excited by what he said: the quantities of gold he had found, his expectations for the next trip. Yet in truth, it still wasn't much. The gold still seemed to elude him; tease him and vanish.

On the last of his trips, out of nostalgia or desperation, he'd moved downstream, to the very bottom of his concession. It was an area where logic always told him that he ought to start every trip, for it felt like the last chance saloon: one more flood and any gold there would be swept on, out of his reach. And he liked working there. It was a mysterious, cerebric place, dark and overhung. Mounds of clubmoss were like green brains in the undergrowth. The tree roots were crinkled veins. Overhead, the branches made dendrites, stretching out, touching, connecting. It seemed to think itself. On sunny days the light arrived in hazy and slanting slats; on misty days, it seemed to hang between the trees like a giant's breath.

And yet it was a difficult place to dredge. The stream was slow and sluggish and the channel often deep. It split, made islands, gravel bars, came together again in muddy pools. The pickings were often disappointing.

This year was no exception. A few tiny nuggets, a quarter of an ounce of finer flakes. For interest's sake, a few gems and minerals, too. It would pay for the diesel for the truck, the fuel for the pump. Not much more.

But still he contrived to hope, and his spirits remained high. The weather was good. The days were still long. He enjoyed his time there: the freedom, the solitude, the birdsong and the sounds of the bush at night. Wekas squawking, quails squabbling, frogs croaking, the trees exchanging stories of their long and arduous life. And there was plenty of claim yet left to explore.

'What have you found?' she asked this time, as he unpacked.

He told her and she gave a small yelp of congratulation. 'Clever boy.' Then: 'Show me,' she said.

'It's not very impressive.'

'Show me anyway.'

He agreed, and later selected some of his finds – not just gold, but other material he'd found, collected out of curiosity or whim, things he thought might interest her – and laid them out on the table. It seemed a meagre haul. Four small specimen boxes, two phials. He felt a wave of embarrassment, as though it belittled him – his skill as a prospector, the smallness of his passion.

Addie, though, seemed impressed. 'All these boxes?' she said. 'Is it all gold?'

He smiled. 'No. No, I'd be a bit more excited than this if it was.'

'So what are they? What's in that one?' She pointed at the largest box.

'Have a look.'

She gasped, as she looked inside. 'Diamonds?'

'No. Quartz crystals. That's all. Not worth anything. You find them all over the place.'

'They're lovely,' she said. 'They really look like diamonds. I'd buy them.'

'A couple of dollars, that's all.'

'Are you sure?'

He nodded, took the box back, selected another. 'And these came out, too. Here, use this.' He passed her a hand lens. She fumbled as she put it to her eye, and he leaned over, showed her how to use it.

'They're red,' she said. 'Rubies? Are they?'

'Garnets,' he said. 'Not valuable again, I'm afraid.'

She tipped one of the crystals on to her palm, tilting it slightly so that it caught the light. 'You could make me a ring with this one. Just a small one, to fit my pinkie.' Carefully, she put the crystal back in the box, returned it.

'This might be better.' He reached for another box, but kept it shut, taunting her. 'You won't often see this.'

'What is it?'

He opened the box, passed it to her. The stone in this one was larger – irregularly shaped, a swirling mixture of pink and turquoise, small patches of black, half a centimetre long. 'It's goodletite,' he said. She repeated the name, unconvinced, and he said: 'That's right. Named after a Mr Goodlet, who first found it, I think. That's got ruby in, sapphire, too. There's a little bit of tourmaline in it, as well – the black. It's rare. The only place it occurs is around here. Nowhere else in New Zealand. It's just the fourth one I've ever found.'

'Ruby, sapphire? This one must be worth something,' she said. 'You could make something out of this.'

'Maybe. It's not really gem quality, I'm afraid. It would break if you cut it.'

'It's lovely, just like this.' Then: 'And what about that one.' She pointed to the last box.

'Ah, that's even more special.' He picked it up, opened it with a flourish. Inside was a single pebble, greeny grey in colour, with a strange soapy sheen. 'This one's greenstone – nephrite. What's often called jade. Maori call it pounamu. It's pretty rare up here. Mostly it's found down on the beach – around Barrytown, for example. Have a look. Take it out.'

Tentatively, she did so, ran her finger over it, smiled, held it up to the light.

'I'd give it to you,' he said. 'If I could. If I'd found it on the beach I could have done so, but up here, you have to declare it, because it belongs to the Ngāi Tahu. So I'll hand it over to a Maori cutter I know, on the way out. Still, it feels special just to touch it, to hold it in your hand. Don't you think?'

She nodded. 'Yes. It's beautiful.'

He waited for her to hand it back, stowed it in the box, slipped on the lid.

'The gold's in those,' he said, pointing to the plastic phials. 'The small stuff in that one. An ounce or so. But this one's more interesting.' He picked up the second phial. 'Here. It's yours.'

She unscrewed the lid, peered in. 'A nugget?' she asked, then laughed. 'Fools' gold! I've heard of that. Just for people like me.'

'No. The genuine stuff. A real nugget. Only a little one, but again, you don't find them too often like that. It probably weighs a fifth of an ounce, a little less.'

'How did it get there?'

'The stream brought it. Where exactly it came from, I don't know. It's mainly placer gold around here, washed down thousands of years ago, or carried by glaciers.'

'What's it worth?'

'I don't know. Two hundred dollars maybe. No more.'

'Two hundred?' She thrust it back towards him, as though it were burning. 'You can't give me that.'

'I want to.'

'Why?'

'Because –' A fair question, he thought: why did he feel this need to gift her something? 'Because you've had a tough time, I suppose, and I wanted you to have something good to make it seem better.'

'You are making it feel better,' she said. 'Just by letting me be here, letting me stay. You don't know how good that is. You really don't.'

For a moment, they sat there, side-by-side, locked into what might have been hostility. Then he said: 'I like having you here, too.'

She looked down, as if chastened.

'I know,' she said. She reached out, took his hand. 'I know Evan. I know you're trying to help. I know that you want to make things better for me. But please, don't try too hard. I can't take too much kindness. I can't deal with it. It's not what I deserve.'

Six

Think of her differently, he'd told himself, as he worked on the claim. As a niece or a daughter, or the wife of a son or of a close friend. Someone he should care for, had responsibility for, could share intimacies with, yet to whom lust and sex did not apply.

Whether it was necessary, he wasn't sure. When he was with her, he knew that his eyes followed her more than they should, but he could still feel that he was in his own control. Out in the bush, it all seemed less ordered, more confused. Memories and stolen glimpses of her, his own longings and imaginings, jumbled together, crowded his thoughts. Anything seemed possible.

Why, what drew him, he couldn't say. Not her looks, he'd told himself; not the raw attraction of her body, for physically she seemed to him too stark, too thin. His taste for women was more old-fashioned than that; he preferred them with some flesh on them. And yet he watched her. He watched her as she sat with Viva, hugging the dog to her cheek, whispering words to her that he couldn't hear. He watched her as she wandered around the clearing, gathering flowers for the vases. He watched as she worked in the kitchen, slicing vegetables, chopping herbs, skinning a rabbit, filleting a trout – doing everything she could to make their meagre meals more interesting and wholesome. Sometimes, he watched her as she read, sitting on the sofa, legs curled beneath her, lips moving as she shaped the words in her mind; or as she lay there and slept, her bottom lip lightly gripped between her teeth, a tic at the corner of her eye twitching irregularly.

Partly, he could blame the way she dressed. Still, she seemed to prefer his shirts to her own jeans and top. She wandered about in them loosely, bare-footed, bare-legged, looking elfin, mischievous – a sly gamin. And she moved in the way a gamin would, slipping silently, silkily from one place to another, so that he never knew quite where she was, where she would appear next.

For that reason, he sometimes caught unintended glimpses of her. In a moment of abstraction as she stood in the kitchen, deep in thought. A brief panic, as she batted wildly at a wasp. Sudden compassion, as she stooped to pick up an injured fledgling from the veranda. A bare foot, a leg, a thigh. The dark tuft of unshaved hair beneath an upraised arm.

When they happened, they felt innocent, natural – the fortuitous sights and sounds of life lived with someone else. Yet when he thought back on them, they disturbed him, and he wondered just how much chance had been involved. Whether he was being voyeuristic, engineering them; whether he could trust himself any more. How to protect her from himself.

His pretence had been the answer. Shape her as something else. Someone he cannot touch.

Yet now, as he drove back, he wondered again: was it necessary?

Didn't he want to touch her? And why not?

He was a man, after all, and she was a woman. And he'd not had a woman in his life for far too long.

*

She greeted him with food again. She seemed to know that it was the proper language between them, affection in its safest form.

She'd been collecting mushrooms, she told him as she ordered him to the table, served him with a glass of red wine. There were horse mushrooms in the clearing, she called from the kitchen; morels as well. 'Have you ever eaten them?'

'Not knowingly.'

'You'd know,' she said. 'They're delicious.'

She brought the meal in: mushroom risotto, rich with herbs, laced with red wine. She picked out a mushroom, held it out. 'This one's a morel,' she said. 'Try it.'

He looked at it dubiously. The stem was pale, the cap dark, honeycombed where she had sliced it lengthways. She saw his doubts and laughed. 'It's alright. It's edible. I ate some while you were away – and I'm still standing, aren't I?'

Tentatively, he nibbled it from her fingers. The taste was strong, earthy, almost meaty.

She took it away, popped the rest in her mouth.

'Good?' she asked, and he nodded, though in truth he still wasn't sure.

'There aren't many in it,' she said. 'But enough to make it interesting.'

She was right. A complex of flavours he couldn't quite pin down, but which grew on him as he ate, so that he all but licked the plate clean.

While he ate, he told her about his prospecting. As he'd prepared to leave for the claim, Addie had leaned through the window of the truck, pinched his arm, told him: 'That's for luck.' It seemed to have worked. The gold was coming at last. He'd been dredging a thin bar of gravel, from a rocky section of the stream, not far from where he'd found her. It was a tricky area, in a small loop of channel, that only carried water in flood. The gravel was coarse and cobbly, and between the cobbles was a maze of fibrous tree roots. He spent most of his time clearing large stones from the nozzle of the dredge or unclogging vegetation from the hose. But it had been worth the effort. He'd found half a dozen small nuggets, a quarter of an ounce of grains. It would bring in almost a thousand dollars when he sold it. The claim was yielding its treasures at last.

When she picked up the plates, went into the kitchen, his eyes followed her, as if seeking some claim of their own.

He watched her as she moved around with that languid stride, her bare feet, padding firmly across the floor. The stretch of her legs as she bent at the stove, to pick up the dish. He watched her return.

She held up the dish, as if in triumph. 'Just for you,' she said. 'Plum crumble. My special recipe, with a touch of thyme. And this one comes with a guarantee not to poison you.'

He laughed, raised his glass and toasted her, and for a moment, their eyes met.

'To us,' he said. 'To the luck you've brought me.'

They touched glasses, drank.

'I've a toast, too,' she said. 'To good hunting, good food.' Again, they toasted. 'Talking of which,' she continued, as she sat down, tasted the crumble, nodded in approval, 'I've found something that might help.'

He asked her what she meant.

'While I was tidying up the outhouse. An old rifle. Did you know it was there?'

'No. It must have been my father's.'

'Did he shoot?'

He hesitated, thinking: another discovery, even after all this time. Will he never cease to surprise me, scorn me for my ignorance?

'I've no idea,' he said. 'I didn't know him that well.'

She nodded: 'Yes. I'm beginning to realise that.' She glanced at the mantelpiece, where the clock still steadfastly refused to tell the right time. 'Anyway, let's hope that it's more reliable than some of his other possessions.'

'Reliable? You want to use it?'

'I don't see why not. It looks good. If I shooed the spiders out, oiled it, I think it would work fine. We could shoot rabbits then. Much easier than snaring them.'

'Can you shoot?'

'Of course. I told you. All farmers' kids can. It's in our blood.'

'Anyway,' he said. 'We'd need ammunition, and a licence, and we haven't got either.'

She glanced at him, smiled: 'Oh, I forgot. Not allowed.'

*

The next morning, she had changed. She woke late, arrived in the kitchen looking wan, pained. Evan was immediately concerned. 'Are you alright? It's not those mushrooms, is it?'

She shook her head. 'No. It's just – just me.'

'What?'

'You know. Time of the month. I've been waiting for it.'

'Ah –' And he didn't know what else to say.

'I'm not used to it, not really prepared. I've been on the pill for years. I feel like shit. I'm sorry.'

'I've got paracetamol,' he said, then stopped, realising the other implications of her news. 'Do you need anything; do you want to go to town?'

'It's alright. I can manage. I'm improvising.'

'I can take you,' he said. 'I have to go soon anyway, to get some more supplies.'

She grimaced, apologised – assuming the blame for eating all his food.

'Not really,' he told her. 'And either way, I've got to go. It might as well be today. We could buy you some clothes as well.' He grinned. 'Maybe I'd get my shirts back then.'

And so it was decided. Yet when he invited her to get ready, she shook her head and said she'd rather stay. 'I feel lousy. Maybe I'll just curl up in bed. I'm sorry.'

He offered to delay the journey, tried to persuade her that a trip to town would do her good – that she could go to the bank and the police if she wanted and sort out about her lost backpack.

'I've told you,' she said, irritation in her voice. 'Stop worrying about my pack. The only thing important was my pills.'

Instead, she gave him a list. Reading it, he realised how out of touch he was with women – their bodies, their needs. As well as tampons, some obvious clothes, there were cosmetics that he'd never have thought necessary out here: shampoo, conditioner, hair dye, hair remover, eye-liner.

'Don't embarrass yourself,' she said. 'Just give the list to the shop assistant and let her choose.'

He agreed, though he felt embarrassed already.

'You could get some cartridges as well,' she said. 'For that rifle.'

He shook his head. 'No. I've told you. I've no licence, and anyway, it probably doesn't work.'

As he was leaving, she caught his arm, thanked him, apologised for her mood – 'I really do feel crap' – looked away. 'One other thing, though. Don't talk about me, please. Don't mention that I'm here.'

'Why on earth not?'

'Because my boyfriend might find out, and come after me.' She saw the doubt in his look, and went on: 'I know that doesn't sound likely, but it's like that in a rural area such as this. Everyone knows everyone else. They know their business. Word gets round. And I'm not ready for him yet. I'm not sure what to do; I'd probably make the wrong choice.'

He was still not convinced: wasn't that what she'd wanted, when she set out – that he'd follow her, try to win her back? Then a different emotion gripped him – jealousy or something like it, possessiveness.

'Don't worry,' he assured her. 'I won't say a word.'

*

'Enough here to feed an army,' the woman at the checkout commented, as he stacked his purchases on the conveyor.

In Greymouth, he'd found a supermarket, toured it, piling up his trolley. To his own unwritten list of staples – more rice, pasta, potatoes, onions, oats, coffee – Addie had added a longer written one of her own, hinting at the meals that she had in mind for them both: fresh vegetables (carrots, pumpkin, kumara, parsnip), couscous, garlic, flour, dried fruit. He put in half a dozen bottles of wine as well, a dozen-pack of Speight's.

'Looks like that,' he said. Then he remembered. 'I've forgotten something. I'll be back in a moment.' And he dashed off to the clothing section, selected a mixed pack of women's pants and two bras.

'That should keep the navy going as well,' the woman said.

He went to the pharmacy, handed over Addie's list, asked the shop assistant to choose what she thought was appropriate and added, unnecessarily: 'It's for a friend.'

As he left, he saw a small clothing store across the road with a display of women's tops outside. He flicked along the racks, looking for something that might be appropriate for her. The storekeeper came out, asked if he needed help. 'For my daughter,' he said, improvising. 'Just something casual.'

'What size?'

He shrugged. 'Small. She's petite.'

'Ten?' the woman asked. 'How about this?'

She took down a blouse. It was bright green, sleeveless, low at the neck.

'A bit less bright?' he said. 'Maybe more – well, modest.'

'How old is she?'

'Twenty-five.'

'Married?'

'No.'

'Not too modest, then.'

Eventually, he let the woman choose, took two tops, a pair of shorts to match. For the amount of material in them, they seemed to cost a lot, but he paid with a smile. Fashion, he guessed, came at a price even out in the bush.

Finally, exhausted by the whole performance, he found a café, had lunch. The only newspaper available was the back section of

The Star. He took that, read the sports and financial news as he ate. The price of gold had risen again, he saw. Good news – if he could find enough for it to matter.

As he went to the door, he saw the rest of the paper, abandoned on a table, swivelled it round to catch the headlines. *Police spread net wider* the main headline said, and then beside it, a photograph and another article: *Toddler found safe and well.* It was the missing child in Westport that the trampers had mentioned. She'd been discovered, it seemed, with a relation, in a caravan near Haast. There were hidden undercurrents in it all, Evan guessed – of paternity or familial rivalries, or something more wretched – but for the moment, the story seemed to have found a happy ending. One piece of death and destruction avoided, at least.

*

He heard the pop of the guns first. He thought it was the engine misfiring, wound down the window to listen. But the sounds were coming from ahead of him, where the cottage stood.

He rounded the corner, into the clearing, and saw the vehicles, the men.

The cottage looked as if it were under siege. Utes and trucks, trailers and quad-bikes, scattered across the grass. A Humvee, in camouflaged greens and browns, parked in the middle, doors wide open as if it had been abandoned in a hurry. Half a dozen men, grouped together in the lee of the outhouse, in earnest conversation.

The cottage was shut up, the curtains drawn. There was no sign of Viva.

There was another burst of gunfire from the broom and gorse at the edge of the bush.

Evan drew to a halt, leapt out, looked around.

'Evan, my friend.' A man detached himself from the group, came across. He was tall, stooped as he walked. His hair was thin, combed backwards; he wore glasses, looked like a university professor – if people looked like their professions any more. He was, instead, a Swedish butcher, and given the money he'd admitted earning, presumably a good one.

'Klas!'

They shook hands, exchanged a brief, manly hug.

'We're here,' he said, simply. 'Well, most of us are. We're one man – and the dogs – short.'

'I'd forgotten you were coming.'

'So your daughter said.'

'My daughter?'

'Addie – is that her name? We talked to her when we arrived. We scared her a little, I think, turning up like we did, unannounced. She thought we were taking the place over.' He laughed. 'She tried to send us away, but when I explained, she agreed we could stay. She said it was just like you to forget to warn her.'

Evan shook his head, struggling for the words to say – to correct Klas's misapprehension. But Klas continued: 'Since you never told me you had a daughter, I was glad she introduced herself. I thought she must be your, what shall I call it – your lucky strike.' He punched Evan lightly on the chest. 'That would be good for you, too, a woman around. But perhaps this is better. A daughter coming home after all these years.'

Evan smiled, confused, silenced by events that had somehow parodied his earlier, inner conceit.

Klas looked around. 'Some of the boys are down in the scrub, as you can hear, after rabbits. The others are putting up the tents. There are twelve of us this year – or there will be when Gordon and the dogs catch up. He's been delayed by work. He'll be here on Monday. If it is alright, we would like to stay until then.'

'Of course. You know you're welcome. You always are.'

Klas and his party were regular visitors, had rights to the place going back longer than his own. When he first encountered them, Evan had challenged them, much as Addie had: 'What are you doing here? What do you want?'

'The same as every year,' Klas had said, amicably. 'A place to camp. A friendly welcome – like your father used to give.'

The words had shamed him, and he'd apologised, but Klas had waved the embarrassment away. 'No. I could see that you were his son. I knew that you would have his nature.'

They were down from Auckland, Klas had continued in explanation, on their annual trip. They'd been coming for years, and had got to know his father well: he was always kind, accommodating. They always camped by the cottage for a night or two on their way in.

They were an eclectic group, Evan had soon learned, changing each year, with nothing in common but their home city and their enjoyment of hunting. Young and old. Pakeha, Maori, occasionally Islanders and Asians, too. Businessmen, craftsmen, artists, labourers. In some years even a woman or two.

He had soon discovered that these weren't the only transients to whom his father had given visiting rights. During that first year, a succession of groups passed through on their way into the hills: hunters after pigs or goats or deer, sometimes chamois; trampers trying to get off the well worn paths, geologists or botanists or bird-watchers out to find something they'd never seen before. Some were regulars, like Klas and his gang; others were ad hoc groups who got together for a trip, asked around, were told that the hunting or the walking or nature was good in the hills north of here, and that if they did go, they should call in at Dafydd Cadwallader's house on the way. To the world outside, Evan thought, it was still that, his father's house; probably it always would be. They came, he knew, even when he wasn't there. He'd see the evidence when he first arrived: a circle of charred stones where the fire had been, tracks in the grass where a ute had got stuck, sometimes a scatter of beer cans or other litter that those less practised in back-country ways had left. As often as not, a twenty- or fifty-dollar bill tucked beneath the door as anonymous payment.

'So where's Addie?' he asked.

Klas nodded towards the cottage. 'In there. Sleeping, I think. She said she had a migraine.'

Later, when Klas had left to join his party, he went to her room, knocked. She answered dully, words he couldn't hear, and he called through the door: 'I've brought you your things.'

'Thank you. Just leave them there.'

'Are you alright?' he asked.

'Migraine. Tired. That's all. I'll be OK.'

'I'm sorry about the hunters,' he said. 'I forgot them.'

There was a mumbled response: 'no worries', or 'it doesn't matter', something like that. He left her packages, tiptoed away.

In the evening, as always while Klas and his group were staying, there was a barbecue in the field. It all seemed to happen spontaneously, almost by magic. A fire was suddenly lit, a pile of wood beside it. Logs appeared for seats, and impromptu tables from the tailgates of the utes. Then a pile of beer-crates, a ghetto-blaster playing rock songs from the seventies and eighties. The air filled with the bittersweet scent of sizzling fat. Smoke wreathed the clearing.

Evan joined the men beside the fire, accepted a can of beer, a sausage almost too hot to hold. Klas came and sat beside him.

'So is your daughter still unwell?'

'It seems so.' He grimaced. 'You know how it is with women.' It was meant to be solicitous, sounded dismissive. 'Still, they make a better fist of it than any man would.'

Klas nodded. 'That's true.' He looked around. 'But I hope that we don't disturb her. The boys can be a little enthusiastic at times – especially on the first night. No wives or girlfriends to keep them in order.' Then he said: 'You must be pleased to see her, after all this time.'

It took Evan a moment to understand what he meant, and to find a reply: 'Yes. Yes I am.'

'It happens with children these days, doesn't it? They come, they go. You never really know where they will be, when they will turn up. The good thing, I suppose, is that they come back.'

Evan nodded, feeling uncomfortable. How easy it was, he thought, to dissimulate, to add to the deceit, without ever actually lying.

To change the subject, he asked about Klas's plans: where his group would be hunting, how long they'd be here. Who Klas thought would win the competition, this year, for the most kills. It was another question that discomforted him, for as he'd admitted to Addie, he was squeamish when it came to killing animals – wild ones especially. But he knew how seriously they took the challenge to outshoot each other, piling the carcasses up.

'Young Todd, I think,' Klas said, indicating one of the men by the fire a languid, louche man, with broad shoulders, large hands. 'He pretends to be a tearaway, but he has a good eye when he wants to use it. If not him, it will be Marty. He's steady; he takes it seriously. He doesn't like to be beaten.'

They talked about hunting and prospecting – the similarities and the differences. They were both quests; why didn't those who pursued the two sports have more in common, Evan mused – why did prospectors and hunters seem to be different breeds?

'Are we?' Klas asked.

'I think so, for all that we play in the same wild places. To me, it seems that hunting is a team sport; prospectors like to do it on their own.'

'Food makes you friendly,' Klas suggested. 'Gold makes you mean. Do you think that might be the difference?'

Evan nodded. 'The latter seems true, sometimes, I admit. I even feel it in myself – you know, miserliness. A possessiveness about the claim.' He thought about Addie, his response to her when she had talked about her boyfriend. 'About other things, too. I don't like it.'

They were still discussing the matter, waxing increasingly metaphysical as the beer flowed and the food kept coming, when the mood in the clearing seemed to change. A sudden tension had emerged, a small sense of expectation.

The focus of it was associated with three of the men by the fire. They stood in a half circle, beer cans loose in their hands, bodies leaned in slightly, as if drawn together by an invisible magnetism. They were talking, laughing, not only to this unseen focus of their attention, but against each other, as if in rivalry. They shuffled, swayed, posed, like cock birds vying for a mate. Others were watching, smiling at the scene. Klas leaned towards Evan, nudged his arm.

'Your daughter's joined us, I see. I'm glad. Perhaps she's feeling better now.'

The men by the fire moved slightly, stepping apart, as if to separate themselves more clearly. Addie stood, facing them. At least, he knew it was Addie. She stood like Addie, she had her build, her features. But it did not look like her.

For a moment, he thought it was just the trick of the flickering light. Shadow and fire. Turning her hair from black to different shades of gold and brown: iron, auburn, burned ochre. Drawing it like a curtain across her face, so that it half hid one side. Deepening her eyes into peaty pools of darkness. Making her skin shine. Changing, too, her body – her waist narrowed, hips made stronger, bust raised. Her bare legs made long.

Then he realised, it was not the fire that had transformed her, but what he had done – the purchases he'd made. She'd dyed her hair, put on eyeshadow and blusher, was wearing the clothes he'd chosen for her.

She was transformed, indeed. She looked doll-like and synthetic – and he didn't like it.

The three young men most certainly did.

*

Over the next hour, Evan watched Addie from afar. He watched her as she performed – for that is what her behaviour seemed to imply: a performance, an act. Strolling around, carrying her small entourage of admirers in her wake, playing one against the other, teasing them, flirting, eyes darting first to that one, then the next, then into the fire in silent contemplation. As she reached out with a hand, to touch an arm, lay her hand on a back. A giggle, a shrug. Then moving away to talk to one of the older men, no doubt sparking new dreams and more imaginings. He watched with a sense of growing unease. Like a real father, he thought more than once, or a jealous suitor, and chided himself for the notion, blamed it on the beers for making him not just drunk but maudlin.

But he felt himself flush with pleasure when she came to him, stood beside him, her shoulder close. He laughed when she told him about Jimmy, only seventeen and already smitten: 'Silly boy.' He let her stroke his arm lightly, as she thanked him for what he'd bought her – 'It's made me feel like a woman again' – and had to resist touching the place her hand had been when she left his side; felt abandoned once more, when she did not soon return.

And later, as the party gradually subsided into a gentler, more contemplative mood, and the radio was turned off, and a guitar brought out, passed around for a few inexpert tunes, he called out: 'Addie can play. She used to be in a band. Let her have a go.'

He called for reasons he'd rather not have admitted, not honourable ones. Not out of fatherly pride. He called because her claim of daughtership had unsettled him, as if it had been a jibe. He called to get her away from the attentions of the men, and because he knew that she would not wish it: would not want to leave their attentions, would not want to play, would not want to be exposed there, centre stage, not in this way anyway, with all the men focusing their collective thoughts on her, their imagination. She preferred them singly, or in competition, one balancing out the other, so that she held them in her hand. He called out of jealousy.

That at least, is what he thought, or had made himself think. What seemed to explain his calling.

At first, she refused, as he'd known she would. But weight of numbers soon prevailed – the cries of encouragement, demand, the whistles – and she took the guitar, strummed it for a while, bent over it, frowning, as if in despair at the quality of the instrument, then all of a sudden slipped into a dark and unsettled song – the guitar chords rumbling, thrumming, like a storm that could not develop, an epiphany that would not come, her voice gravelly and almost untuneful, the words rolling into each other so that they had no meaning other than a deep sense of desperation and doom. Until, without a pause, the tempo changed, and she was playing something light, taunting – half Irish jig, half barcarole. The music danced away into the darkness, carried on the smoke that billowed from the fire, by the shadows that the flames made, on the wings of unseen owls, on the unfelt breeze. It was primordial, organic. It seemed at one with the place and the night.

Evan found Klas beside him again. 'She plays well,' he said. 'But she is a chameleon, your daughter. She changes colours with a click of her fingers, a flick of her head. Though whether to hide or be seen, I cannot tell.'

He, too, was drunk, Evan thought. Alcohol always turned him into yet one more moralist and philosopher.

Addie played two or three more songs, complex rhythms without words, in which one melody seemed to vie and toy with another, as if trying to resolve some ancient debate. Evan suspected that they weren't tunes at all, just improvisations that her fingers made as her mind roamed in some place where she was alone. They had the effect that she perhaps wanted, for the men turned aside and began their talking again, or just stood, silently watching.

Then he noticed that the music had stopped and she'd slipped away. Soon afterwards, he went too, and lay in his room trying to rid himself of the strange altercation that was still ringing in his thoughts, those two different yet entangled versions of the world: young, old; falsehood, truth; daughter, lover. For everything, he thought, brought its opposite.

Seven

Addie said: 'He's found lots. Gems, gold. You ought to see the stuff.'

She was trying to help, he knew – to compensate for deserting him all day, perhaps to demonstrate her loyalty. But she was making it worse.

He'd hardly seen her since the previous night. At first he thought she was in her room, sleeping late, and left her to her slumbers. When she still did not appear, he worried that she was ill, and went to her room, knocked on the door. There was no answer. He knocked again, called: 'Addie.'

Still she did not respond.

He'd opened the door cautiously, afraid of what he'd find – not just Addie, but a man, too? There was no one there. But the bed appeared to have been slept in, the sheet and blanket thrown back as if she had woken and pushed them aside; the shorts and top she'd been wearing at the party discarded on the bed. A book that she'd borrowed from him – landscape poems by Brian Turner – lay splayed open, face down on the floor. On the windowsill, the makeshift vase filled with flowers, drooping now. It had seemed like a message, just to him. He closed the door, went out.

From the veranda, he heard her voice, scoured the clearing with his eyes shaded against the sun before he saw her. She was standing by the outhouse with Todd and Jimmy. Even from a distance he could read what was happening, the contest that was taking place: Todd leaned against the wall, the picture of easy charm; Jimmy, brimming with young ambition, trying to catch her eye. Addie seemed to be enjoying it, playing them each along.

At lunchtime, he searched for her again, but could not find her. He counted up the men: Jimmy was there but Todd was missing. He asked Jimmy if he knew where she was, received a moody shrug in response. Klas didn't know either, and smiled at Evan's evident concern.

'Don't worry so much,' he said. 'I know you haven't seen her for a long time, but she needs to have some fun. Let her enjoy herself. I'm sure she'll come to no harm.'

He was right, Evan had told himself. She's a free agent, a grown-up woman; not your property. Not your daughter at all. Yet somehow his admonishments made him feel worse, not better. He ate alone, warmed up leftovers of beans and ham he found in the fridge.

Then Addie came in. She had the rifle in her hand, was flushed and excited. 'Look,' she said. 'We've been in the shed. Todd helped me get the rifle working. We've stripped it down, cleaned it, oiled it. We've adjusted the sights. He's given me some ammunition. We're going to take it out this afternoon and give it a try.' She laughed. 'He bet me I can't hit a can at twenty paces. He doesn't know me!'

'Just be careful,' he said, and thought: the father's prayer.

'I will be.' She turned to go, stopped, grinned. 'I'll bring you back a rabbit.'

Throughout the afternoon, he heard the pop and bang of gunfire from the other side of the clearing, or in the bush. Each shot made him tense, thinking: has someone been hit? Then he yearned to hear the next shot, to know that they hadn't.

Now, the whole group had gathered on the veranda. The weather had changed: showers, a cool breeze. It had brought them all back from whatever diversions they'd been pursuing. Todd and Addie had returned each with a brace of rabbits.

'That one's for Evan,' Addie had said, pointing to the biggest. 'I promised.'

She had won her bet, too, peppering the beer cans, not just at twenty paces but fifty and beyond. She'd brought a can back to show. The men were impressed: 'She's a real pro,' Marty had said. 'Heaven help anyone in her sights.'

Perhaps as a consequence, no one wanting to be outdone, the chatter had become combative. The men boasted in turn about their shooting prowess, about how many reds they'd claim this year, or how many pigs they'd be taking home; exchanged banter about previous trips, and how others had made fools of themselves; argued about which were the best guns or knives or boots.

Then someone said: 'We should take the young lady with us. She might teach some of you a thing or two.'

'I look forward to that,' Todd said, and they all laughed.

Addie shook her head. She couldn't possibly go; she had no clothes. Bringing a leer from Todd, the obvious riposte: this is sounding better and better.

Someone else suggested that Evan come along, too, and when he declined, that led to another debate – about which was more rewarding, hunting or prospecting. It was the antithesis of the quieter, reflective discussion he and Klas had had the previous evening. Scornful, confrontational. Todd jeered at Evan, trying to provoke him to defend his sport: how could it be fun when the stuff just sat there waiting to be found; and what skill was there in it, when it was all just luck? Evan refused to be drawn, said passively: 'Different folk like different things.'

'Fuck me,' Todd, said, 'You're not one of those, are you?' Earning more laughter.

Then another jibe – about how much money one could make hunting. Thousands of dollars on a trip. Could he ever match that?

He had shrugged. 'Sometimes.'

'What's your best?'

Another shrug. 'For one trip? About five K, I guess.'

'Five thousand dollars? Bullshit. I bet you never have.'

'You don't have to believe me.'

'So what have you found this year?'

'It's early days,' Evan said.

'Oh – you mean nothing, then. Just dirt.'

'A little more than that.'

He had hoped that would be an end to it, that they would change the subject. Instead, Addie had stepped in, her voice hard and defiant.

'You should believe him. He's shown me some of it. He's found lots. Gems, gold. You ought to see the stuff.'

Now, the men regarded her, silent. Addie glared back.

'You don't realise what gold is worth,' she said. 'Just one little nugget fetches hundreds. He wanted to give me one.'

The silence deepened, became what might have been embarrassment, a smirk or two at what it seemed to say about their relationship. But Addie didn't seem to notice. She turned to him: 'Go on. Show them.'

Evan tried to refuse, but at once the clamour started. Just as Addie had found when he'd challenged her to play the guitar the night before, it was impossible to deny. Reluctantly, he went to his room, pulled out the box-safe from under his bed. For a moment, he stood there, caught in the grip of the dilemma: what to take, how much to show? Too little, and he'd simply fuel their ridicule; too much, and who knows what jealousies and wild notions he might spark?

He took the whole box.

'Is that it?' Todd demanded, as he returned. 'All of it?'

'I'm afraid so.'

'Show them,' Addie said. 'Show them the nuggets. Show them the new ones you've found.'

He took out one of the sample tubes, held it up for them to see.

'It's not much.' Jimmy said, disappointment in his voice. 'It can't be worth more than a few dollars.'

'I guess it depends what you mean by a few. There's probably an ounce there. So fifteen hundred at today's prices.'

Jimmy was impressed. 'Christ! I wish pigs were made of gold.'

'They're beautiful as well,' Addie said. 'Much nicer than your pigs.' She took the tube, toured it round the group, showing them. Todd peered at it, as if he couldn't quite see. Then with a quick move, he snatched it from her, hid it in his hand.

'Gold?' he said. 'What gold?'

She asked for it back, but he shook his head.

She stood, scowling at him. 'Prick,' she said.

'Rich prick now, though.'

He opened his hand, taunting her. She made a grab for it, but he closed his fist tight shut again, laughed as she tried to peel it open. She dug her nails in.

He gripped her wrist, holding her at bay.

For a moment, there was stalemate. Addie looked wild, angry; Todd smiled back at her, innocent and mocking.

'Let her have it,' Klas instructed, his voice quiet, insistent.

'I'd love to,' Todd said, eyes on her.

But he relaxed his grip, opened his hand.

'Thank you,' Addie said.

'Any time.'

She returned the tube to Evan, apologised.

As she turned away he caught her expression. She looked humiliated, distraught. He wanted to call her back, talk to her, tell her that it didn't matter but knew that he couldn't. Soon afterwards, she slipped away.

Yet by the evening, as they ate from the barbecue, all seemed friendly and good-humoured again. Addie had reappeared, dressed in the second top he'd bought her – more demure than the previous evening, he was glad to see, its neckline less revealing, looser across her breast. Her face, too, was made up less provocatively, her hair tied back, elegant rather than coquettish. But she was welcomed as enthusiastically as before, with a wolf-whistle, a cheer.

She returned the greeting with a small bow and a smile, talked briefly to Jimmy and Marty, then went across to Todd. She stood in front of him, looking tiny against his tall frame. But her body was taut, whip-like, her eyes bright and when she spoke to him, he looked down, as if sheepish, and nodded. An apology? If so, well deserved.

Now, the two of them sat together on the grass, chatting, laughing, their bodies close. Friendship restored, it seemed.

Evan moved away, sat in his chair on the veranda, Viva at his side. Young people, he thought, ruefully: they had an advantage, seemed to skate more easily across the surface of life than he did. They did not snag in the same way. With him, Todd's earlier behaviour still rankled, had left him feeling surly and sour. For Addie, the annoyance had been brief, was easily forgiven.

His thoughts drifted. The claim, the gold, the next trip. Addie's pretence that she was his daughter. All the questions she provoked; the strange web of ambiguity that she seemed to weave about her.

Klas's words: like a chameleon. Always changing.

So many questions that he wanted to ask. He yearned to be alone with her, just to talk, to understand. To know her properly.

'I've brought you some food.'

He looked up. Addie stood there, a plate in her hand.

'It's as wholesome as I could make it with what's on offer. I've added some salad.'

He took the plate, thanked her.

'You don't join in much,' she said. 'You've been sitting here brooding for the last hour, now.' She perched on the arm of the chair. 'Don't you like parties?'

'I'm happy.'

'You don't look it.'

'I enjoy just watching,' he said.

'Of course,' she said. 'Keeping your distance.' She regarded him steadily, and he wondered what message he was meant to be reading: daughterly affection or womanly disdain?

'Anyway, it's good to see you having fun,' he said. 'I was worried at first, yesterday, when I got home.'

It was intended to be an invitation, for her to explain herself, her claim to be his daughter, but she seemed to miss the deeper meaning.

'I've you to thank for that. The clothes you bought me, the make-up and everything. It's good to feel human again. I feel like a changed woman.'

'You look good,' he told her, and this evening it was almost true. The clothes suited her. He liked the way she'd tied her hair, the way now a strand hung loose, though the colour still worried him: he preferred its natural black. 'But changed, yes. I hardly recognised you at first.'

She smiled. 'I'm glad of that. You'd not exactly seen me at my best.' Then she looked down, smoothing a finger over her hand. 'I've a favour to ask. Another one. Some of the boys want to take me out hunting tomorrow. I said I'd go, if I could find some gear. Jimmy's already said he'd lend me his spare coat: he's the smallest, and the poor boy was so pleased to help; he blushed like a beetroot when I asked him. I guess my trainers and jeans will be fine. But I need to take a sleeping bag. Can I borrow yours?'

'You're staying out?'

'Just for one night. They'll lend me a tent. I told them I wasn't sharing.' She grinned. 'I think that's what they were hoping. Do you mind?'

'Why should I mind?' It was said stiffly.

'Todd thought you might. I think he sees you as the doting father.' She grinned.

'That's something we need to talk about.'

Again, by either accident or design, she seemed to misunderstand. 'Todd's alright,' she said. Then, smiling, winsome: 'So can I?'

'What – take the sleeping bag? Of course.' Still there was stiffness in his voice, and he tried to disguise it with further generosity. 'You can use my pack as well if you like. And take a jumper; it will be cold at night.'

'Thanks.' She slipped off the chair, seemed about to go.

'And take care,' he said.

She paused, regarded him gently. 'Don't worry, Evan. I'll be fine. Marty's coming as well – to chaperone us I think.' She laughed. 'Todd needs a chaperone.'

She touched his arm, let her fingers linger there as she turned.

But as they prepared to leave the next morning, he couldn't help repeating the advice: take care.

*

They had the place to themselves now. They sat together outside Klas's tent, enjoying the sudden silence and stillness, drinking, chatting about old times.

Gordon and the dogs had turned up soon after Addie and her small hunting party had left. For a brief hour the clearing had been filled with a cacophony of yaps and barks. But then, they had left again – the whole group this time, off to reconnoitre the land up on the hills, blood the dogs. They had taken the Humvee, were no doubt having fun somewhere, following the dogs; charging through scrub and peatbogs and mires, bouncing over the rocks, slithering their way up muddy slopes, trying to take the vehicle beyond its limits. What happened if they did – if they rolled it or got it stuck – Evan wasn't sure. But Klas seemed unworried; no one had managed to do so yet. He seemed to have more faith in the Humvee than their driving.

'Do you think they'll be alright?' Evan asked.

'I've told you. You can do anything in that Humvee.'

'No, I mean Addie. She's never been hunting before. Not in country like this, anyway. And Todd and Jimmy, too. Neither of them is very experienced.'

'She'll be fine. Jimmy's green but he's got a good head on his shoulders, and Todd's not as crazy as he pretends. In any case, Marty will make sure they behave.'

Evan nodded, but the doubt remained, and he couldn't contain it. 'I just worry about her with that rifle,' he said. 'I know that she's a good shot. But it's different in the bush. It's so easy to have an accident.'

'She'll be alright, I'm sure.'

They talked for a while about firearms accidents, the ways they seemed to happen. Pure foolishness, mainly, not even deserving the title of accident. And whatever might be said, always the shooter's fault. There was no excuse. People not thinking, not checking, being too trigger happy. All you had to do, Klas argued, was live by the simple rule: don't shoot unless you're 100 per cent sure.

He'd sent men home early from his trips before now, he said, because they wouldn't abide by that rule. He told them at the beginning, never gave them a second chance. Whatever they shot at – a bird, a dog, or nothing at all – if it wasn't a legitimate target, they were out.

The subject found its own end, in silent reflection. Evan gazed out, across the clearing, up towards the saddle, the mountains beyond. The thought of his claim, waiting there, unattended, nagged at him. The thought of Addie somewhere in the hills behind him, with Todd, tugged in opposition. He felt caught in the small space between, the fulcrum on which the world was balanced. Which way, he wondered, did his real desire lay?

'Look.' Klas touched his arm, pointed.

At first, Evan could see nothing of note. Just the grass, scribbled over by rabbit-runs, etched more deeply here and there by the wheels of the trucks; the backdrop of the trees at the edge of the bush. But then, twenty metres away, amidst the dappling shadows of the ferns, he caught a movement. A deer, a young hind. Her coat glowed bronze against the greens and blacks of the enclosing trees, seemed to tremble where the sunlight touched it.

He had seen deer in the clearing before, though usually amidst the mist and glinting sunlight of early morning, or like a ghostly presence at dusk, and rarely now, in the summer, when the herds gathered on the open tops. He wondered what had brought the hind here, felt a stab of gratitude at the thought that it might be to her good fortune, might preserve her from the hunters' guns.

He glanced at Klas. He was as rapt as Evan was. Did he share the same sense of privilege?

The deer moved slightly, raised her head, testing the air. The world seemed to freeze to stillness and silence, holding itself for whatever decision she made. To come or to go.

He imagined the same scene, being played out now, up on the hills, but with a different audience, a different end. The hunters crouched, ready. Addie's finger on the trigger.

Would she take the shot? Did she have that in her?

She'd proved it, with rabbit and trout. Could she do the same with a beast as sentient and regal as this? He hoped not.

And then he saw another movement. A small flash of white. The hind had a fawn with her, tucked against her flank. It twitched again, and he could see its outline, the lines of pale spots on its side.

He thought again of Addie. At least now, she would not shoot.

The nostrils of the hind flared, her ears bristled. Then she kicked, and in a moment seemed to dissolve from sight, the fawn with her. Brown hides melting into shades of green, white to sunspots, flick and flash of ears and nose and eyes to shivering leaves.

'Magic,' Klas said. 'Don't you think?'

He wanted to ask: why do you shoot them, then; why do you make a sport of the act? But he had asked the question before, knew the answer he would get. Because, in truth, deer are pests and in too large a number cause so much damage to the land; because hunting is the kindest means of control; because the killing, for the purpose of the meat, at least gives some value to the necessary death. And as for the enjoyment of the sport, why not take pleasure in the beast alive, the special intimacy of the culling, the meal to come?

He had heard the arguments, and knew that they had reason to them, were difficult to refute. Yet he could not bring himself to accept them, all the same. There had to be another way.

Perhaps to break the moment, the small and unspoken tension between them, Klas opened another beer, passed it across. 'Tell me about your life,' he said. 'The one when you are at home.'

'Home?' he asked. 'Where's that? I live where I am. I don't have deep roots.'

'Your other home, then,' Klas said. 'Your winter home.'

It took an effort to think about it, to stretch his mind that far. Away from this glade, this view, the forest and the mountains, the high dome of sky. Christchurch, his life there, seemed so implausible, so alien. It was the counterpart to this world here, was what made it possible, yet it felt more like an antithesis. A life of discomfort, urgency and need. A life of denial and lack. Last winter especially. It had been long and hard. Rain and snow and storms. He'd been kept busy, working on the lines. There'd been call-outs most weeks, to remote valleys or hills where a pole had gone, or the lines brought down by the weight of snow and ice. On top of that, repairing the repairs – going back to places he'd been weeks before in a blizzard or a gale, patching it up just to get the power back on; now, time to do the job properly, see if you could finish it before the next call-out. Day after day, night after night, hardship and struggle.

'With that plus the long-term contracts on the Kaikoura coast – all the earthquake repairs – I could work most weeks twice over, if I wanted to,' he said. 'It's getting more difficult to get men. They don't like that kind of work, out in the cold, wet through, fingers frozen up, ice in your beard. Nor the irregularity of it, not knowing when the next job will be. They want predictable work in nice conditions, tea-breaks every other hour. Even the money won't tempt them. We rely on migrant labour more and more. Islanders, Asians. Everyone's happy to welcome them when there are dangerous and unpleasant jobs like this to do – as long as they go back where they came from afterwards, of course.'

'We migrants are a problem, aren't we?' Klas said with a grin. 'Bringing all our strange customs and diseases with us, putting people out of work. Raping and pillaging. Stealing all the best Kiwi women.'

'Having met Julia, I'd suggest that you're guilty of the last of those,' Evan replied, 'even if not the rest.'

There was justification for the claim. Klas's wife had accompanied him once, on one of the hunting trips – to see what he gets up to, she'd said. She was a wife any man would have chosen. Laughing, lively, yet at the same time calm and self-possessed. She had poise and stature, one of those women, Evan guessed, who had the luck to get ever more beautiful as they got older, or who somehow contrived to stay young.

Klas laughed. 'I'm sure there are one or two good ones left; I didn't take them all.'

They were silent. To Evan it seemed the companionable silence of two friends who did not need to speak. But then Klas said: 'I would never have guessed.'

'Guessed what?'

'That Addie was your daughter. Not if she hadn't said.'

Evan looked away, made no reply.

'You know, I've been watching her since we arrived. Forgive me for that, but I am interested. I have been looking at her, trying to convince myself I can see you in her, or she in you. A likeness, traits that are yours. But I cannot.' He laughed. 'Perhaps she should be relieved about that, don't you think? I know my daughters are that they don't take after me.'

Still Evan did not reply, his mind racing, weighing up the choices: to tell the truth or to continue the deceit? The consequences either way. Humiliating Addie, betraying his friendship with Klas.

Klas turned, regarded him quizzically: 'I am sorry. Do I offend you, my friend? I do not mean to do that.'

'No. Of course not. But it's just – complex.'

Klas nodded, was silent, drank from the beer can, placed it carefully beside his chair. Then, in the same cautious manner, as though venturing on to dangerous ground, he asked: 'So what is she? A long-lost daughter, that you never talked about? Or a recent discovery, that you did not know?'

Neither, he wanted to say; she's not my daughter. But the words would not come. Dissimulation was easier, less embarrassing. 'Both I suppose.'

'So did you find her, or she find you?'

Evan frowned. Each question took him further into falsehood and guilt, made any retracing of his steps more difficult. But in this at least, he consoled himself, he could respond with a semblance of truth.

'I found her.'

'Recently?'

'A little while ago.'

Again, Klas was silent, reflecting. Imagining, no doubt, how it had happened – the search for a daughter from a life before, perhaps a daughter Evan had never seen. The happy reunion. The long journey of rediscovery, each of the other.

All untrue.

Once more he thought: should he tell him, could he?

'It's not what you think,' he said.

'And it's not my business, I know. I am sorry.' Klas stood, hesitated a moment as if there was more he wanted to say; instead, touched him on the shoulder, patted it. 'Good luck my friend,' he said. 'Good luck to you both.' He walked away.

*

Her absence, now, was palpable. He lay in his bed, unable to sleep.

It made no sense, because on other nights he would have been in his room alone, and she in hers, and there would have been the same walls and space and silence between them. And when he was away, on his claim, she could have been anywhere, doing anything she pleased. Pleasing herself, his mind echoed, maliciously.

Yet now, because he knew where she was – or rather, where she wasn't – he felt the emptiness, felt what seemed like loss.

How can you lose something you've never had, his thoughts asked; what trickery is that?

He turned over, facing the grey square of the window, the sliver of sky where thin moonlight skipped and danced between the clouds. Playing the same game: here then gone. Behind him, the dog stirred, sighed, complaining about his restlessness.

He worried too much, he told himself, then thought: what father doesn't?

It had been a device, of course, a fiction, and one Addie had blatantly invented. And he could understand why. It was as Klas had said: she must have been frightened by the hunters' sudden invasion, believed that she needed to send them on their way. To protect his property and privacy; perhaps to preserve their time together, not have it invaded by people she did not know. The claim of his fatherhood must have given her the authority she required.

He knew, too, why he had connived as he had. Out of loyalty to her; to avoid embarrassing her, to cover up her deceit.

Yet weren't they just excuses, his mind now asked; wasn't there another reason?

That he wanted it to be true.

Could it be? Was it?

Is that what had brought her here – the search for her father?

He turned again, stared at the ceiling. It was impossible, of course. It would be too much of a coincidence, too much like a trick of fate. A trick, too, of Addie's; all her stories about her boyfriend and background false.

It made no sense.

And yet he'd thought it himself, and in that moment so had she. Wasn't that coincidence, too?

Could she be, he asked himself again; despite what Klas had said, were there likenesses?

Not much in stature, that was true. Yet in her character, in her manner, there was a familiarity that he could not quite touch, so that all too easily he seemed to know her thoughts, and she his.

In the way she sometimes regarded him, too. In that sense of doubt and enquiry, almost disbelief. He'd been told it himself as a child: don't look so quizzical; don't you believe me?

In that nub of determination and denial.

And if so, she could only be Lisha's, for her age matched. Twenty-five. He'd made that calculation the instant Addie told him how old she was, testing her against his own life. Nineteen ninety-two or three. When he had been with Lisha, and life seemed like an ocean wave that could carry them anywhere.

The carefree way they had lived then, the way they had loved would have made it possible. The way they had parted, too.

And he would not have known. For Lisha would not have told him, would not dare. She had a husband, a son. There was honour at stake. Catholic honour at that. Better to remain silent; better to pretend.

She would have known, too, that he would prefer ignorance, would not want to deal with the responsibilities a child brought.

It was possible.

Is that what he saw when he looked at Addie, he wondered: not just his likeness, but hers, Lisha's? That darkness in her. The physical darkness – Mediterranean rather than Maori, Greek blood. The darkness of spirit, mixed with the light. The two extremes: happiness and despair, wildness and desolation, always in contest. Between them, balancing each with the other, that stoic streak.

And yet it couldn't be.

But he wished it was. Or feared that it might be.

Eight

The play of lights on the window alerted him. Then the bark of the engine. He dragged himself from his mix of thoughts and shallow dreams, the wash of sleep, peered at the bedside clock. Gone midnight. He went to the window, looked out.

One of the quad-bikes stood in the centre of the clearing, its headlights making a bright, white pool. In the blackness around, he could make out nothing. Then a shadow ballooned across the grass, like a winged monster snatching at him. It shrank, became a man dismounting from the quad, stepped forward.

Another figure strode into the light. Klas.

There was what seemed to be a hurried discussion. Arms waved. Klas put a hand to his head, then turned, disappeared again into the darkness.

Evan grabbed his shorts, ran out.

'What's happened?'

Marty turned. In the starkness of the headlights, his face looked stretched, pale, as if he had been confronted by a ghost.

'There's been an accident.'

He knew immediately what the words meant. Someone had been shot. Addie.

'Who? Where?'

'Up the side-valley. Where the track runs out.'

He did not know where Marty meant, yet could picture the scene all the same. The dense bush, the elusive trails, small clearings. Obvious places for a hasty shot, an accident.

'Who?' he said again. 'Is Addie alright?'

'It was Todd.'

Shooter or shot, he wondered. 'Todd?'

'Yes. He rolled the quad.'

He was struggling to understand. Not a shooting then. A different accident. But Addie injured all the same?

Then the lights dimmed as the engine of the quad-bike stilled, and Jimmy dismounted, came towards them. 'It was a washout on one of the tracks,' he said. 'He didn't see it. It just went off the edge.' His voice was animated, almost brimming with excitement, as if the whole experience had been a game.

'Jesus.'

'He was lucky,' Jimmy continued. 'He's not too badly hurt. He was thrown clear.'

'What about Addie? Where is she?'

'We left her there.'

'Left her?'

'Yes, we left her with Todd. She's looking after him.'

'Looking after him? You mean she's not hurt?'

'No. She wasn't on it.'

Evan felt a surge of relief, almost joy. 'What's wrong with Todd?'

'His ankle's damaged. Hopefully it's not broken, just a sprain. Addie's bound it up.'

'Yes. Yes, she was a nurse once. He'll be in good hands. And the quad?'

'Not a write-off. But we couldn't get it out. We tried, but our rope wasn't long enough, and in any case, this thing probably doesn't have enough grunt. We need a winch and one of the trucks. Klas has gone to get them.'

As he said it, there was an answering roar of an engine, and new lights flooded the scene. The truck drew up beside them, Klas at the wheel. He leaned out, threw them all orders. Jimmy to come with him, Marty to lead off on the quad; Evan to stay there in case the others returned – to brief them if so. And if they hadn't got back with Todd by then, to send the Humvee out.

They were gone for what felt like an age. It was almost four in the morning before they reappeared. As the vehicles drew back into the clearing in a blaze of noise and light, Evan ran out to greet them.

Addie stepped down from the truck. He put his arms out, wanting to hug her, hesitated, then thought: isn't that what a father would do? She let him envelop her, yet seemed eager to escape, wriggled free.

'Are you hurt?' he asked.

'No. I'm fine.' Like Jimmy, she sounded fired up. 'Don't worry, Evan. I really am fine.'

Back in the cottage, she told him her story. From what she said, it had been one of those chains of events that seem innocent at the time, yet with hindsight have disaster written in them. It was late evening, almost dark. She'd been riding pillion to Todd, on the lead quad, as they forged their way along a narrow and overgrown track through thick bush. There were washouts and slips. Todd had signalled to Marty and Jimmy to wait, while he explored ahead. She clung to him as they nosed their way forward, ducking as branches whipped at her face, tearing her arm free from bramble-snags. But after a minute or two, the going had got too difficult even for Todd, and he'd admitted defeat. He told Addie to get off while he reversed to somewhere that he could turn round. She was following him on foot, eyes shaded against the glare of the headlights when it happened. Where the track was narrowest, he'd misjudged his line, hung one rear wheel off the edge. All she'd seen was the sudden arcing span of the lights, the front of the quad, its handlebars like a startled horse, rearing; Todd's body lurching. Then the quad had slipped, rolled, 'just fell,' she said. She'd screamed, scrambled down the bank after him, expecting the worst. What she found when she got there was almost comical. Todd was lying in a pool of mud and water, just below the lip of the slip, lit up by the lights of the quad. He was face up, looked winded and dazed. The quad was on its back thirty metres down the slope, seemingly mimicking him, wheels spinning. She'd clambered down, helped him out of the mud. He'd winced, cursed as he put weight on his left foot. By then, Marty and Jimmy had appeared, carrying searchlights. Together they got him back to the road. She'd checked him over, bound his ankle.

'What's he done?'

'To his ankle? Just a sprain, nothing worse, though he'll be hobbling for a few days. It's his pride that was hurt worse.'

'And you're alright?' Evan asked, yet again.

She grinned. 'Stop worrying. I'm fine. Except that I need a shower; we all do, I guess. But I'm going first. The men can form an orderly queue.'

Klas came in, calling his thanks after Addie as she scuttled away, then told Evan the rest. They'd managed to haul up the quad. Surprisingly it was not too badly damaged; it would still run. As for Todd, maybe he would learn something. 'We have a saying about people like him,' Klas said. 'Han lär sig bara från hur han lider av sina misstag. In English, perhaps: his only teacher is the pain of his errors.' But he deserved some credit, he admitted. 'He did the right thing, and jumped. But for that, it would be his head in bandages – assuming it was still attached.'

*

She stood in the corridor, as she had that first day, after he had found her, looking sleepy and pale. As then, she was dressed only in one of his shirts, her legs bare. She rubbed at her eyes.

'What time is it?' she asked.

'Eleven-thirty.'

'Shit. Did I sleep that long?'

'You needed it.'

She went past him, walking slowly, touched him with a hand. He half reached to take it but held back.

At the window, she looked out.

'Are they going?'

'Soon,' he said. 'The others came back an hour or so ago. I'm surprised you didn't hear. They found chamois up on the ranges. They're keen to get off.'

She was silent, and he watched her, wondering what was in her thoughts. Regrets that they were leaving, that soon it would only be the two of them left? Todd gone?

As if in proof, she asked: 'How's Todd?'

'Sleeping it off, I think. Like you.'

She nodded.

He went to her side, watched the scene in the clearing. Most of the tents were furled now, stacked in piles beside the truck. The utes were being loaded, the engine cowling of the Humvee was up, two of the men leaning inside, making adjustments.

'Last night was a cock-up,' she said. 'I'm sorry.'

'Not your fault.'

'No. But I'm sorry all the same.'

'I hope it was worth it – that you enjoyed the hunting.'

'It was OK.'

'Did you see anything?'

'Game you mean? A little.'

She seemed reluctant to expand, and he had to prompt her before she would say more. They'd tracked some wild pig, she said, had followed them for over an hour, but then had lost them in a ravine. After that, they'd found a small group of deer. Several hinds.

He remembered the deer he had seen with Klas, asked: had she shot any?

She shook her head. 'I never got the chance. Jimmy got trigger happy, scared them off.'

'And that was it?'

'More or less.'

Again, he had to prompt her.

Todd wanted to get up on to the tops, she said, so that they could hunt at first light. That's why they were driving so late. There was a place he knew, a good campsite near the bushline. He had other plans as well, she implied, just for him and her; he fancied his chances. As it was, he'd scotched them, too. She shook her head, as if clearing some memory from it – one she wanted to lose. 'Christ, he's a fool. He's a born loser, that guy.'

Was it disappointment, he wondered, or annoyance?

'You'll be sad to see them leave,' he said, testing her.

'They've been fun,' she said, with a shrug.

He told her what Klas had said: Todd would only learn from his mistakes.

She nodded. 'He's probably right.' Then she gave a grim, ambiguous smile. 'Though some men don't manage even that, do they?'

Whether it was aimed at him, or her boyfriend, or men in general, he could not tell. He thought of his conceit during the night – that he could read her mind – and mocked himself for it. She was a closed book, a blank script. Yet the residue of his imaginings remained: was she his daughter? He sneaked a glance, hoping it would tell him in some way.

'There he is anyway,' she said. 'Now, let's see if he can still walk.'

In the clearing, Todd had emerged from his tent. About his own ability to walk, he seemed unsure. He stayed for some moments, yawning, stretching, as if tied to the spot. Klas called across to him, words they couldn't hear, but the message evident: pack your tent. Slowly, he began to do so, limping as he moved from peg to peg. Evan felt a stab of satisfaction. There was justice in the world, after all.

One of the hunters came over, said something, laughed, then began to help.

Evan watched, suddenly impatient for them to complete the task and go. He wanted to be alone with Addie again, wipe away all the jealousies and rivalries that their presence seemed to have brought. He wanted to be able to talk to her, question her, have her to himself. He wanted to settle their relationship once and for all – though how he could broach the question he still did not know. So he stood in silence, half a pace from her, the distance between them like an impenetrable wall.

There was a knock at the door. He pulled himself back to the moment, called: 'Come in.'

Klas entered, holding his hat like a supplicant. 'We're ready now,' he said. 'We'll be off.'

Evan went to him, extended a hand, but Klas brushed it aside, and instead reached for his shoulders, pulled him forward in an embrace.

'Our apologies,' he said. 'We've disrupted your life more than visitors ever should. Forgive us.'

'You're welcome any time. You know that.'

'Will you come and say goodbye to the others?'

'Of course.' He looked around. 'Addie. You, too?'

She shook her head. 'I'm not quite dressed for it yet, am I? I'll just wave from here.' But she went across, gave Klas a chaste hug, a kiss on the cheek.

He regarded her gravely, seemed about to say something, then changed his mind. 'Good luck,' he said.

Outside, the men were finishing their preparations for departure. Straps and bungees tested, tarpaulins tucked tight, a feel of the pockets to make sure that wallets and keys and cigarettes were safely stowed. Then the slamming of doors, the cough and growl of engines, the acrid taste of diesel smoke.

Evan stood at the foot of the steps, waved.

Klas leaned out of the window of his truck, gave a small salute.

'Good hunting,' Evan said.

'Hunting is always good, whatever trophies we win.' He grinned. 'Thank you again my friend. And thank Addie for us. For some of us, I'm sure, she rather than you or me – or even the hunting – will be what they remember from this year's trip.' And with that he pulled away.

The next ute circled in behind, Brian at the wheel. Todd was in the passenger seat. He leaned across, yelled in the direction of the cottage: 'Love you Addie.' Then he called to Evan: 'Tell that girl of yours, she can't escape. I'll be back for her soon.'

Indulgently, Evan smiled, raised a hand of farewell.

*

'I need to know,' he said.

She shook her head, as though the question did not matter, or had no answer that she could give. She looked moody, petulant, like a schoolgirl wrongly blamed.

As soon as the hunters had gone, he had tried to have his wish, to be with Addie alone. But she had contrived in some way to avoid it. She had spent what felt like ages showering, getting dressed, tidying her room. Then she had been busy, stalking the kitchen as she made herself something to eat, never still. But at last, he had managed to corner her with a cup of coffee, steered her to the veranda, persuaded her to sit down. She had perched on the balustrade, legs drawn up, head on her knees.

He had settled himself in his chair, Viva at his side, regarded her for a moment. Then his question had burst out: 'Why did you tell them that you were my daughter?'

She had answered with a shrug, nothing more.

'I need to know,' he said again, now. 'Tell me.'

She shrugged once more. 'I just did. It seemed – I don't know, the best thing to do. Does it matter?'

'Of course it matters.' He tried to explain why, somehow failed to say it clearly, so that even to his ears it seemed no more than a petulant bleat. He tried again.

'I don't like lying to friends. That's why.'

'So why did you?'

'Because – .' It was his turn to stumble, to give a wave of his hand. 'Because I wanted to protect you. Because I didn't want to embarrass you.'

'In which case I'm grateful.'

'So why did you say it, then?' he asked.

She grimaced, seemed about to refuse his question once more, then relented.

'They spooked me,' she said. 'That's all. They came in, in their trucks and bikes, all smoke and noise and bravado, and I was scared. OK – that's silly. But I was. I didn't know what was happening, who they were, what they were going to do. When Klas came banging on the door, I just wanted them all to go away. I told them they weren't welcome. When he asked me who I was, almost as if he was laughing at me, I told him I was your daughter, and you'd left me to look after the place. That's all. And I'm sorry. Does that satisfy you?'

He nodded. It was as he'd guessed. No mystery, no scheme. Just simple panic. He should have trusted his instincts, trusted her.

'Anyway,' she said. 'It's your fault. You should have told me they were coming.'

'Yes. I should have done. I'm sorry. I forgot.'

She regarded him from her perch, her eyes challenging, as if seeking more.

He wondered whether it was an invitation. Whether she knew what was really on his mind, was offering him the opening he needed to ask. Not why she'd said that she was his daughter, but whether it could be true. He reached for the words he might use, a light phrase that could lead them into the topic or be dismissed with a laugh.

But she forestalled him. 'Well then, let's call it quits, shall we?' And when he didn't immediately answer: 'Agreed?'

He nodded. 'Agreed.'

She held out a hand and he took it, helped her down. Standing there, looking up at him, she seemed small, guileless, yet unknowable, too. The armour of innocence, the most protective armour of all.

Who are you, he wanted to say; what are you?

'You're a chump,' she said. 'Did you know that?' Her voice was affectionate, gently scolding. A daughter's voice, he thought.

'It's been said.'

She pointed a finger at him. 'Well chump. No more brooding. It's a mess out there. We've work to do. Let's get to it.'

They started on the cottage. They swept it out, rearranged the furniture on the veranda, picked up the cigarette butts. He was glad of the task. It felt homely, intimate – a task that father and daughter might naturally share in the wake of a party.

After lunch, they moved on to the clearing. Evan gathered the various logs and pieces of timber that the men had hauled out to use as chairs or tables, and stowed them behind the shed. Addie collected the ashes from the campfire, carted them round to the back of the house to add to the soil where she was extending the herb garden. Then, while Evan burned the rubbish, Addie searched the ground for any litter or possessions that the men might have left.

She showed him what she'd found where the tents had been: two tent pegs and a wrap of silver foil. She threw the foil into the incinerator. 'Drugs,' she said. 'Coke.'

'How do you know?'

'It's obvious,' she said. 'You're not that innocent, surely.'

He shrugged. 'Maybe. It's not my area of expertise.'

'A good guy, eh? I'm impressed.'

'And you?'

She ignored the question. 'It'll be Todd's I bet. Any money you like. He's that sort of dickhead.'

In the evening, she offered him salad, the remains of the bread the hunters had donated to them. 'We've eaten enough animal flesh for a lifetime in the last few days,' she said.

He volunteered to help prepare it, but she shook her head. 'No. Leave it to me.' She gave him beer. 'Here, take this. Chill out. You deserve it.'

He went out on to the veranda, leaned back in his old armchair, feet on the balustrade, supped from the can. Across the clearing, the shadows were merging, the forest growing dark. It might have been an amphitheatre, he thought, after the play was done, the lights dimmed. The dark wings, the shadowy shapes of the backdrop, the air left strangely taut in its sudden silence.

He thought of the hunters, and their time here. All the hustle and bustle and noise. The dramas played out. The analogy amused him and he let his mind pursue it, imagining their visit like that of a group of second-rate travelling actors who'd happened to pass. Their performance, a Shakespearean comedy, perhaps, light and rich in repartee on the surface, but with an undercurrent of deeper meaning that he had not quite grasped.

Yet if so, he wondered, who were the players and who the audience, and where was the division between? For they had all colluded. Addie, sole heroine, temptress, goad; dressed for the role in her dyed hair, heavy eyeshadow, hamming it all up. Todd the villain, like a figure from a children's pantomime. He, too, the classic fool, though less wise than the part should imply.

All of them, strutting and fretting.

*

'So are you going back to the claim?'

She had been first up, this morning, had breakfast waiting. She seemed primed, intent, as if ready for the day. Her hair was held back with a simple band, her face was unmade. She was wearing her jeans again, a checked shirt. She looked more like the real Addie, the Addie he knew.

'Do you want to?' she asked.

He did not answer, did not know what to say.

During the days that the hunters had been there, he'd heard two voices calling with equal insistence, two different questions begging for his response. His claim: where was the gold, could he find it? Addie: who was she, how could he know?

Yesterday, working alongside her, they had teased him still, though more gently. Cloud shadows racing across the hills, the scent of the bush on the westerly wind, drawing him back to his claim. Addie's voice, her quick smile, a toss of her head, the touch of her shoulder against his, beckoning him to stay.

During the night, the questions had returned, fierce and malicious once more: gold or Addie; daughter or lover? Which did he want? Until they merged in some strange manner in his dreams, and became inseparable – Addie and the gold, a daughter, a lover, all one.

And now, facing her across the table, in the spotlight of her gaze, he wondered: would getting away from her, going back to his claim, help? Might distance give him perspective, make her just a chance-found friend again.

Was that what she wanted, for him to leave?

She seemed to read his uncertainty for she said: 'You mustn't let me stop you. You know that.'

And yet, with that same look, he knew that there was no real doubt. He didn't want to go. Not yet. He wanted to stay here, enjoy her company again, whatever she might be.

'No,' he said. 'I thought I'd hang around for a few more days. Sort a few things out.'

She grinned. 'Good. I'm glad. Because I've something planned for you.' Her eyes danced across him, light, mischievous, and for an instant he wondered what she meant. Then she continued: 'Some jobs that need doing on the cottage. Things I can't do without some help. The roof especially. Are you game?'

He nodded. 'Sure. If you are.'

'You bet. It'll do me good. Blow the cobwebs away.'

She was right, of course. The cottage needed some attention. It was old – a century or more if you allowed it the deceit of the grandfather's axe and ignored the amount that had been replaced over the years. Even with that help, he knew it wouldn't last another century. The structure was growing weak, sagging. There was a bow in the roof, a tilt to the floor; the veranda was coming away from the frontage. Each year, the weather and the wasps and the worm claimed a little more, and the ground seemed to receive it. In response, he'd mended what he could, ignored what he couldn't. He'd replaced two of the piles under the veranda and been pleased with his efforts. Occasionally, he'd patched the weatherboarding, though hadn't bothered to paint it. But the roof always concerned him. If the wind got under that, if the rain got in, the whole place would soon be uninhabitable. With another pair of hands, he'd have worked on it years ago. Now he had them. It was a chance he could not miss.

He fetched the ladder from the outhouse, collected together hammers, jemmy, tin-snips, a box of grip nails, then hauled a couple of spare sheets of roofing from the store-space under the veranda, washed them off. He found gloves for them both. By the time he'd assembled everything, Addie had the ladder raised, and was up on the roof, scampering over it, light as a cat.

'Careful,' he called.

She looked down, grinned. 'Oh, I forgot. You're a professional at this climbing stuff, aren't you? You'll want to do it properly, with scaffolding and security harnesses and full risk assessment.' She stood up, threw out her arms, twirled around. 'Me. I just dance.'

'Not between the trusses, you don't,' he told her. 'You'll dent the roof.'

'I don't dent things,' she said. 'I glide, I float.' And she gave another twirl.

They worked together on the roof all that morning, into the afternoon. It might have been a precious interlude, snatched from the tumult of life. It might have been what her fiction had implied – a reunion after long years apart. In the wake of all the rumpus and hubbub of the hunters' presence, it certainly seemed like an oasis of calm, despite the banging and prising at nails, the heaving at roof sheets. The metal grew hot in the sun, so that he fetched some old blankets for them to kneel on. Flies and bees buzzed around them. Swallows dived past, harriers circled above. Across the valley, the bush steamed and the hills dissolved into haze.

They spoke to each other quietly, in brief phrases: requests to hold this, pass that; words of thanks for tiny acts of unasked for help; small curses when the hammer slipped or a sharp corner of roofing metal bit. They exchanged glances, nods of satisfaction, smiles. They slipped into a rhythm of understanding and trust, each knowing what the other would do, or needed, or was thinking.

As they took a break, sitting together on the roof, he pointed out some of the features in the landscape. The ridges, the folds where the river went, the saddle into the valley where his claim lay. The line of a miners' track, the scars of some of their workings, absorbed now back into the landscape.

He gave the hills their names: each one, an explorer, a general, a politician, otherwise forgotten.

She repeated them, said: 'Not many women, then.'

'Just one,' he said, and pointed to a smaller, rounder summit on the ridge opposite.

'What's that called?'

'Mount Hera.'

'Hera?' she asked. 'Who was she?'

'She was the Greek goddess of love – of women and marriage.'

'Well, two out of three,' she said. 'Just a shame about the marriage.'

'She was married to her brother, Zeus.'

'There you go, then.'

'We could do it tomorrow, if you liked.'

She glanced at him, sharply. 'Climb it, you mean?'

He nodded.

'OK – why not? But only if we finish this first.'

Yet neither of them seemed in a hurry to finish. When they'd nailed down the roofing sheets, tapped down the flashing, cleaned out the gutters, Addie insisted that they scrape the worst of the lichen off the spouting. Then she fetched a bucket of water and washed the skylight above his bedroom.

'There,' she said. 'Everyone will be able to see what you get up to now.'

But finally there were no more jobs to do. They gathered up their tools, and Evan stood on the top of the ladder while Addie passed them down. He saw again, or thought he did, the marks in the crease of her elbow where she'd cut herself, in those troubled times before. Times he could only guess at. But there were new marks, too. Scratches from the roofing metal and nails, a small stain of blood from a wound above her wrist. Life wounds us all, he thought, every day.

Her fingernails, which she'd varnished when the hunters came, were flaking as well, pink between the painted blue. But to him that seemed the opposite, a healing of sorts. The real woman emerging again, untainted.

He took the tools, carried them down the ladder, then waited for her to descend.

He allowed himself one small act of chivalry and professional concern: he put a hand on her waist as she reached the final step, guided her to the ground. She smiled, thanked him.

*

'Why didn't you?' she asked. 'Marry I mean.'

He shrugged. 'It just didn't happen.'

They were sitting together at the bottom of the veranda steps. The evening was quiet, still, as if the world was holding its breath. Even the bush had fallen silent. Matching it, they spoke in hushed tones.

'Did you never find the right woman, or did you find her and not ask her? Or did she say no? One of those, at least, must be true.'

'Maybe,' he said. 'For whatever reason, it never happened. And I'm OK with that.'

'OK?' she repeated, doubtfully. 'In that case, what have you done instead? How many women have you had?'

Her question shocked him and he gave a nervous laugh. 'I'm not sure you can ask that.'

'I just have. And you can tell me. Or do you want me to guess?'

'Not really.'

But she did. Wildly, perhaps provocatively so, veering to either extreme. Twenty, thirty? Then just one. None? Too many to remember.

'A few,' he said.

'Tell me about them. Tell me what it was that attracted you. Why you chose them. Or you let them choose you.'

He shook his head. 'It wasn't like that.'

She frowned at him. 'No choosing you mean?'

'Not always.'

'Never?'

'Occasionally,' he admitted.

'OK. Tell me about those.'

So he did, or tried to in some way that might make sense. Not always the whole truth – the avarice or self-indulgence on his side or theirs, the simple opportunism – but the simpler and more romantic versions, with love and longing and loss. He told her about Juliette and Rana. He talked about Yasmine in Canada, a story that seemed like a warning to him, and might be an explanation to her. The way in which it was meant to be a brief interlude as he passed, yet he'd found himself instead returning to her again and again. The way he had criss-crossed the country to be with her, no matter what the cost, as if he'd snagged in some way against her, and couldn't break free. The times with her that – if he'd added them up – would have been measured in no more than days rather than weeks, yet which had seemed to fill his life then, and still occupied a space in his memory.

'Just three,' she said. 'Is that all?'

He hesitated, thinking of Lisha and of the trap she posed. If Addie was truly her daughter, then she would surely know. And if so, not telling would seem like an act of denial, both of Lisha and of her.

But if not?

'One, perhaps,' he said.

'But you're not telling?'

He shook his head.

'Someone special you want to remember? Or someone you want to forget?'

'Special,' he said.

She seemed to think, her lips pursed, then nodded. 'Good. I'm glad there's someone like that. But – but none of them wanted to marry you? Or you them?' And when he didn't reply: 'Most women still do, you know, want to marry. It's usually the men that don't.'

'Maybe one,' he said, at last.

Again, she regarded him, thoughtfully, assessing, saying nothing. He wondered what she was thinking, what she already knew. Then she shook her head sadly and grimaced – like the daughter despairing at her father's unfathomable ignorance or obstinacy. 'Poor Evan,' she said.

Nine

She climbed hills, he thought the next morning as he followed her up the trail, like she climbed ladders and roofs. With that same lightness, that same agility. All balance and flow. Her hips moved freely, with an easy rhythm. Her bare arms swung loosely at her side. She never seemed to miss a step. The only sign of effort was the dark triangle of perspiration at the centre of her back. It was allegorical, intimate. It drew his eyes, teased at his thoughts.

They were above the treeline now, out in the open. The sun was high. Luckily, though, today there was a breeze and a scattered flock of clouds – white lamb-tufts that scampered eastwards, as if racing eagerly to some event that they didn't want to miss. They afforded some relief from the glare and the heat.

He stopped, whistled for Viva. She emerged from the tussock grass ahead of them, bounding enthusiastically down the slope, spittle flicking.

He pulled the water bottle from the side of his pack, offered it to Addie. She accepted it, drank, her head tipped back, the tendons on her neck tightening and relaxing as she swallowed. A dribble of water trickled from her mouth, ran down her neck, left a tiny trace on her skin.

She handed him the bottle. 'How much further?'

'Half an hour.' He pointed to a bluff of rock on the ridge above them. 'As far as that again.'

He drank himself, drawing the water in deeply, feeling its coolness in his throat, sharp enough to scald. He recapped the bottle, slipped it into the pouch of his pack.

Suddenly each movement, each detail seemed to be seminal, have a significance beyond its scale.

'Ready?' he asked.

She nodded.

'After you.'

Then he was following her again, watching her hips, the dark stain of sweat, the cloud of insects parting to let her pass.

What did it remind him of? Why this sense of knowing and expectation?

Still it tantalised him. Still he could not pin it down.

Ahead of him, Addie stepped on to a boulder; her calf tensed, and she eased across. No calculation, no effort, just motion at its most primitive.

She turned, looked over her shoulder, laughed. Her mouth wide, a dark cavern, her eyes creased.

A loose buckle jangled against the water bottle in the pouch of his pack.

The grass sprang slowly back from the place her foot had been.

And he remembered.

Another day, another time. Another place.

The Auvergne, the Puy Mary, the day hot like this one, the path steep and winding. Sweat in his eyes, flies buzzing at his head. From below them, in the meadows, the contrapuntal clunk of cowbells. And five steps ahead of him, Lisha, deliberately leading him on. The same stride, the same easy movement. The same mark: follow me.

Might it have been then, he wondered, even that very day?

He could not recall the occasion, the love-making in the grass, but knew that it must have happened, for the proof of it was in her eyes and in her laugh. And it happened, in any case, every chance they got; and where better than in the sun, on a carpet of orchids and lady's bedstraw, mobbed by butterflies of every colour and shape.

Yet if it had happened, it might have been almost any day during those last few weeks together, as time slipped from their grasp.

He'd wanted in some way to preserve it, that time, and as they lay together had fought to etch the memory into himself, deep into his loins. He'd tried to hold that picture of her, beneath him, above him, pressed close to his face – every detail of it, each pore, each hair, each mole and blemish, every fold of her skin. The taste of her, smell of her, the sound of her voice and breath, even her silences.

Yet his efforts had failed as such endeavours always do. Weeks later, he had to conjure her up within his consciousness by force of will, every time a new act of creation. Months later he remembered her more from his few photographs of her than from any reality. Now, there were only memories of memories left.

He wondered again: had she found a better way?

Addie stopped, looked back again, grinned. 'Race you to the top,' she said.

Lisha's own words.

'OK. But no cheating.'

Which is what he always used to do himself, trying to grab her and wrestle her to the ground. Tickling her until she was helpless, exploiting the opportunity.

Now he simply padded in Addie's wake.

But old habits die hard. Near the summit, as the ground levelled out, and he was still two paces behind and struggling, he dived for Addie's ankle, caught it with a flick of his hand. She sprawled into the grass, laughing, cursing. He ran past her, then her silence snagged him and he abruptly halted, looked back. 'Are you alright?'

She sat, shaking her head, nursing an elbow, holding it tight against her ribs.

'I'm sorry.' He went back to her. 'Christ, I'm sorry. That was silly. Let me look.' He knelt beside her, held out a hand.

She raised her arm, shoved him in the chest.

'Mug,' she said, and leapt up and ran to the summit.

*

Not his, then. Not his daughter.

Whether he'd ever believed it, he wasn't sure, but even so the knowledge was bittersweet. He'd wanted it to be true, or at least had been seduced by the possibility, and by its implications. A young woman in his life, perhaps there to guide him through his later years. Who wouldn't want that? Someone to care for and love. Meaning and purpose to his existence, replacing the blankness of a world in which she was not. Lisha returned, living and whole, all his memories of her given substance, all his regrets wiped away.

Perhaps that more than anything. Something he thought had been wasted and lost, transformed instead into the most wondrous act of creation.

And yet there was a sense of reprieve as well, though at first he could not understand it, nor see from where it came. Relief at a more complex future avoided, perhaps: one where he would have to accommodate himself to someone else, trim and tune his life to match hers. Or something deeper, more convoluted. The way it would have altered the past. Made Lisha as treacherous as the rest. The mother of his daughter that he'd never known, that she'd kept to herself. All those years denied.

Addie had told him on the hilltop, lying there amidst the hum of flies, the dust of pollen, legs loosely crossed, one arm thrown out, the other beneath her head; hair flared around her, like a fire in the dun dry grass.

He'd stood, seeming to tower above her, seeing her from afar. She looked so fresh, so guileless, so different from everything he was: not just by sex, by age, by stature, but by the simple wholeness of her – the way life had failed to touch her, however rough it had been.

Beneath the hem of her shorts was a stripe of pale skin, stark against the bronze of her thighs. Her shirt was twisted, exposing a small sliver of waist, the dimple of her belly button.

He was doing now, he realised, what he'd done with Lisha all those years ago. Mapping every moment. Fixing the memory.

Did it all mean so much?

Then he realised that she was looking back at him, through narrowed eyes. Was she doing the same, he wondered, or just seeking his thoughts, trying to work out what his own look meant?

She moved a hand, cupping it on her forehead. 'I can hardly make you out from here,' she said. 'You look like a statue, of one of those explorers perhaps, stuck up here to claim his discovery. All pomp and stone.'

He laughed. 'I've been called worse.'

She sat up, drew up her legs, hugging them to her; rested her chin on her hands.

'Thank you for bringing me,' she said.

'Thank you for coming.'

She rocked against her knees, sucking at her hands. From above them, a skylark scattered its song, all trilling cadences, rippling notes, a musical kaleidoscope.

He sat down beside her. For a long while, neither spoke.

'What did you think?' she asked at last. 'About me saying I was your daughter?'

Once more, the swerve of her mind surprised him, and he struggled to respond.

'You were angry,' she said. 'I know that. You've told me; you've made it clear enough. But what else?'

'I'm not sure. Surprised. Mainly confused, I think. About why you said it – and well, yes, about how I felt.'

She regarded him solemnly, her brow furrowed, as if she were struggling against her own thoughts. 'When I said it, I felt – I felt as though I was. Just for those moments. It didn't feel like a lie. Does that sound stupid?'

He shook his head. 'No. Not stupid.'

'It wasn't that I wished I was, or believed it; it just *felt* true.'

He made no response, unsure what to say, how much of his own imaginings to reveal, and she asked: 'Did you think that? That it might have been true?'

He shrugged. 'Not think it, not that it was true – but imagine. I tried to imagine how I'd feel.'

'And how was that?'

'Strange.' It was not an answer, he knew; not the real answer. But he did not know how to tell her that: the swirl of contrasting emotions, hope and need and fear.

'Do you still think it might be?'

He was silent again, trying to analyse his thoughts, searching for the truth.

'It would be possible, wouldn't it? You must have had women then. One of the women you told me about. The one you didn't. One of them must have been about the right time. And I bet you didn't always use something, and they weren't all on the pill.' She smiled, that kindly, mocking smile that seemed to be her trademark, or her repeated message to him.

'Don't,' he said. 'Don't talk like that. Don't make fun.'

'I'm sorry.' She was immediately contrite, hung her head. 'It wasn't meant to be funny, or cruel. It was just – it just made me think how odd life is, how arbitrary. What made me "me", rather than someone else? Whether I'd be the same person if I'd been born a few hours earlier or later, or a day, or a year. Or to different parents. If I'd been your daughter instead.'

A small blue butterfly jagged through the air around her, fluttered in front of her face.

Evan thought of Lisha.

Gently, Addie wafted the butterfly away.

'I'm not, though,' she said. 'I'm really not.'

He nodded. 'I know.' And all the imaginings vanished, as though they had never been.

'It's not just unlikely, it's just not true. I knew my dad. I know he wasn't you. Though I admit, I didn't know him for long. Not long enough. He left when I was young. But I can remember him.' She bit at her knuckles, frowning. 'I look like him, I know that. I've seen photographs of him, I've still got one. He was small, like me, like a jockey. Short and skinny just like me. He's half Maori: that's where I get my blood from. And he's got my eyes – that look I know I have, fierce and quizzical, though it's not meant. My mum says he had the same temper, too. She used to blame him for that.'

She glanced up at him, grimaced. 'Sorry,' she said, though whether for her temper or the truth of her fatherhood, he wasn't sure.

He said nothing, and she rocked again on her knees, her thoughts seemingly far away. Then she began to speak dreamily, as if drawing from some deep memory. 'The thing I remember most is sitting with him in a big chair as he read to me once. And walking with him, hand in hand along a road, on the verge, with the grasses up to my knees. I was singing and brushing my hands through the grass. It's ever so clear, even now.' She paused, then continued: 'There must be other times, locked in there somewhere. But I can never quite find them. Just the sense of – goodness, happiness, of being with him. That's all.'

'Didn't he beat you?' Evan asked. 'I thought that's what you'd said.'

'Did I?' She shrugged. 'Perhaps sometimes he did. All kids get a beating, don't they? Most of them deserve it? I'm pretty sure I did.'

'What happened to him?'

'They separated.' She shrugged. 'Like people do. I was at school by then, but I can't remember quite when it was. You'd think I'd know, wouldn't you? You think I'd remember my dad walking out. But I can't.'

'Is that what happened? Did he walk out on you?'

'That's what my mum said, whenever I asked her. And later on I asked her quite often, until she got sick of me asking and got angry. But I don't know. I think she might have told him to go. Maybe he was having an affair.' She gave a grimace, ironic yet sad. 'You know what men are like.'

'So what happened afterwards – after your father left?'

'My mum found someone else. It must have been two years later, maybe a bit more. I was nine, maybe ten. He was another farmer. There's never any shortage of those, looking for wives. Especially ones with a farm as a dowry.'

'That, at least, was good,' he said. 'It kept you on the farm. Kept it going.'

She nodded. 'It wasn't so bad. I suddenly had two brothers, and that was good, though they teased me and hurt me at first. But I'd already learned to stand up for myself, to be more like a boy than a girl. Eventually they seemed to accept that – that I wasn't just a soppy girl they could boss around. And in those days my dad – my step-father – just ignored me and let me do what I liked.' She pulled at a stem of grass, chewed on it.

'We never got on,' she said at last. 'That is, I never felt anything for him, nothing daughterly. He was just there, in the house with us. That's how it seemed. To me, I think, he was just a lodger. Someone we allowed to live there with us, but who'd one day leave. He might as well have been. He didn't do anything for me, didn't seem to think I mattered, and that suited me. Not until I was twelve or so, anyway; then it began to change. He started to take notice of me. He became – solicitous, attentive. He'd spend time with me, used to take me out. He'd drive me somewhere in his car, or we'd go for a walk. Sometimes, he'd meet me after school and walk home with me, taking the long way. He'd sit with me, doing my homework. I thought he'd become a real father at last.'

Again, she paused, as if reflecting, trying to decide what to say next, what was worth telling. Evan waited, his eyes idly running across the line of the hills on the other side of the valley, tracing their shape, seeing in them as he so often did, the gnarled heads and faces of old men, who might have been the men after which they were named.

'Then he raped me,' she said.

*

The knowledge had changed them, rewritten their world. Neither, now, seemed to know their roles. That, at least, is how it felt as he followed her down the hillside; that evening as they sat together on the veranda, silently watching the sun bleed itself into the land; over the next few days as they tried to pick up the threads of their lives in the cottage again.

They were divided now, made separate by what they both knew. He felt it every time he looked at her, every time they came face to face. The division of age and sex and experience of life – what it had done to them. He on one side, she on the other, a world of difference.

What they were to each other, he did not know. Not his daughter, that was clear, nor even a surrogate daughter of any sort, nor any other proxy relation that he might invent, for each implied more intrusion, more abuse. Yet nor could he call her simply a friend, for wasn't that, too, full of dangers, of yet more assumptions and possibilities?

At the same time, the intimacy that she'd granted him seemed to invite just that: friendship, concern, interest. It defined her, that brutal act; it must have made her the woman she was.

He looked at her, therefore, expecting to see its mark in every feature and in everything she did. And it gave him the excuse and the obligation to look. To watch her, search for the signs, study each action, each change of expression or mood for warnings of what might lie beneath, what had happened to her, the scar it had left, the hurt that might still erupt.

But what of that attention, those glances and looks? Wasn't each of those just another violation? For when he looked, she seemed to stand there: a young woman, vulnerable, exposed, laid bare by his eyes.

In mitigation, he tried as much as possible to avoid her – to give her space. But in the way of such things, the more he tried, the more fate seemed to throw them together in clumsy and ambiguous scenes. He'd meet her half-dressed on the way to the bathroom, or catch a glimpse of her through the window of her room. He'd bump against her in the kitchen, or their hands would accidentally touch as they each reached for a knife in the drawer, a plate on the table, a book.

Their time together seemed brittle and laden with new dangers. Every thought and exchange full of unstated intent. Pull and push. Fondness and fear. Care and confusion. Everything was in contradiction.

Perhaps she felt it, too, though he could not tell. The way she looked at him seemed to change by the minute. One moment hard and refusing, another warm and full of fondness or need, the next wild and challenging; then yearning, then with coldness and blame. It added to his sense of bewilderment and guilt, and he did not know how to react.

He wanted to get away, to get back to his claim, but could not bring himself to suggest it. He felt trapped. Tied by what she had told him, her secret, by the guilt he somehow seemed to share. So he stayed, and smiled at her, and nodded, and talked to her when he could of safe and neutral things. The weather, the house, the dog.

In between, he thought of what she'd said, and over and over again replayed the conversation with her, picked at it for things he'd missed, new insights, other meanings.

'Afterwards,' she'd said, as they sat on the hilltop, 'it was better. After he'd done it.'

He'd glanced at her, shocked.

'Before,' she'd continued, 'it was all just pestering. Touching me, groping, stolen kisses. Odd things he'd say – about how I looked, what I was wearing. Coming up behind me, or into my room without knocking. I hated it, but I still didn't really know what to make of it. What was natural, what was just him, doing his best. And none of it seemed worth making a fuss about. So I just let it go. Then he did it – raped me. That changed everything.'

'How old were you?' he'd asked.

'Fourteen. Just – two days after my birthday. "My birthday present," he said.'

'What did you do?'

'What, then? I couldn't do anything. He was three times my size.'

'No. I mean afterwards. Did you tell your mother?'

She'd shaken her head.

'Why not?'

'She loved him, or thought she did. He'd rescued her, after my dad left, or he'd married her despite me. I don't know. But I wasn't going to destroy everything she thought she had, was I? I couldn't ruin her life.'

'And you didn't tell anyone, do anything?'

'No. Not then.'

'But later? You did something later?'

She was silent, and he'd asked: 'Do you want to tell me what?'

Again, she'd shaken her head, more slowly this time, a gentler denial. 'No. It's not for telling.'

He'd waited, but she said nothing. He'd reached for her hand, but she'd withdrawn it, looked away.

After a while, she'd stood up, and started to walk down the slope, but stopped, looked back. 'I've told you,' she'd said. 'You're the only one I've ever told.'

Now, a day later, she confronted him, stiff and assertive.

'Shouldn't you be getting back there – to your claim?' she asked.

He didn't immediately answer, and she scowled. 'You can you know. You don't have to stay here with me, like a nursemaid. I'm fine.'

And when he still didn't commit himself one way or another, she shook her head and told him to wait and keep Viva with him and went back into the house. A few minutes later, he heard the pop of the gun from the bush, then another after a pause. Soon after that she reappeared in the clearing, with two rabbits hanging from her hand.

She held them up as she approached. 'Rabbit pie,' she said. 'If that's what it takes to get rid of you.'

Ten

When he'd set out, his goal had been clear. He'd work down the claim systematically, from one end to the other, sampling until he could see the pattern the gold made. Then he'd target the best area, dredge it to the bone, take out whatever gold was there. He'd had enough of darting around in response to some vague and futile instinct, trying here, then there, always missing what he sought. It was time to be analytical and thorough.

Now he was on site, though, that goal seemed both ambitious and naïve. The gold didn't seem to be laid out like that, in a simple pattern, which he merely had to deduce. It was patchy, erratic, disorderly. It hid.

On his first afternoon, he'd started at the very top of the claim. It was an area he didn't often come to, for the terrain up here was complex and difficult to work. Three small tributaries, draining the ridge beyond, came together in a tumble of mossy boulders and rocky cascades, dense bush.

The gold ought to have been there in abundance, because the glaciers that had torn it from its original source somewhere high in the mountain ranges had left ridges of moraine on the hillsides and in the valley heads, and it was from these that the gold was now being washed. Each spring, each snowmelt, fed the rivers, brought in a new influx. This was the first place in his claim that it found, the first place it could rest

Yet the area had failed him in the past; that day, did so again.

At the end of the afternoon, he stood by the marker post that Jeb must have set up years ago to define the limits of the claim, gazing up the valley, wondering what might be up there, just beyond his grasp. The land was part of another claim, owned but never used as far as he could tell. Not for the first time, he was tempted to trespass – just this once, to go a little further, see what he could find. Who would know?

Not for the first time, he banished the idea. There was an honour in prospecting, a code, and he was not the one to break it. He turned, made his way back to his camp, empty-handed. Sitting outside his tent, he ate the first half of the rabbit pie that Addie had given him – compensation of a sort – and fretted. It was not the start he'd wanted, seemed to bode ill for the days to come.

That night, he slept fitfully. He tossed and turned, chased shapeless quarry in his dreams. Gold or hope or love: he could not tell which.

Somewhere in the early hours, Viva tired of his fidgeting and padded off to a corner, circled several times on whatever clothes or tool-sacks he'd thrown there, settled down with a sigh.

Not long after, the blackbirds started to sing, welcoming the first rays of dawn. Then the thrushes joined in, soon after that the tuis. At five o'clock, he gave up his attempts to find sleep again, got dressed, made a cup of tea. He sat outside drinking it, listening to the growing bird chorus, watching the day come. It soothed him, stirred the optimism that he'd been unable to track down in his dreams. The gradual lightening of the sky, the sudden glint of sun, like a shaft of gold between the mountains. Moths and hoverflies skittering in the liquid air. The stream laughing to itself as it danced by. Who could deny hope on a day like this?

After breakfast, he went back to the top of his claim, stood again, gazing up the valley, tempted once more. Is that where his fortune lay? Out of reach, in someone else's hands. Biding its time.

If so, it seemed like a moral for life. Keep waiting, keep hoping. One day it would come.

Just not yet.

He turned his back on the hills, headed downstream, scanned the channel, seeking somewhere that called him, a new place to pan.

Here, at least, the river was more orderly, seemed to have found its purpose. As it emerged from between the roots, from behind the boulders, out of the puddles and pools, it gathered, deepened, became a determined, bubbling flow. More water dripped from the banks, crept in from small side-streams. A larger tributary joined, added its contribution.

While he explored, he tried to picture the way it must have been during the storm. Where the current had twisted and turned, where it had spread out, where it had pooled. The shuffle and roll and bounce of the gravel, the quartz grains, slipping and sliding, leaping in long arcs, the grains and nuggets of gold amongst them all, shambling and creeping as if they were hobbled or reluctant, as if they dare not stray too far. Hugging the bed, always choosing the deeper ways, always lagging behind.

And as he explored, he sought out places the gold might have found. The low places, the sandy places, the gravel lenses and bars, in the lee of boulders, in the cuts and channels left abandoned as the flood subsided.

When he identified one, he swept up a sample, panned it, peered into the residue as though at oracular tea leaves or bones.

Yet the pan continued to disappoint. Prophecies there might have been; gold there was not.

The morning passed. The sun rose higher, beat down through the trees. The air was hot and sultry. He found himself instinctively panning in the shade. Around mid-day, he came to a cut-off where the stream had dumped a mass of boulders, diverting its own flow, leaving its old channel as a pond, the still water dark, smooth as a mirror. Beneath the surface, mosquito larvae hung, jerked away at the touch of his shadow. He dipped in his pan. The reflected trees rippled, bent, broke into shards of green and blue and white. He scooped up the sand from the bed, took it to the main channel, panned it. Two tiny nuggets: his only finds. Welcome relief from the barrenness, but poor pickings for a morning's work.

Doubt nagged him. He counted up the days he'd spent on the claim so far, made a guess at how much gold he'd found. Twenty days, perhaps an ounce and a half of gold. Say 2000 dollars in total. One hundred a day. Twelve dollars an hour at best, not counting travel and preparation and the intervals spent in the cottage. As Todd had said to him: a fool's game. How he would laugh if he knew.

When he reached the camp again, he stopped for lunch, perching on a log on the river bank. Viva sat beside him as he ate, pretending a patience that was belied by her dribbling jowls. In return for her efforts, he shared the final crusts with her, then fondled her ears, found a few burrs in them, sat holding her against his knee, ignoring her protestations, as he picked them out. 'Poor design,' he told her, not for the first time. 'An inbuilt imperfection.'

For a while, he pondered on the gold – or the lack of it. A theory had begun to form. It had been a wet winter and had lasted late. The river this year had run high. He could see the marks it had left in the trees that overhung the stream bank: tangles of debris caught in the branches, chest high above the ground. The flow had been strong, erosive; it had scoured the bed; any gold that it had picked up or brought with it had been swept right through, out of his claim. There was nothing worth finding left.

Gold above, gold below, he thought; just no gold here, in the middle.

Was it worth continuing? Or should he give up now, go back to the cottage and wait for the next rains? Whenever they might be.

But Addie would be there, bristling with all the contradictions she posed.

Yet, even with that thought, the picture of her changed. She seemed more innocent, less intimidating. Standing outside the door, as she did in the mornings, arms stretched, yawning her greeting to the day. Coiled on the sofa in the evenings, as the room shrank into shadows around her. Like a nautilus, like a snail, he sometimes thought, drawn back into herself again, safe from the world.

As she'd been when they worked on the roof together. All lightness and movement. A bird, a mouse, a mischievous chimp.

Which was the true Addie, he wondered; did even she know?

The hurt young woman on the hilltop, telling him of her past. A secret only he knew.

Did he want her secrets? Were they the most special gift she could ever give, or the unkindest curse?

Viva came up to him, pawed at his lap. He tipped the last coffee dregs from his cup into the grass, stood up. The gold was summoning him. Time to go.

That afternoon, he worked steadily, intent on finding something – anything worth dredging. Yet still there was nothing: just rare flakes, mere hints that there was any gold in the valley at all. He reached the top of the gorge, skirted it, following his usual path over the bluff to the stream below, made his way another fifty metres down, chose a spot on a gravel bar, near the rocky cut where his only real finds this year had come from. Squatted by the river, scooped up a sample, panned once more.

And there, late in the day, he found success at last. A few small grains, a penny-weight or two. But proof enough. He tried in another spot: at the top of the next gravel bar, where the pebbles lined up, neatly imbricated, like a packed rugby crowd, each one straining to peer over the shoulders of the one in front. And amidst the gravel, he found a little more; and when he panned again at the lower end of the bar, more again. Here, below the gorge, there was gold.

That night, he finished off the rabbit pie, slept better, and his dreams were sweet.

He woke just once, with a full bladder, went outside, peed. Above him the sky was a dark canopy, pricked with stars. The Milky Way made a broad river, splitting the heavens in two. *Te Ikaroa*, an old Maori man had told him once as they stood outside a hut, on a clear, crisp night. Or *Whiti-kaupeka*. A great fish, and the guardian of the night sky, whose task it was to protect and cherish all the smaller suns, the stars, and to lay down the courses of the heavenly bodies, so that the seasons would come when they should.

He stood outside his tent for long minutes, staring up at it, seeing it as if for the first time. It spoke of eternities of time and distance. A world without end. His own presence there, in the darkness of the land, seemed so meaningless, so infinitesimal that it could not be real.

He looked for a plane or a meteorite to give movement to the panoply, but none came.

He thought of Addie, back in the cottage, pictured her at that moment, curled tight in bed, and saw how small and lost she must be, how alone in the world. He wished he could be with her, wished she would want him there. For her sake and his.

The next day, he went back to the area below the gorge, set up his dredge. It was another hot day, sultry and still. From early morning, the sun blazed down, reflected from the water and the gravel, seemed to pick him out as he worked. He felt trapped within the intensity of its grip. Viva retreated to the shadows on the bank, ventured out occasionally to stand in the stream, panting, or for a long and eager drink.

He was wearing shorts, was stripped to his waist. Sweat gathered in his eyes, in every crease of his body; grit seemed to etch itself into his skin. Flies crowded at his face, and he repeatedly swept them away with his hand.

The metal of the sluice burned every time he touched it.

And the gold teased him. A scatter of grains, a smear of yellow on the pan when he sifted the finer residues. A few tiny nuggets.

He did the sums again – quantity won times market price over time spent – and came to the same sad conclusion. A fool's game, indeed.

Yet he worked on, for this was the place he belonged, not back at the cottage with Addie, with a woman barely half his age, hurt and abused. A woman he could not read or look at or touch.

As he did so, other thoughts swirled in his mind, other memories. Drawn, it seemed, by the rhythm of his body and the dredge and the pump, the tug of the water against his knees.

He thought of Juliette, so much Addie's opposite – and still, more than two years later, the last woman he'd known. Juliette, calm, self-possessed – a lawyer's poise. Juliette, wild and wanton. Juliette who promised him so much, left him with so little.

She'd been introduced to him by friends. The sort of contrived introduction only done for a friend in need. He'd liked her immediately, and she seemed to like him, but the enthusiastic encouragement of his friends had been too much for both of them. Before they left the pub that night they made a whispered plan. To his friends' disappointment, they left separately, he first, she later, with casual farewells – but a block away he waited for her, and she found him there. They kissed hungrily in the shadows, managed to stave off anything more until they got to her apartment, though not much longer.

A few weeks later, they'd gone on holiday together, and when they returned could no longer deny that they were lovers, were fond of each other, could share some part of their lives. Yet the sharing remained balanced, conditional. They slept equally in her house and his without ever feeling that either was a mutual home. Sometimes, they talked about life ahead, and surprised themselves by imagining that it still contained them both.

He began to believe. The life they'd constructed wasn't perfect. When they were apart, he missed her and wished she were there; when they were together, he felt their parting loom. But he could believe that it still might be love. Perhaps this time, he could yield to it, let himself fall.

Though the doubt never left him. Would she be there to catch him, when he did?

And then, with no warning, it happened. She'd been offered a job in Australia, she told him; it was too good to refuse. She'd already accepted it, would be leaving soon.

He waited for her to ask him to join her, to give up his own world and become part of hers, wondered what his answer would be. Could he do it? Could he make himself leap?

But she didn't ask. There were phone calls, emails. Vague plans about meeting again. Afterwards, nothing. He'd never heard from her since, made no effort to find her.

Now, he realised how much he missed her – or rather, missed what she'd given him. Bodily comfort, sex. The love, he admitted, he could do without, for that had always been a fiction. But the sex was real, and he yearned for that.

A fly buzzed him and he swatted at it, as much as anything to bat his memories away.

He thought of Addie, felt a surge of lust. Fierce and raw.

He stopped, stretched. He needed a break.

An idea came, and he called to Viva: 'Come on, girl. Playtime.'

He turned off the pump, waded upstream, into the gorge. Halfway up, below the bench where they'd found Addie, there was a deep pool that stretched from one wall to the other and was thirty or more metres long. It would be cool, shady. Where better for a swim?

He reached it, stripped off his boots and shorts and pants, waded in. The water lapped round him, fresh and limpid and slow. It felt silken around his naked body, voluptuous against his skin. He ducked down, stretched out, swam.

Then Viva bounded in, paddled out to join him, nose up, ears flat against the water, fur extended like tendrils of gossamer, her body and the water one. When she was close, he flicked water at her face. She turned, snapping at the droplets. He tried to grab at her, and she twisted away. He chased her, and tweaked her tail. When he rolled over and swam on his back, she nuzzled against him, as if to turn him over the right way.

Eventually, she tired of his games, and swam to the edge of the pool, pulled herself on to the bank, shook in a rainbow of spray. When he next saw her, she was standing on the rocky bench, looking down at him, her tongue lolling, body still dripping. He called to her to come back, but she remained there, wagged.

He lay on his back, floating.

He thought again of Addie, imagined bringing her out to the claim, showing her what he did.

She'd like that, he thought, and realised that he'd like it, too.

It would be innocent, a way of reuniting with her.

He could teach her how to pan.

He tried to picture her, as she might be, in the water beside him, swimming lithe as a fish, or standing on the bank, towelling herself. He turned over, dived into the darkness of the water.

Here, at the top of the pool, the bed was bare: rock, smooth and fluted, like the ribs of some ancient beast. He felt his way along one, enjoying the glossy feel of the stone. He circled a boulder, arms brushing it, his skin tingling with pleasure at its touch.

Then to his surprise his hand touched gravel. He swam on. There was more. He scuffed it, stirring up the sand, so that he had to shut his eyes. His lungs were beginning to ache. He kicked upwards, surfaced, spluttering as he gasped for air.

He dived again.

*

It all made sense now. The lack of gold upstream, its teasing appearance below the gorge. The pool where he'd swum. He could see it all, carved in the rocks around him, told by the shape and texture of the stream.

He was standing on the bench above the gorge, the same place he'd stood all those weeks ago when he'd found Addie. He was naked, still wet, dripping, making a stain of dark water around his feet.

He'd splashed out of the pool, clambered up the muddy slope, as soon as he realised, as soon as the truth dawned. He'd been greeted by Viva, excited by his sudden enthusiasm, the excuse to jump and splash. To protect himself from her scrabbling, he'd had to scold her, push her down.

It was obvious, now, he thought. Why hadn't he seen it before? How blind could he be?

He looked again at the place where Addie had been. There, slumped against the low palisade of rock.

Quartzite, pale, glassy, harder and more massive than the sandstones and gritstones of the rock around. It protruded from the crags at the back of the ledge, ran across the bench obliquely, towards the gorge. More resistant, making a wall.

He went to the edge of the bench, looked down. He could trace the line of the quartzite on the face below. It slanted upstream at an angle of about seventy degrees, met the water just above the pool where he'd swum. He could follow it through the water. A shallow ridge, forming a small cascade, where the stream frothed and boiled. He could see it mirrored on the opposite wall.

And he could read the story, imagine the way it had happened. The young valley, gradually deepening as the stream cut down. The hard band of rock, remaining defiant, snagging at the water, holding it back. For hundreds, perhaps thousands of years, the two battling – water and rock – in close contest. The water seeking its natural level, the rock resisting. Yet slowly, the water won. It nibbled and gnawed and grated and scythed. Beyond the quartzite, where the rock was softer, it carved a gorge. The hard band of quartzite became a waterfall, standing proud, yet even in doing so sealed its own demise. The water surged over it, tumbled, threw down boulders and rubble, sometimes gripped the rock-face in an icy grasp. It dug, swirled, undermined. And slowly, at the base of the waterfall, a pool formed.

A plunge-pool, cut deep and smooth.

Until, at last, the quartzite yielded, crumbled, broke, and the waterfall became a chute and the chute a cascade, and then just a jumble of boulders, and the plunge-pool slowly clogged with gravel – and became what it was now, a shallow dip in the bed, sediment filled.

The depression in which he'd swum.

The sort of place that every prospector searched for: a natural sink; a place that caught the river's sediment. A place where the gold gathered, year after year after year, became trapped.

A place that harboured its treasure, kept it to itself. A glory hole.

He called Viva to him, hugged her to his side. 'We've done it,' he whispered. 'We've found it. We've found a glory hole!'

*

'That's it,' Addie said. 'All we need is a bottle of champagne.'

All tensions were forgotten now. There was just gaiety and excitement.

'You'll be rich,' she'd said earlier, when he'd told her, and gave a clap of her hands. Then she flung her arms around him, planted a kiss firmly on his nose. 'You clever, clever man. Congratulations.' She'd kissed him again. 'You deserve it. You really do. It couldn't happen to a nicer guy.'

'It's still not certain,' he'd warned her. 'It's just a notion at present. I might be wrong.' After his moment of elation in the gorge, that truth had weighed on him, countering every wild and optimistic thought.

'You won't be wrong,' she'd said. 'You know it all too well. You know how it all works.'

'And I know I might be wrong.'

'I'll bet you,' she'd said, grinning. 'I'll bet you all you find that you were right.'

He'd laughed. 'Nice try.'

'When will you dig it out, or whatever it is you do. Dredge it? Is that the word?'

'As soon as I can.'

'How long will it take?'

'I don't know. Weeks, months. Probably the rest of this trip.'

'Can I help?'

He had laughed, laced his arms around her waist in sudden abandon, pulled her to him, kissed her on the forehead. 'You already have. I wouldn't have found it, if it weren't for you.'

'But can I?'

'Of course. You can help me right away.'

The difficulty, he had explained, was not just the depth of the water, but the gorge as well. There was nowhere nearby where he could set up the pump and sluice. He could put them up on the ledge, where he'd discovered her, but it was twenty metres above the stream; the pump wasn't powerful enough to lift the gravel that far. Or he could set it up on the bank downstream, but that would need extra hose far more than he had – and would just increase the problems of blockages. The only alternative was to put it all on floats – the pump and the header box and sluice, too. That was how some people did all their dredging, he told her: usually, with the aid of wetsuits and snorkels, so that they could lie in the stream with their heads under water as they dredged. He had none of that gear – no floats, no wetsuit, no snorkel.

'What will you do?'

'I don't know. I might be able to hire stuff, or buy it. In Hokitika maybe, if I'm lucky. More likely Christchurch. But the weekend's coming. It would cost me two days, at least.'

'Can't you build it? There's wood, and some old oil drums in the outhouse. We could build a raft.'

'That's what I was wondering.'

'I can help with that. Rafts are easy. We used to make them when I was a kid.'

So that is what they had done. Two rafts, a larger one for the header box and sluice, which he could tether a little way downstream; and a smaller one for the generator and pump. They were expertly made, so that he could break them down for transport, reassemble them with ease. Addie had added some decorations, too. The bulwarks ornamented with lengths of fretwork she found in the woodpile; on the prow of the larger one, a painted figurehead – a mermaid, big-breasted, long blonde flowing hair. 'A bit of womanly encouragement for you,' she said.

Evan added names on the stern of each one: *Daniel Erihana*, *Hākaraia Haeroa*.

'Fancy names for boats,' Addie observed: 'Why those?'

'They were early gold miners,' he told her. 'It's a classic tale. Their dog got swept overboard. One of them swam after it to rescue it. When he caught the dog, he found gold dust in its coat. The river must be full of gold, they realised. By the end of the day, they'd collected eight kilos or more from the nearby rocks.'

'Clever dog,' she said. 'What was she called, I wonder?'

The emphasis, Evan noted, was on the 'she'.

Now, Addie said: 'We should give them a proper launch. We just need a bottle of champagne.'

'I've a bottle of supermarket plonk.'

'That'll do. But I warn you. It's just to drink. There's no way I'm going to waste good wine by smashing it on silly boats, however fancy their names.'

Eleven

He'd been right about the site: the waterfall, the plunge-pool. In the first day back, his sampling across the area had soon shown that. At the upstream end, he'd uncovered the hard band of quartzite, dipping at seventy degrees or so up-valley, matching what he'd seen from the bench above the gorge. At the edges, the gravel was shallow, underlain by bedrock. In the centre of the pool it was at least two metres deep. At a guess it must contain over a thousand cubic metres of gravel – two thousand tonnes at least to shift. Working every hour, every day, it would take him all the time he had left – four weeks – maybe longer, for as he got deeper the difficulties of dredging would increase. He wasn't even certain that he could get to the bottom without diving gear.

How much gold it might contain he still could not tell. From the samples he'd gathered, it seemed that near the surface the gravels were barren, but with depth the gold gradually increased. Close to the bedrock there were nuggets to be found. In one place, he'd hit a pocket carved into the rock. It contained half an ounce of gold: more in one small hollow than he'd found in a week of dredging before. That's where the real treasure would lie, he told himself: in the swirl holes and cavities that the water had carved at the base of the pool. How much would depend on how many there were; how many he could reach. But the numbers enticed him. Twenty ounces, perhaps thirty? Maybe forty if he were lucky? Even at a conservative fifteen hundred dollars an ounce, he'd be looking at tens of thousands of dollars' worth of gold by the end. A year's wages, more.

Addie had already asked him what he would do with it all – the money he'd earn. He still didn't know. He'd have to share it with her in some way, of course, though in what proportion, he couldn't yet work out: time to worry about that later. But he'd have plenty left. What was it that he desired? What were the bounds to his greed?

Addie had come with him to the claim. She'd insisted, given him no choice – or none that he either dared or wanted to assert. He welcomed the thought of her company, yet worried that she'd be unable to cope with the conditions, the stress of the work, that she'd be in his way. He wondered how they would manage living together out in the bush, where facilities were basic and they couldn't help but find themselves together, in close proximity. Where his own simmering desires would be put to the test.

But his concerns seemed to have been misplaced. She'd already proved her worth. She'd hauled and heaved with him to carry the rafts up to the claim, helped him assemble them and drag them into the stream, then stood waist deep in the water as he positioned the pump, got everything balanced. She'd shown her inventiveness when the limits of their original design became clear, and the pump threatened to shake itself off its raft: cutting lengths of supplejack from the trees and using them to lash everything in place.

As he put together the dredge, he'd shown her the layout, explained how it worked. A main hose, running from the nozzle to the header box; feeding into it a narrower hose, which linked to the pump. It was all very simple, he told her: the pump forced water into the main hose, creating a suction that drew in material through the nozzle, and shot it out into the header box. There the force of the jet broke the material up and carried it on to the sluices, where baffles trapped the heavier material while the lighter sand and silt were washed out.

He assigned her the task of standing by the sluice and watching the header box. If no gravel came through, he told her, she needed to yell, for it meant that the hose was blocked. She could watch the trays as well, and warn him if they got overloaded. 'But whatever you do,' he said, 'don't put your hand in front of the jets. The gravel will take your fingers off.'

She'd nodded at his instructions, said: 'OK boss.'

Living together, too, had proved less fraught than he'd anticipated. He'd brought the small tent that he always kept in the truck in case of need, and she slept in that. For the rest – the roughness and make-do of bush life – she showed no concerns. And out here, where everything was done by necessity, not choice or planning, the inevitable awkwardnesses they encountered, the accidents of immodesty were natural and easily laughed away.

Even with her help, though, the dredging was proving hard. He'd never tried to dredge on this sort of scale before, and was learning the technique as he went along. To give him extra reach, he'd extended the nozzle on his dredge as far as he could, using additional pipes, but it took all his effort to hold it in place, and as he disturbed the bed, the silt clouded the water so that most of the time he was working blind, feeling with his hands to ward off larger pebbles that might block the hose. Often, he was working at the limits of his reach, up to his nose in water.

Blockages happened often, and he got to dread Addie's sudden shout of alarm: 'It's plugged!' Then, he had to abandon the suction nozzle, splash across to the sluice, remove the rubber bung from the front of the header box, and stab at the obstruction with the metal probe. Occasionally, the hose blocked. Then it was a game of trial and error, trying to wriggle or bang it free; when all else failed, he had to stop everything, break the hose down, curl and twist the blocked section, slap it against a rock, rootle it with the probe in order to clear it. More than once, they both missed the early signs, and he kept dredging after the blockage had occurred, so that the gravel backed up, clogging the whole line.

But as time went on, he was getting more skilled at it all. He had an instinct, now, for which pebbles might cause a blockage and should be avoided, when to divert the nozzle to prevent more getting sucked in. Addie was also learning to interpret the flow of water through the header box, the sounds of the jet, and to give early warning of problems. He became more adept, too, at chasing the beds of gravel, so that the process of dredging became smoother and more natural, less frenetic.

Even so, the work was tiring and cold. Every thirty minutes or so, he took a break. By the end of the day he was aching and exhausted. And yet the companionship of it all was pleasure and lightened the day. In the evenings, after they'd washed in the stream, eaten, they would sit together in the darkening glade, while the gas lantern made a small pale pool at their feet, and they would talk.

They talked about anything. About the dredging and how it was going, how much gold they'd found. About the gold itself, how it had got there, how it was made. About places they'd been. The world, politics, religion. Books and films and music. There seemed to be nothing that they could not talk about. She told him of teenage heart-throbs – Dev Patel, Cam Cigandet, Chingy – people whose names meant nothing to him. He talked about philosophy and some of the great thinkers he admired: Twain, Rousseau, John Stuart Mill.

One evening, she tried to instruct him on theories of dance. The views of Anna Pakes and Monroe Beardsley: that dance is expression through action and that any action can be dance in the right context. He didn't really understand it, and she stood up, told him to watch. Then she began to dance, moving silkily in the darkness, her body a shifting curtain against the shadowy trees, so that sometimes she was the light and sometimes the dark, sometimes both, then neither. He watched, entranced.

'So was that dance?' she asked, when she stopped.

'Yes. Of course.'

'Why? Why wasn't it just fidgeting, or exercise-taking?'

He thought for a moment, trying to grasp the essence of what he'd felt. 'I suppose, because it spoke to me,' he said at last. 'I felt a connection with it.'

'What did it speak to you about?'

'I'm not sure. A snake, a serpent. Maybe the river. Maybe something else.' He wanted to say 'beauty, love', perhaps 'desire', but didn't dare. 'Life,' he said.

'You see. They're right.'

'Is that what it was meant to be?'

She sighed. 'Oh you clod. You literalist. It's not *meant* to be anything. It's just a pathway, a journey, which takes you somewhere, to wherever you want it to go.'

He nodded, though he was still not sure that he understood.

*

The next evening, she danced for him again.

They were sitting in the camp once more, washed and fed after another long and tiring day. They'd reached the bedrock now, and he was dredging in the swirl holes, his arms stretched, his body bent. The holes seem to wait, cowering against his approach. A smooth hollow, a cusp in the rock. A cluster of cobbles, rounded by the water, like birds huddled in their nest. And beneath them, amidst the gravel and sand, the treasure they protected: nuggets of gold. In truth, he rarely saw the gold until he'd finished and panned the residue in the sluice, but he imagined it as he worked and sometimes thought he'd glimpsed it, winking at him through the dappling waters, before it was obscured by the silt, gobbled up by the hungry dredge.

When at last they'd stopped, he'd fetched his towel, gone to the small pool below the camp that he used for bathing, lay there in the dark waters, feeling his aches and his tightness slowly drain away. He tried to work out how much gold they had found that day. Each nugget weighed three or four pennyweight – a fifth or a sixth of an ounce. Each one was worth another two or three hundred dollars. There must have been a dozen today, maybe more. Two thousand dollars or more for the day's work? Riches beyond dreams.

Addie said much the same when he got back to the camp. She stood waiting for him. Her skin glistened from her own bathing in a pool further upstream, her hair – almost black again now, its false colour leached out by the sun – seemed to dance in the low evening light.

He fetched the two beers that he'd put in the stream to cool that morning. They fizzed as he opened them.

'To another good day,' he said, passing her one, raising his own in a toast.

'To a fortune beyond imagining,' she replied, and the cans clinked.

But after she'd drunk, she put the can down and moved a few paces away, stood there for a moment, looking around.

She might have been sizing up the place she'd found, or perhaps matching herself to it, though for what purpose he could not deduce at first. Then she began to hum, softly, a wandering, tuneless sound; and then to turn, treading the grass flat. She turned again, repeating the process. Four, five times, she turned, and then, gradually, she began to shrink. With each rotation, she became smaller, bending lower, slowing, until she seemed to curl into herself and became still and silent.

He watched, waiting for her to move again, to break the spell. But she remained motionless, wrapped tight, the curve of her back making a shape that he struggled to name. An apple, a foetus, a bud, a hidden nest of gold.

She stayed that way for several minutes, not moving, making no sound. He kept his eyes fixed on her, counting away the seconds until the change that he was sure would come. Thinking he saw it, realising that it was just the rise and fall of her body as she breathed, his own eyes playing tricks. Until, almost imperceptibly, her body seemed to reshape itself, her back straightened, her neck stretched, her arms extended, twisted, wove, reached up, and the sound of her humming grew. A worm, he thought, emerging from the apple, becoming a snake? The foetus unfolding; the bud opening out? The gold giving itself up.

She stopped, stepped forward, became herself.

'What did you see?' she asked.

'A dance.'

'Yes,' she said. 'A dance. But you see, all that stuff I told you, about dance being movement. It's true. But it's not the whole truth. Dance can be stillness as well, so long as the stillness contains the movement within it. The promise of movement. The seed.' She came across and sat on the log she used as a seat.

'Maybe that's true of other things as well. That you don't have to have the real thing, just the possibility of it, the anticipation.'

He nodded, knowing that there was truth in her words. A truth about him.

He told her that he'd liked what she'd done, and she smiled in acknowledgement.

'I'm glad. It was mine. I wrote it, performed it for my finals. It was called *Still Life*.'

And later, after they'd eaten, she sat motionless and silent for a long time, and he wondered whether it was another performance, another dance. But then she stood up, came across to him, laid a hand on his shoulder and said: 'Thank you, Evan.'

He looked up at her, asked: 'What for?'

'For letting me stay, bringing me here with you. Putting up with me. Caring.'

He reached up, gave her hand a squeeze.

'You're welcome,' he said.

'It means a lot,' she continued. 'More than you can imagine. Far, far more.'

He started to say something, searching for words, but she silenced him with a shake of her head.

'I feel safe here, secure. I like that – the way you give me space and freedom, yet care about me, too. I feel – I feel loved. Am I allowed to say that?' He nodded and she continued: 'It's alright. It's only – what do they call it? – only platonic, I know. But I like that. It's what I need.'

And she bent, kissed him on the head, slipped her hand free, and said softly: 'Goodnight, Evan. Sleep well.'

*

It was, he knew, the sounds and patterns that trapped him, made his thoughts swirl and vortice around the same small point. The rhythms of the stream and his body and the machinery. Each day it happened. And though the trigger for it all changed – some unexpected event, something he'd seen or heard or said, some memory stirred up from long ago – in a way, the focus was always the same. Life, and what it meant. Addie.

He wondered about her, tried over and over again to fix her in some way, put shape and boundaries around her so that he might know what she was. Yet always she eluded him. Always she led his thoughts on.

And as she did so, his thoughts seemed to fuzz and fade, dissolving into the interplay of his own movements, and the water's, and the sound and pulse of the dredge, the vacancy of everything else. The repetition. The ache of his limbs. An impressionist's world, he imagined: light in fragments, light and colour in their most primal forms, flash and splash as they tried to find their shape. Even his own body, he could believe, no longer one, but dabs and drips of matter, each with its own degree of hurt, but held together by that – the ache and the pain.

The world in paint and pain, he thought. Life as a dance.

Everything reduced to this.

Another day. Another few ounces. All the noise, the movement, the cold, the hurt, compressed within what he held in his hand. A cluster of metallic grains that glistened when he turned them against the light; half a dozen small nuggets, warty and misshapen. Could it mean so little?

Could it be worth so much?

So the days came and went, each one written to the same template as the one before. Rising at dawn, stiff and still tired, yet eager to get out on the site. A simple breakfast. The walk along the bank, beside the rippling stream. When they reached the gorge, splashing through the riffles and pools, making the droplets dance and the young trout dash for cover in the shadows of the nearest overhang. Then the floats pulled into position, anchored, the sluice checked, fuel added to the generator. One last look around, and the motor heaved into life, complaining. And then the hours of bending, bracing, crouching, reaching, stretching to the demands of the dredge. All the while, working his way up the pool, in slow lines, a half metre at a time. Addie, stationed by the sluice, an expert now, keeping the header box clear of debris, picking out the rocks from the trays, checking them, saving those that she thought might contain the hint of gold for him to check later. Sometimes, giving a quick yell of triumph when she saw a nugget amidst the grit and sand. Calling him over when she thought that the trays needed emptying, or if there were problems of any kind.

Two or three times in the morning, again in the afternoon, he'd wash the trays, take the residue downstream to the end of the gorge, and perch there on the bank, pan the sands. As he did so, she'd crouch beside him, tense with excitement.

'What have you found?' she'd ask. 'There's some,' she'd say, pointing. Or: 'What about that?'

In the evenings, he'd sort through the finer residues by the light of his lantern, running a magnet over the black sand to draw the magnetite out, check what was left with his hand lens, bottle it. Then, she would sit apart, knowing that he needed to concentrate, that her shadow looming over him would be a distraction. But when he'd finished she'd hold the phial in her fingers, against the lamp, and try to guess how much there was. Always too much, for she was no judge of the tiny volumes that the glass seemed to magnify, and let her enthusiasm carry her away.

And slowly the gold came. Not in a steady flow, but as he knew it would, in surges and waves. Some days, there was hardly any at all. They'd struggle for hours to shift boulders or to get into the deeper crevices that reached into the rock wall, and end up with nothing. They'd move huge mounds of gravel, and be rewarded with just a few grains. But on other days, he'd hit a swirl pool or a rich pocket in the lee of a rock, and the gold would pour out.

How much now, he wondered: a dozen ounces, fifteen? Nearly twenty?

But as the work went on, it became harder still. By the second week, he was dredging at the limit of his capability. Plug-ups became a bane, for he could no longer see the end of the nozzle, nor reach down to feel it and keep it clear. And the deeper they went, the coarser the gravel became.

In desperation, he tried a new strategy: clearing areas of coarser pebbles, dredging it for a while, then clearing it again. It was a slow business, and at times he had to resort to ducking down beneath the water, operating almost blind, his lungs near to bursting as he tried to shift the cobbles and boulders from the deeper sections. But it seemed to work.

Addie demanded to help and eventually he allowed her to have a try. She quickly showed herself surprisingly skilled. What she lacked in strength, she made up for in her agility and guile. She swam just as he'd once imagined – like a fish. She seemed to be streamlined like one, too, so that she moved with silky ease. And she could hold her breath for half as long again as he ever could. So she shared the task of clearing with him, giving him a break – a chance to warm up, rest his limbs, watch.

He enjoyed watching her. The dark shape of her body as she hung below the surface; the sudden bubble of disturbance as she rose from the stream, water cascading from her shoulders; the quick shake of her head, scattering droplets in the air. The way the water received her as she ducked down again.

After five or ten minutes, she'd signal to him, and pad across to where he waited in the shallows, and stand in front of him, dripping, her shorts and shirt clinging to her body like a skin, hair glistening, her face made smooth and shining, eyes bright. As she stood there, she'd explain what she'd managed to do – whether he could yet start dredging again, where to aim, or whether it needed him to do more clearing. Then she'd make her way downstream, or up on to the ledge above the gorge, and lie there for a while to warm in the sun, recover. Sometimes, after a while he'd go and join her, check that she was alright, and on occasions he'd discover her, sprawled like a child, asleep.

Yet as the days passed, the work and the time they were spending in the water began to take their toll.

Their evenings became shorter, they went to bed earlier, slept longer. There was no more dancing, not much talk. Most mornings, when Evan emerged, Addie was still in her tent, and he let her stay as long as he could. When she appeared, she always looked ragged and bleary, shocked by the brightness of the world, and he would wonder: will she stand the pace? A few weeks earlier, she'd been traumatised, battered, near to death. Was he demanding too much?

Their skin became chapped, peeled; their hands were calloused, their legs sore. Both of them complained of burning eyes.

And amidst all the endeavour and effort, mistakes began to happen, tensions emerged. Most were minor, cause for no more than a curse, a shrug, a laugh. But one afternoon, after he'd stripped the sluice down, cleaned it out, rebuilt it, he'd mis-set the angle of the trays so that the water gushed through too fast. He didn't notice for nearly an hour, wondered idly as he worked why Addie hadn't called to warn him that the trays were filling again. Eventually, he stopped dredging, went across to the sluice to check. Except for a few pebbles, fragments of rock, the trays were empty. He turned on Addie: why hadn't she noticed? She spat back angrily: 'Hey – you're the bloody boss, here. I just do what I'm told.'

The following evening, another mistake. Addie had blundered into him as he was crouched by the tent, serving the food. Pasta sauce went everywhere: over his trousers, in the grass, on to the burners of the stove where it charred, filling the clearing with its acrid smell. Viva had fed well in consequence, doing her bit for tidiness. He and Addie had shared what was left in the pan, filling it out with flat, stale bread. Not what they wanted at the end of a ten-hour shift, and eaten in silence.

The next day, he called a halt at lunchtime.

'What's wrong?' she asked.

'Half-day,' he said. 'We need a break. I know I do.'

They spent the afternoon in the camp, tidying up, reading, doing small working repairs to clothes and gear. Evan took out his box-safe, opened it up, showed Addie what they'd found.

'How much, do you think?' she asked. 'What's it worth?'

'I don't know. It must be over half a kilo – seventeen ounces, maybe eighteen,' he said, deliberately under-estimating as ever. 'That's 25 000 dollars or thereabouts.'

'Christ. And how much more is there left?'

He shrugged. 'I can't tell. If we're lucky, as much again. Probably less.'

'And you just keep it all in that box, in your tent?'

'Out here, yes.'

'You must be mad. What's to stop someone finding it? They'd think they'd won the lottery.'

'Who'd find it out here?' He spread his hands, indicating the expanse of bush.

'People like you,' she said. 'Mad prospectors. And people like me – people who get lost. Hunters, too; people like Todd. Any one of them might come past while we're out dredging, poke around, find it. It wouldn't take much intelligence to work out what you're here for, and guess that there might be gold around. For goodness sake, put it somewhere safer. Somewhere it won't be found.'

For a while, they argued about it. She was right, he knew. There was a risk. He'd fretted about it before when he'd been working here alone. Usually, though, there was far less gold to worry about, and he stayed out here for only a few days at a time. In between, he took the gold back to the cottage, hid it there.

'And where's that?' she asked when he told her, in surly self-defence. 'Let me guess. Under the mattress? Under the bed?'

He shrugged. 'It's been fine until now.'

'Fuck me,' she exclaimed. 'Don't you know what the world these days is like?'

Her question hurt him, made him feel belittled, reminded him of the difference in their age and knowledge of life.

'I'll think about it,' he said.

'You should. You should hide it properly. For both our sakes. Because if anything happened, and it got taken, the first person you'd suspect would be me.'

'I wouldn't.'

'Believe me, you would. You simply couldn't avoid it.' She stood up, looked down at him, her features taut. 'Please,' she said. 'Just do it. I don't want to know where. I'm going for a walk. Just do it while I'm gone.'

He did so. He waited until she'd had time to move out of sight, then found the spade, took it a short way into the bush behind his tent, dug a hole, and put the box in. He covered the spot with a rock that he hauled up from the stream, and stood gazing down at it.

His own attitude puzzled him. It was out of character, he knew. He regarded himself as a cynic, as a doubter. Trust nothing, trust no one. Why then, was he so willing to trust the world with his gold?

And yet, perhaps, he knew. Because to do otherwise felt like the admission of distrust. Not just of the world in general, the odd passer-by – but of Addie, too. As though he were being made to protect it from her. As though she didn't trust herself.

He didn't want that. He didn't want to think it. He wanted to trust her, and wanted her to know and see that trust. He wanted her to be trustworthy, and to prove it every day. It was the bargain he sought: her trust and restraint in return for his.

Later, when she still had not returned, he went down to the stream, Viva at his side. There was no sign of Addie. He wondered where she'd gone, and on an impulse turned downstream, made his way to the bluff above the gorge. He picked his way up through the scrub, the way he'd gone when he first found her. He came to the boulders, looked down. She was lying on the ledge in the sun, legs splayed, arms stretched, head back, like an ancient sacrifice to the gods, left for the birds to scavenge. She was naked.

She'd been swimming, he guessed, had lain there to dry, enjoy the warmth of the sun.

For five minutes, perhaps longer, he stood in the shadows of the trees, watching. Reading her like he would the landscape. Belly and breast, rib and hip, dark tangle of bush. Then she stirred, rose, picked up her clothes and started to dress.

He slipped away.

*

If Addie's gesture of abandonment above the gorge had been a sacrifice, then the gods had been appeased, for the next two days brought rich rewards: nearly four ounces of clean nugget gold. Most of it came from a single swirl hole at the base of the pool. It was long, curved, made up it seemed of two holes that had become linked. From the contours of the rock, he guessed that it had been fed by a loop of water that had cut its own path, separate from the main flow. For whatever reason, it seemed to have been a magnet for the gold. There were a dozen nuggets, clustered together, the largest perhaps a quarter of an ounce. He'd never found gold in such proliferation before. It seemed too good to be true.

It had been won against all the odds. Fuel was running out, and on the second morning he'd poured the last dregs of the supply he'd brought into the generator. All the time he was working, he'd been listening to the motor, waiting for it to cough, stop. He was worrying, too, about the sluice. It had had a hard beating this year, running hour after hour, day after day, carrying loads far beyond what it usually did. There were dents in the trays, the framework was twisted, on one section one of the wing-nuts that held it all in place had sheared off. He needed time to repair it before it broke completely. There was no time now.

But the biggest challenge had been the hole that contained the gold. It was almost inaccessible: in a tight cleft, behind a large mass of rock that must have fallen off the edge of the gorge. From the angles he could work at, it was impossible to get the nozzle into the space. He'd had to fit a smaller bore, then lie, arm extended as far as it would go, face pressed against the rock to reach into the cavity. In that position, his mouth and nose were under water, so he'd had to improvise a snorkel with a piece of tubing. Addie stood by him, trying to support his head, massaging his back, feeding him with drinking water from a bottle whenever he paused; checking the sluice and encouraging him with reports on what she could see: 'Two nuggets, good ones . . . another – and one more . . . oh, wow, that's a beauty . . .' It helped, that commentary, her enthusiasm. Each cry was a spur to continue for another minute or two.

Somehow, the minutes extended, became hours. He spent half a day like that, in four shifts. When he extracted himself after the last one, he could hardly straighten up enough to stand. Addie put her arm around him, helped him to the boulder that they used as a base, hugged him gently.

'You're a hero,' she said. 'A real hero.'

He hobbled across to the generator, switched it off, went to the sluice. Even as he approached it, he knew that there was a problem. It leaned drunkenly; water spilled from the side. He inspected the frame. One of the pieces of angle-iron had sheared, allowing the trays to collapse.

He swore.

'What's wrong?' Addie asked.

'That last dredge; we've lost the lot. The sluice has collapsed.'

'Oh, Evan. I'm sorry. I should have noticed. I'm so sorry.'

It wasn't her fault, he told her; she couldn't be in two places at once. 'Anyway,' he said. 'That's it. Tomorrow, I have to take some of this stuff back, do repairs. I'll bring more fuel as well. Another rest day for you.'

He asked her if she wanted to come, but she shook her head, said she'd rather stay. 'I want to try my hand at panning,' she said. 'Is that OK?'

He was happy to oblige. There was not much she could do to help, for he could easily carry the sluice rack and empty fuel cans to the truck, and whatever she might carry on the trip back, it would still take two trips from the car park. He yearned, too, for a day alone – not to get away from her, but just to have a chance to think: about her, about himself, and with distance between. She'd become too entangled in his life, too tied up with everything he did and thought. It couldn't last, he knew. He needed to know again what life would be like without her.

On the way to the cottage, therefore, he tried to feel the space opening up between them. Each step, each jolt of the truck, another unit of separation.

He tried to analyse how it felt. Not release, not that. Not freedom or a return to some older self. Instead, like a journey reluctantly completed, a dream fading and the reality of the day ahead. Edging towards the inevitable – three or four weeks away now at most – when the trip would be over, he'd be back at work, Addie would be gone.

The thought lay over him like a cloud. The summer retreating, dull autumn waiting in the wings.

He reached the cottage, stood regarding it from the bottom of the steps. Even from this distance it felt abandoned, neglected. Like something unfairly blamed. He went to the door, pushed it open, easing it the last part of the way with his knee. Silence greeted him. In her absence, he realised, it was a place that did not wait there, anticipating his return. It was just an empty building, shut up.

He spent the rest of that day repairing the damaged sluice rack, bolting on a length of aluminium to hold the broken frame-piece together, finding new nuts for those that had been lost. He refilled the fuel cans from the dwindling supply in his tank, loaded them on to the truck. By the time he'd finished, went indoors, it was already getting dark. The days shortening, he thought; the future seeping in.

He hadn't told Addie, but he'd brought the gold with him. He thought it was what she wanted, for him to spirit it away to somewhere safe and unknown. Somewhere that took it out of her realm, beyond her concern and care. Quite where to hide it, though, he wasn't sure. There were dark corners and cupboards in the outhouse, but that had no lock and anyone could wander in. He could hide it in the bush, but the same applied; rabbits, too, might uncover it as they burrowed, or pigs dig it up as they rooted for fungi and bugs. He looked around the cottage.

There was a narrow loft: too obvious, and the entrance was in Addie's bedroom, so putting it there seemed like a deliberate test. There were drawers in the kitchen, and a space behind the cabinet in the living room, but neither felt secure. He opened the wood-burner, looked inside, but other than the grate or the ashcan there was nowhere within it that would take the safe. He stood in his bedroom, but as she'd already indicated, that seemed the first place that anyone might search. He went on to the veranda, felt for a loose piece of weatherboarding that he might hide it behind, found none. Suddenly he realised how difficult it was to conceal some part of yourself within your own domain, something that defined you, for everywhere seemed to speak of what you were and advertise its knowledge.

In the end, he returned to the kitchen, moved the table and pulled back the rug. Near the wall was a place where the floorboards had been renewed when the wiring for the generator had been laid. They'd been refixed with screws. He undid them. Below was a small cavity, containing a junction box. The space beside it was just big enough to take the safe. He slid it in, relaid the floorboards, replaced the rug, dragged the table back. It would have to do.

He slept that night in his own bed, and slept well. But the house around him was empty and he dreamed of its vacancy in different guises – as wide-open spaces, as darkness, as something once held and now lost. And in the morning, as he sorted through his remaining provisions, tried to decide what he could take with him, what he should leave, he realised again how close the end was. Soon, the story would be finished, and Addie would be gone.

He drove back over the saddle slowly, trying to stretch the journey out. He wanted to delay his arrival, knowing that it would feel like a departure, too. He wanted just to think of her ahead of him, awaiting his return; time with her, still his to spend.

But as he walked from the car park carrying the trays, a can of fuel in his pack, his self-control gradually slipped. He began to hurry, almost to run, stumbling beneath the weight of his burden, cursing it for holding him back. Every minute seemed like a waste. As he approached the camp, he listened for some sound of her, then scoured the clearing, trying to see her, afraid that she would not be there.

Her cry of welcome greeted him, echoing Viva's bark. They both ran towards him, reached him together.

He put down the trays, slipped off his pack. Viva had claimed priority, was jumping at him, licking his face: I've missed you, I've missed; you've been gone so long.

Addie waited.

'There's more to come,' he said.

She nodded, smiled. 'Yes, there is.'

Then she stepped towards him, took his hand. 'It's this way,' she said. 'A surprise.'

He imagined it was a trout or rabbit casserole, magicked up in his absence, or perhaps a small nugget of gold she'd found while she'd tried panning in the stream. Instead, she led him to his tent, pulled back the flap, ushered him in; slipped in behind him, sealed the flap. And there, in the light of the lantern, she drew him down to his bed.

'I've had enough of Plato,' she whispered. 'Haven't you?'

Twelve

How had it been the first time, he wondered, all those years ago? Had he walked to school the next morning, as he walked through the bush today, his step light, his body lifted, his mind aglow? Had the world then – the drab Christchurch streets, the smoky buses, the brash young men on their way to work in the estate agents and banks and car showrooms in Sydenham and Waltham – seemed as vibrant and vital as the river and the trees and the chattering tuis did at his passing now? As though every one of them knew his secret and commented about it to each other admiringly behind cupped hands. Had he felt so smug?

Such adolescence, he thought, with a laugh. Such madness. This yielding, this abandonment. He wouldn't have believed he still had it in him. He could not believe his luck.

Sometime, in the night, he'd woken and wondered whether it had all been a dream, imagined himself alone in his makeshift bed. But then he felt her, nestled beside him, her body curled to the shape of his. His hand on her breast, as it had been when he woke that first night, weeks before – the night he'd first discovered her. This time, though, he did not withdraw, but left it there, and was content.

Yet the morning brought new doubt for when he woke again he was alone, and though he waited, convinced that she would soon return, she never came, and when he at last got up, went out, he found her sitting on a log by the stream, staring into the water, and imagined her regretting what had happened, or worse, indifferent to it all. Just another small pleasure, just another man. Then she turned, saw him, and smiled warmly and said: 'Hello dream-boy. You looked so sweet lying there, far too peaceful to wake.' And she took his hand, gently kissed it.

And later, when he told her he needed to go back to the truck to get the fuel, she'd insisted on accompanying him, had to be dissuaded.

'I need you to get the sluice rebuilt, get everything ready,' he told her. 'We can't waste any more time.'

Her face darkened. 'Oh, so that's what we were doing, is it? Wasting our time. Well, don't worry. I'll make sure it doesn't happen again.' And for an instant he had thought she meant it, but then she laughed, reached up, kissed him. 'Go,' she said. 'But no dallying. I want you back by bedtime.'

So he whistled as he went, and replayed her words and the night in his mind and imagined the night to come, and the forest sang its chorus to him, full of admiration or envy or pure happiness.

At the car park, however, all was quiet. It was late morning now, and even the birds had stilled. He unloaded the truck, strapped the cans to his pack, sat on the footrest drinking coffee from his flask, savouring the silence, the sense of a world that was sated, lulled.

He looked around, seeing suddenly features in the place that he had never noticed before. A pile of stones, like a cairn, at one edge of the clearing. A rusted post, which once perhaps was part of a simple footbridge across the stream. A ragged piece of paper, pinned to a tree, the words long ago bleached away. Each seemed apocryphal, full of unregarded meaning; each part of a story that ought to be known.

He scoured the ground, looking for messages there. The footprints of birds, the spoor of deer, the scuffings where pigs had been.

The line of his wheel-tracks, from when he had driven in, leading back towards the saddle and the cottage, and the world beyond; back to his old life. In the other direction, the trail through the bush that he'd just followed from the camp. Different destinies, different worlds.

He closed his eyes. He imagined himself a blithe spirit, able to go where he willed. To the cottage, to Addie, anywhere on the wild hills. A strange contradiction, he thought: that loneliness shackles you, that love makes you free.

Is that what it was: love? It seemed difficult to deny it now; Addie had used the word herself. And yet it hung beyond his reach, a word he could not say. He had thought he had found it before, been disabused. He had learned the lesson. Better not to name it; better simply to enjoy it while it existed, whatever it might be.

A sound reached him. He opened his eyes. It had come from behind him, somewhere up on the ridge, beyond the bush. He turned, listened. It came again. A crackling rumble. Thunder, he wondered, then dismissed the notion. Gunfire; rifle shots – two or three in close succession, muffled and distorted by the distance, the echoes from the surrounding hills.

Hunters in all likelihood, he guessed. Klas and his group should have gone by now, but one or two of the men might have stayed. Marty, perhaps, or Todd? Or just a new group, come while he'd been on the claim. Hunting for pigs, if he'd heard right, for deer and chamois would scatter at the first shot if they did not fall, might offer a second chance, never a third.

Good luck to them, he thought – the deer or the chamois, not the hunters. And perhaps this time his wishes would work, because just for once he had luck in abundance to spare.

*

Addie swished the pan, threw the residue into the stream. 'There's no gold in there anyway,' she said. 'You've taken it all.'

Her petulance, he knew, was feigned. She was enjoying herself, the challenge of panning, the excitement, the strange physical satisfaction in the act, the intimacy in the learning. But like all novices, she was impatient and tried too hard. She wanted to make the gold appear, wanted to conjure it out of the sand and silt, rather than let the pan do its job.

'Here,' he said. 'Feel how we do it.' He filled the pan again, set it in her hands, then leaned around her, one arm on each side, and gently began to guide her.

She leaned back, twisted up, trying to kiss him.

'It would help if you concentrated,' he said.

'It would help if you weren't such an old stodge.'

The water in the pan swirled, drawing the sediment with it. Already, he could see the grains begin to separate out, the larger and heavier ones drawn to the centre, the finer and lighter washed to the side.

'See?' he asked.

'I see,' she said.

But the softness of her hair against his cheek, her bare skin against his, the weight of her against him, won again, and he nuzzled her neck, ran his lips down to her shoulder, over the sharp edge of her scapula, tasting the salt on her skin.

They seemed to live like this, now, in a state of perpetual dance. His body and hers each aware of the other, responding to its presence and pulse. They woke in the morning in the cocoon of his bed. They ate their breakfast, side-by-side on a log in the clearing, as if still not ready to let their bodies part. They worked together in the stream, separated by a dozen metres or more of noise and swirling water, yet minds and limbs tuned to each other, so that they seemed to know what they were each thinking, could summon one another with a single cry, would often turn towards each other at the same moment and share a glance. They hurt together, sometimes bled together, shared the same bruises and disappointments, the same moments of joy.

And in between, when they took a break from the work, they swam naked together in the placid pools above the gorge, or sat on a gravel bar, bodies close, talking. And in the night, they lay together again, and shared themselves more deeply.

'Now you show me,' he said, and withdrew his hands.

'Spoilsport,' she muttered, but she tried, and this time she moved more fluently, without jerking the pan, and seemed to sink into the rhythm of her movements, almost as if in a trance, and when she at last stopped and peered into the residue, she gave a small cry of delight.

'I've got some!'

She showed him the pan. There was a single nugget, the size of a peppercorn, amidst the grit and mud.

'It's all mine,' she said. 'This one is. You can have all the rest, but this one is mine.'

'I'm going to share it all with you,' he said. 'You should know that.'

‘What do you mean?’ She spoke sharply, suspicion in her voice.

‘All of it. Everything. We share it between us.’

‘That’s stupid. Don’t be so silly.’

‘You’ve earned it,’ he said. ‘It wouldn’t have happened without you. I wouldn’t have found it. I couldn’t have done the dredging.’

‘I’ve told you before,’ she insisted, ‘I don’t want it. I really don’t.’ She held up the nugget. ‘This is all I want.’

That evening, she shared with him gold of her own. She took him to the stream below the camp, played a torch across the water. Small golden sparks blinked back at them. ‘Crayfish,’ she told him. ‘Koura.’ Then she showed him how to catch them with a simple line and hook and twist of bacon, and cooked them for him – boiling them until they turned orange, and the flesh was white, then serving them with herbs they’d brought from the garden behind the cottage.

The next night, she made him try his hand with the line, laughed when he came back empty-handed.

‘Were they too smart for you?’ she asked. ‘Or was your heart too soft?’

‘A bit of both,’ he admitted.

She laughed again. ‘You’d never survive in the wild,’ she said. ‘Do you know that? You’d starve rather than hurt anything. You’re too kind-hearted for your own good.’

And so the days passed, and the nights, and her affection for him, what seemed like her need, wove itself around him, and filled his dreams.

Once, as they lay together, she asked him when his birthday was, and when he told her the month and day, she asked for the year as well.

‘You’re fifty,’ she said, as if in wonder. ‘You don’t look it.’

'Do you mind?'

She laughed. 'Should I?'

'It's twice your age.'

'So – what are you suggesting. That we shouldn't be doing this?'

He didn't answer, and she regarded him with what felt like scorn. 'You worry too much,' she said. 'Age isn't everything. There are plenty of people like you and me happily married, or happily fucking. It's no big deal.'

Her response, crude though it was, soothed him. That word, love, flickered again at the margins of his mind, and he let it in. The hope kindled: that there might be a future somewhere, beyond the span of his time here on his claim, where she still existed, which she might somehow share.

And all that week, into the next, the weather seemed to echo his mood. Still days, with cotton-wool clouds, stretched blue skies. The air sweet with the scent of tea-tree and cedar and lemonwood, the honeyed hint of fungus and gorse. Bellbirds and tuis making the bush ring with their chiming songs.

And all the time, the gold came. Not in any steady flow, but in the same teasing pulses it had from the start.

He might almost have ignored the next challenge, yet knew he could not.

So far they'd excavated three-quarters of the plunge-pool. They had just the last quarter to go. It was the area next to the band of hard quartzite, tight against one wall of the gorge. It was here that the waterfall must have paused the longest, where the pool would be at its deepest, the swirl pools and crevices at their largest, the gravels the least disturbed. Buried within them, he knew, would be the richest finds of all.

The problem was how to get at them.

Dredging in the way he'd been doing wouldn't work. It was inefficient, would take far too long, and would leave the best deposits of all still out of reach. It was exhausting him, too. His body was battered and worn, Addie's the same. As he watched her, he'd seen the way she had changed with the work. Her muscles thickening, her legs and shoulders gaining strength, her face now almost berry-brown. When he held her at night, explored her, he could feel the tightness of her sinews, the roughness of her skin, the blisters and scars. He worried for her. How long could she go on?

He had to find another approach. He puzzled over it for days, thought of solutions, dismissed them. He talked it over with Addie, was mocked for his lack of trust in her stamina and strength. 'I dance, remember,' she said. 'Nothing is as hard as that.'

Another concern growing all the time. The weather, changing.

It had happened subtly, and at first he'd hardly noticed, dismissed it as just imagination and doubt. But one evening, as they sat outside his shelter, reflecting on the day's work, Addie suddenly rose, crawled into the small tent that had once been her own, pulled out her sleeping bag, wrapped it around her, then sat by his feet, snuggled tight against his legs.

'Cold?' he asked.

'Cosy,' she said.

Two days later, there were more signs. The wind shifting slightly, from the south. In the morning a bite in the air. Ragged clouds over the mountains all day, making small forays as if reconnoitring, trying to decide: is it time yet to invade? In the evening, mist on the river.

When they went to bed that night she wore one of his shirts as a nightdress for added warmth. It seemed to change her in a manner that he could not decipher. Not just clothed, but in some way withdrawn. It made him feel distant, held back, and he wanted her all the more.

But the next morning, there were no doubts. Autumn had arrived. The grass glistened with dew. And on the high ridges, there was a white rime of snow, making wedding cakes of the mountains.

He stood for a moment, beside the camp, calculating. When Addie came up to him, her breath clouding in front of her, he told her: 'We can't do it like this. Time's running out now. We need to make every hour count.'

He was going to divert the flow, he told her, across to the far side of the gorge where they had already excavated. Then they could dredge in the dry. He tried to explain his plan. First they'd build two small banks – wing dams, as the gold-diggers used to call them – running at an angle partway across the stream. The first would be beside the band of hard rock above the plunge-pool; the second downstream, in the area that they'd excavated. Then they'd make a bund – a bank of gravel – at right angles, running between them. It would create a small pond, which they could pump out, work in more easily.

'Clever,' Addie said.

'Maybe. But it will leak – so we'll have to keep pumping the pool out. And as we get lower, we'll need to shore up the gravel face to stop it collapsing. But it should work.'

'Should?' she asked. 'You mean, you don't know?'

'Will. I've never done it before, but it's how they used to work in the past – before they had pumps and dredges. I've read about it somewhere. It'll work.'

'Sounds good to me,' she said.

'But there's a downside,' he told her. 'I need to use the tarpaulin to give the main wing dam extra strength – which means that we're going to have to sleep in the little tent from now on. It's going to get cosy at night, I'm afraid.'

'If that's the downside,' she said, laughing, 'I can't wait to find the up.'

It took all day. He set Addie on moving all his belongings out of his tent, stowing them as best she could. He took down his tarpaulin, dragged it along the trail, back to the dredging site, then paced up and down the bank, working out where to place the dams.

The first wing dam, above the hard band of rock, was the hardest, for they were in the full force of the flow. They hauled in the heaviest boulders they could move to make a core of the dam, found logs and wedged them into place between the boulders. They added brushwood and gravel to help plug the gaps. Next, struggling against the water, Evan heaved in the tarpaulin and wrapped it over the structure, weighed it down with cobbles and small boulders. Then they banked up more gravel and brushwood to complete the job.

Lower downstream, beyond the area they needed to dredge, they made another dam, using boulders and cobbles and logs. Finally, at right angles, they used the dredge to pile up a rough gravel bund, linking the two.

It was crude, makeshift, but the stream seemed to understand. It pooled against the dam, fingered it experimentally, swirled for a while as if trying to decide what to do next. Then it gathered itself, spilled around the barrier, found the bund; lapped against it, shifting a few pebbles, sucking at the sand, and all of a sudden seemed to accept its lot, and settled into its new course.

Evan stood on a boulder, watching it all, proud, pleased. It wasn't a pretty sight. Neither a connoisseur of topography nor an engineer would have found much in it that was attractive.

But any other prospector, schooled in the art of bodgery and make-do and the Kiwi culture of 'she'll be right', would have seen its merits, given a small and approving nod.

'It works,' he said.

'Of course,' Addie shouted, from where she stood on the bund. 'I didn't doubt it. I never doubt you.'

They hauled up the generator, set out the hoses, started to pump the water out from the area behind the dam. Two hours later, the water level had fallen by half a metre. If he ran it all night, he reckoned, it would be dry by the time he needed to start the next day. After that, it would be a delicate balancing act: dredging as fast as he could, then pausing to pump the water out again before it got too deep; in between, shoring up the gravel banks with more logs.

That night, they crawled into Addie's tent, exhausted, aching, but triumphant. Addie kissed him, told him how brilliant he was, and was asleep almost before she'd finished the compliment, her head cradled against his chest. He lay awake for an hour or more afterwards, keyed up by what they'd done, the sense of achievement, and the paradox that now lay ahead. Wanting to hold time, just like this, still in his arms. Wanting to finish the job, get the gold and get out, before the weather broke.

*

Addie's confidence in his engineering had been well-placed. The wing dam held. For three or four hours at a time, Evan could work in its protection, dredging the gravel with the pool never more than knee deep. Then it would take two hours of pumping to remove the water that had seeped in. During that interval, he'd pan the residue or sit with Addie while she panned. Those hours seemed like precious times. Times when he felt like a rock able to withstand the tide, the weather, the gnaw of wind and ice, could deny even the flow of time itself.

But as they worked, as they played in the brief intervals between the dredging, in the evenings as they sat together, at night as they lay woven into one, the imbalance of time's tyranny seemed to loom over him, mock him for his pleasures. On the one side lay all that time in her life that he didn't know other than in the tiny glimpses she sometimes gave him of her past – precise cameos, tattered portraits, blurred landscapes, none of them real. All the time in his own life that had passed before she was even born. And on the other, the short span of their time ahead. A week or two now, a handful of days, then what?

He wanted to ask. He wanted to reason with her, probe to see how far she would go.

He thought of Juliette and the way his time with her had ended, not even with a whimper, just silence, indifference. How could he avoid the same thing again?

Yet how could he ask?

Instead, he lapsed into silences, and his own blank thoughts.

One day, as they sat on the platform above the gorge, waiting for the pumping to finish, he asked her to dance for him again. She hadn't done so for over a week now, since the last phase of the dredging had started, and she demurred at first. But then, without more persuasion, she seemed to change her mind. She got up, took a few steps away, stood poised for a moment and started to move. It was a light, folksy improvisation, which after a short while she accompanied with the murmured words of a song, about buttercups and meadows and soldiers and maids. And while she danced, a fantail appeared, and seemed to dance with her.

'The virgin's lament,' she told him when she'd finished. 'It's traditional.'

The following evening, in the camp, in the half-dark, she danced once more, this time without provocation. She'd been silent for a long time, and he wondered whether she was unwell, or – like him – reflecting on their small and diminishing interlude together; summer going, autumn creeping in. When she stood up, and touched him on the shoulder, he thought that she was walking away from him, perhaps to the tent, to sleep, or for a few moments alone. Instead, she stepped to the edge of the pool of light that the lantern made, and stood there in that pose she always adopted before she danced. Her body loose, her head bent. Her hair – long enough now to reach her shoulders, hair that he loved to stroke and nestle against at night – falling across her face. And she started to move. Her movements were slow, wistful, and seemed to come not from anything she'd learned or practised, but directly from her mind. An improvisation, he guessed, a welling up of something in her that she could not express in any other way. Yet, in a minute or two, it faded, and she stilled, and at the end left him feeling strangely cheated and unsettled, as though her thoughts had dried up or perhaps she could not face revealing the conclusion.

It seemed to speak of the future, of a life she couldn't grasp or thought she might never reach. It seemed almost like a farewell.

That night, in their tent, he needed her comfort and tried to draw her to him, lure her with a caress. But she gently pushed his hand away.

'Too tired?' he asked.

'Too dangerous,' she said. 'Unless you're better prepared than I thought.'

He laughed, relieved more than disappointed that the reason was mundane and biological, and not because of him. 'I'm afraid not. I wasn't really expecting this.'

She touched his chin – the softest of reprimands. 'Well, learn your lesson. Come prepared next time; you never know what might happen out here in the wilds.'

Thirteen

She was dancing again, standing on one of the logs that the hunters had dragged up to the fire. From the west, the low sun angled through the trees, bathing her in its golden glow. A spotlight on the star performer. Evan watched entranced, amused. There seemed no end to her eccentricity and inventiveness, nor nature's willing connivance.

As she danced, she chanted – strange nonsense rhymes that she might have learned in the playground as a child, or perhaps made up herself. 'The savage rabbit is known to inhabit every corner it can find. And the male snail has its house in its tail which is a moral for all mankind . . . The worst curse is a spaniel in the works, or so many people opine. But abusive mooses give no excuses for not getting to work on time.'

After each one he laughed, applauded, and she smiled in acknowledgement, then danced on silently for a while as if trying to remember what followed.

He needed this respite. He needed the distraction. And he needed to see Addie like this, to drink her in, to let her infect him. Time seemed to be racing now, dragging him in its wake. Every breath of wind, every rustle of trees and every leaf that fell carried the message, telling him that soon it would all be at an end. Soon, she would be gone.

Soon, too, the gold would be his.

They had most of it now. There were just a few metres of gravel left, tight against the edge of the gorge, in the deepest section of the pool. It was a small area, hard to get to, but far too good to ignore. It beckoned him like his destiny. For the last week, the gold had been getting more plentiful day by day. This final corner, where the wall of the gorge and the hard band of rock met, making a small overhang, almost a cave, was going to hold the richest deposits of all.

Dredging them, though, would have to wait. Once more, the struggle had taken its toll, not just on Addie and him but the equipment as well. He needed to do more repairs, collect more fuel. He needed, also, to adapt his way of dredging, and to fetch timber and tools to make it work. As they got deeper, the gravel was becoming increasingly unstable. He could hear it slipping, pebbles falling around him in the pool. Once false move, one twist of the stream, and the bank would collapse. It threatened them; it threatened the gold as well. The residues from his sluicing, the remaining gravels, would slump together and become mixed up. The gold that was left would be dispersed amongst it all, lost. It was a risk he couldn't take. He needed to box in the sides.

So they'd returned to the cottage, emptied the outhouse, collected every piece of timber that might serve the purpose, loaded up the truck. Tomorrow they'd portage it all in. Then a day of woodworking and to pump the section dry, and he'd be ready. Two long days dredging after that, and the job would be done.

One more push, he told himself. A few more days. And with the thought came a sadness too strong to hold back.

Addie, he knew, felt it, too. She'd become quieter, more reflective, more subdued. Though love-making was out of bounds, she clung to him more. She seemed to crave his touch.

But now, she seemed to be making a special effort: to lighten the mood, to amuse him, to entertain him. Perhaps to take his mind away from the darkness that overshadowed them both.

'The gander and panda and giant salamander should be treated with respect,' she intoned. 'But felines and sea lions and canny chameleons are never quite what you expect.'

Once more, he whistled his appreciation, laughed, and she smiled in return. Then she danced again, that sylph-like flow of her body, her arms and hips moving in slow synchrony.

And to emphasise her point, she made a rotation, swinging round on tiptoe, one arm gracefully extended, head thrown back, eyes closed.

In that moment, she was a miracle in his life, and he loved her.

In that moment he seemed to hold her in the cup of his hand, and she balanced there, waiting for him to decide.

She wavered, like a leaf in the wind, and perhaps the wind grew stronger, for she seemed to sway and bend. She bent and buckled. Her foot slipped. She recovered, appeared to hang for a moment, defying gravity, still lissom and full of grace.

Then she yielded. Fell.

Watching it, Evan was transfixed. In that instant she had changed. The sprite, the elf had gone. In its place was a rag-doll of a figure, all limbs and floppy torso, disarranged, thrown out. A grotesque parody of the woman she'd been.

Briefly he thought: it's just more silliness, more comedy; just another trick. The archetypal joke. Like the best of slapstick from a silent film: the punchline telegraphed long in advance, so that the audience knew it was coming, yet could not believe that it would. The moment delayed and delayed until it was expected no longer, then acted out in slow and exaggerated mime. Her face, as it disappeared, full of surprise and dismay. Her last words: 'Oh shit!'

He remembered her pretence on the hills, tricking him as they raced for the summit.

But the silence refuted the idea: no joke this. He leapt up, ran across to her.

She was on her knees, head down, as if in pain.

'Addie.' He touched her. 'Are you alright?'

She shook her head, more in confusion, he thought, than denial.

She swore again.

He took her arm, tried to lift her up.

'I'm cut,' she said.

She was holding out a hand, staring at it. Blood oozed between the fingers, dripped on to the grass.

'Fuck.' She beat her other hand against her thigh.

He helped her to stand, took her hand, turned it palm upwards. It was too dark, here, to see the detail or gauge the extent of the wound, but he could feel the blood, warm and sticky on his own skin.

'It looks deep,' he said. 'We need to get you inside.'

'Oh fuck,' she said again.

He led her back to house, up the steps, into the living room, sat her at the table.

The blood still flowed. It trickled down her arm, on to his hand, dripped on to the tabletop.

'Keep it up; hold it tight,' he instructed.

He fetched the medical pack, a lamp, washed the wound, carefully opened it up. It was worse than he had thought. A cut across the ball of the thumb, a wide, half-moon incision. When he pulled the skin back, he could see the muscle, milky white.

There was glass in the wound, small slivers. He found his hand lens and tweezers, used them to search for the shards, pick them out. The glass was brown – beer bottle. It must have been lying broken in the grass. It was from the hunters' visit he guessed, though he could hardly blame them alone; they'd all been complicit in the partying.

Addie had no such reservations. She knew whose fault it was and who to blame. 'Todd,' she said. 'He was always chucking bottles away. It was the same when we went into the bush, like it proved what sort of man he was. He's an oaf, that's what he is. A stupid dickhead.'

Not for the first time, Evan wondered what had happened during that trip. Before, Addie had seemed amused by Todd, half attracted to him. She seemed to respond to his simple advances, laugh at his jokes. Afterwards, there was just this stony and angry disdain.

'You ought to be in hospital,' he said.

She shook her head. 'No.'

He searched the wound again. It seemed clean, but he could not help speculating: what else might there have been in the grass? Would the cut heal on its own or did it need stitches? He doused it with Dettol, dried it, carefully closed the flap of skin, fixed it in place with butterfly strips, bound it tightly.

'It's the best I can do.'

'It's more than I deserve.'

'It wasn't your fault, just an accident.'

'It was stupid,' she said. 'I'm sorry.'

He bent down, touched her fingers with his lips. 'That will make it better.'

She nodded, said nothing.

'One thing's clear, though: that's the end of your prospecting.'

'No. No way. We need to get back to the claim. I'll be fine.'

He wanted to argue, to force home his point, but her face stalled him. It was pale, drawn, not just with pain and the sight of blood, he knew, but her misery. Their happiness suddenly shattered. Clumsy reality, like a thief, breaking into their world.

*

He returned to the claim alone. Addie had wanted to come with him, but he'd refused.

For a while they had argued. Addie tried every ploy she knew: determination, disdain, pleading, moody silence. He still refused. Her hand needed to heal, he told her, and be kept dry and clean. That wasn't going to happen out there.

'You ought to be in hospital,' he said again. 'It needs stitches.'

She shook her head in denial.

At last, a compromise was reached. They had both known it would happen, though neither wanted it. He would go, she would stay. It was the worst of all choices. Time apart. Their brief time together diminished further, just the tatters left.

'I hate you,' she said, as he packed to leave.

I love you, he wanted to reply, but could not say.

Now, though, he missed her. Not just for her body, her companionship, but for the help she could have given, too. Even with only one effective hand she would have made a difference. It took him four trips, a whole day, to carry the timber, the tools, the last can of fuel, from the parking area up to the claim. By the time he'd finished, it was dark and he was working by the light of his head torch. His hands were sore and splintered, his back and legs ached. He slept badly, woke unrefreshed.

The next day, as he tried to build the dam, it was the same. Alone, he battled to hold the timber in place against its own buoyancy and the flow of the stream. He dropped tools and nails as he juggled to position the struts. Everything he needed – his jemmy, the hammer, the next plank – seemed always to be just out of reach. He missed, too, the knowledge that she'd be there beside him in the evening, later as they slept. Without her, all was trouble and toil.

But in the end, working late again with the aid of his torch, he managed, and that night he set the pump running to drain the water out. To his surprise, the next morning, the area was dry and the dam looked secure.

Now, at last, he was dredging, chasing the layers of gravel from between the boulders in the base of the plunge-pool, patching the dam as he went to stop the water spilling back in, pausing to pump it all dry when necessary, yet cursing the interruption. He was wet, cold, tired. He was increasingly anxious about the weather, casting his eyes towards the mountains, looking for change in the sky. He fretted about the dam and whether it would hold. Fretted, too, over Addie – how she was, whether her hand was healing. For the time together he had lost. Yet countering it all were the new finds. Nuggets and grains, lying waiting for him each time he checked the trays, the skim of gold flake when he panned the finer residues.

He took to wondering how much gold he now had, in his mind adding what he had gathered during these last days to the store in his box-safe back in the cottage. Ten ounces here, over thirty in his safe, he guessed, though he still hadn't weighed it accurately. Early in the trip it always seemed wrong, like a test of fate; since Addie had been there, it felt too much the miser's act.

He remembered his conversation with Klas – the difference between prospectors and hunters – and wished himself for a moment in the latter group. If so, perhaps he would be satisfied by now, would have hauled his trophies home, be back with Addie, giving her the care she needed, feeling her love in return.

And with the thought, his mind looped back to that other conundrum. The one he couldn't resolve, despite all his wit and rough wisdom, and his skills in make-do.

Addie. How to keep her in his life.

Once, before he'd left the cottage, he'd tried to broach the subject with her. He did so too abruptly, so that the words gushed out and seemed more like words of dismissal than hope: 'Where will you go when we leave?'

She had been reading, seemed to continue to do so, though her eyes now were fixed. She said nothing.

'I mean, when we've finished here; it's only a week or so. I need to know.'

Still she did not answer, and he felt his spirit weaken, his hope fade.

'I'll be going back to Christchurch,' he said, his voice flat, too demanding. 'If you want, you can come along.'

She shook her head. Was it refusal, or just pity – for his foolishness, his innocence? He could not tell.

He tried again, stumbling over his words: would she come with him, would she stay part of his life? But she put up her hand, cut him short.

'No,' she said, though quietly, gently. 'Please don't ask.'

'Why not? I thought –'

She shook her head again, fiercely this time, silencing him once more. 'Please,' she said. 'No.'

'No, you don't want to?' he asked.

'No, because I do want to, but you mustn't ask.'

But again he asked: 'Why not?'

'Because I just can't think of the future, now. I can't see it, not the way you can. I'm sorry. I want to; I don't want to hurt you or disappoint you or let you down, but I can't. I can only deal with the present. Each day at a time.'

Was it enough? It had to be, he assumed, for it seemed to be all she could give. One day at a time.

Right now, though, he was here and she was there, and their few days together were being wasted. Wasted on chasing more gold.

Why do it, he asked himself once more; why not stop? Declare the job done. Take what he'd got and go.

All he needed to do was put the dredge down, walk across to the pump, switch it off. After that, if he worked into the night, he could have everything hauled in, be back at his camp by midnight. If he took only what was essential, left the rest, he could have his gear loaded on the truck the next day. By tomorrow night he could be with her again.

In front of him, the bedrock curved away beneath the gravel, smooth and sculpted. Another swirl hole. He felt that surge of anticipation that always gripped him when the sediment or the landscape took a turn for the good. Just another half hour, he thought. That's all. Then he'd stop.

*

And so he returned.

It wasn't that day, or the next. But on the day after that, in the late afternoon, he managed to go at last. It was six days, now, since he'd left Addie. Longer than he'd intended, longer than he'd planned. But the gold had led him on, and the weather had held, and there seemed no point in abandoning just a small patch of the gravel undredged. And by using every last drop, the fuel had lasted him out.

Now, though, he hurried back, eager to be there, eager to see her, show her what he'd found. The conquering hero returning. Gold in his pocket, love in his heart.

In his eagerness, he'd cut corners at the end. He'd quickly demolished the dam, dragged his tarpaulin out, left the river to sort out the rest. Back at the camp, he used the tarpaulin to cover up the heavier gear – stuff he'd leave this year, despite the risks. Then he'd loaded himself up as much as he could, and in two trips got the other equipment back to the truck.

Next year, he might regret it: there'd be damage, loss, inconvenience. Now, though, he didn't care. There were six days left. Six days with Addie before the world outside claimed them. Six days to sort the future out.

And for that, he had a plan.

It was simple really. The best plans always were, he'd told himself. That's what life, and all this prospecting, had taught him. Do what you need to, do what works. Don't worry about the rest.

The only surprise was that he hadn't realised it before. It was obvious enough. It seemed to stare him in the face as he dredged the last patches of gravel, as he looked at the bare sculpture of the bedrock.

Tell her. Tell her he loved her. Tell her outright.

It might not work of course. It might not be enough. But if that didn't work, what would? And if it didn't, what would anything matter?

Love, surely, could conquer the years between them; she'd almost told him that, herself. Love and what gold could buy. A clean slate. No debts, no past. A new start somewhere. A new life. Wasn't that why he'd wanted the gold?

'I love you, Addie.' He rehearsed the words as he drove. Or rather, they rehearsed themselves, churning in his mind, carving their place, gathering in the hollow they created, where they belonged. 'I love you Addie.' Now and then, they spilled out, and he heard himself say them aloud. Viva heard them, too, recognising the name, or feeling the joy in his voice, wagging and nuzzling at him.

On the saddle, he paused, got out of the truck, looked back. The valley behind him seemed peaceful now, composed. Beyond, the mountains were muffled beneath white clouds, ready for the snows to come. The air had a grubbiness to it, summer's dust waiting to be washed out.

The whole world was like that, he thought, poised, waiting. Waiting for him.

He turned, looked ahead. The land ran rugged and ridged down into the valley, was lost in a mass of dark bush. Somewhere there, in a cottage in a clearing, she was waiting for him, too.

'I love you, Addie.'

'I love you, Evan,' she replied in his mind.

He imagined asking her to marry him, heard her laugh in response to his old-fashioned attitudes, though fondly. 'I don't need that,' she would say.

From the driver's seat, Viva nuzzled him again.

He climbed in, slammed the door, restarted the truck.

Twenty minutes later he pulled up outside the cottage. The clearing had a sense of stillness and peace. The cottage sat, huddled, silent. The door was open, though Addie was nowhere to be seen.

He imagined her in the garden at the back, picking herbs, or down in the scrub at the edge of the bush hunting for rabbits.

He sat, waiting for her to emerge.

From somewhere nearby, a quail called: 'Where-are-you, where-are-you, where-are-you?'

Or was she lying in bed, ready for him, wondering why he was teasing her in this way?

He got out of the truck, ran up the steps, went indoors, stopped.

The scene that confronted him seemed to strike him like a fist. Unexpected, full of force.

'Addie?'

The room wasn't his, or not the one he knew. It was ugly, disarranged, a room gone mad.

Furniture moved, books scattered, log-pile spilled, the rugs pulled back. Addie's vase of flowers scattered by the hearth.

He strode through to the bedroom, calling. The room that greeted him was the same. The bed had been stripped, the mattress lifted, cupboards and drawers pulled open and their contents flung on the floor. The picture that had hung on the wall lay amidst the chaos. He picked it up, turned it over. It was a photograph from his work: a snowy road in the midst of a white-out, shadowy figures of men perched there like vampires or bats on the poles. The glass was shattered, the image torn.

He went to the kitchen, knowing already what he would find. Not Addie, but explanation: the focus of all this destruction, the frenetic passion that must have been involved. The table had been moved, the rug shifted. The floorboards had been prised up. He looked into the cavity. The box-safe had gone.

For what seemed like long moments he stood there, his mind blank. It was too much to take in, too much even to try to understand. And where, in any case, would understanding take him, except to a place he could not go? The gold taken, Addie gone.

He remembered her words: if anyone takes it, I'll be the first you suspect.

'No.'

The sound of his own voice pulled his mind back.

'No,' he said again. 'Not Addie.'

Who then? Why? How?

Where was she?

He felt a surge of panic, possibilities crowding in, clamouring against his mind. Addie attacked, Addie taken; Addie lying somewhere, injured or dead.

He ran out to the veranda, stood there, shouting, bellowing with all the voice he had. It echoed back at him from the clearing, its power lost, its sound drawn out, like the bleat of a lost and abandoned lamb.

'Addie!'

Fourteen

For an hour he searched for her, called her name.

On the veranda, he had at last stilled himself, forced his mind back to something like sanity and calm. Just think, he told himself; stay calm and think.

Search first. Look for her, look for clues.

He searched systematically, starting in the cottage, moving outward, into the garden and beyond. He looked in all the rooms, in the loft, in the undercroft beneath the house. He found nothing other than more of the mess and devastation that he had already seen. No message, no signs of Addie. Just rooms in turmoil, belongings broken, clothes cast aside. The small changes and traces that she and he had made together as they lived side-by-side scuffed and trampled now into the debris.

He looked in the shed. Save for a box of ammunition, spilled on the work-bench, it seemed untouched.

But the box made his mind freeze with dread.

He thought of the gun, realised that he had not seen it in the house, looked for it now in the shed. It was not there.

The gun, the cartridges? He felt panic rise again.

He searched the clearing for clues. Wheel-tracks, spent cartridges, blood. There was nothing.

He searched in the garden at the back of the house, amidst the fruit trees that his father had planted all those years ago. He took the lid off the water tank, peered inside, he pushed through the gorse scrub and bush beyond.

He looked for her, he looked for her body. He did not know what form she might take.

He looked for her in his mind, trying to see her, imagine her, conjure her back into existence. Building stories of what might have happened, a way of explaining where she might be.

He let Viva out of his truck and encouraged her to search: 'Where's Addie. Find Addie. Go find.' The dog wagged, sniffed the air, seemed to find her scent in every direction.

Together, they searched more widely, out beyond the clearing, down by the stream, ranging further and further into the bush. Root-hollow and rabbit-hole, crevice and cleft, he searched them all. Piles of branches, mounds of leaf-mould, in the dark overhangs beneath the bank of the stream.

He searched, he called. He could not find her.

He returned to the house, searched again, discovering more details now. The screwdriver beside the floorboards in the kitchen; the spilled cutlery drawer where it used to be kept. The empty hook in the porch where Addie's anorak would hang. The space in the pantry where his spare water bottle used to stand. The kitchen sink half full of water, scummed with soap. On the floor a can of beer, open, spilled. In his bedroom, amidst all the bedding and clothes, a towel, knotted, crumpled, a strand of Addie's hair.

He tried to make sense of it all, repeating to himself: think, think.

The possibilities came back, other wilder notions with them, accusations and fears.

A random thief chancing on the place, finding Addie not there. She was somewhere out in the bush still, hunting for rabbits, looking for mushrooms, unknowing and safe.

Her boyfriend returned, finding her, taking her and the gold.

Todd.

Addie?

Except the last, he told himself, any of them might be true; or none. How could he know, what should he do?

Once, as a child, he had waited for his parents, alone in the house. They had gone away for the day, to a meeting or a funeral or a wedding – he could not remember now – with the promise that they would be home before bedtime. He had enjoyed the day, the freedom it had given, the indulgences it allowed. Biscuits for lunch, a sandwich of bread and sugar for tea, a litre bottle of Cola to himself. The radio at full blast, game shows on the TV. But as the evening wore on, he began to feel lonely and yearned for their return. Worry set in. Whose bedtime did they mean – his or theirs? He went out, listened for them, peered into the night. He boiled the kettle, set out cocoa and milk, in the hope that it would lure them home. He lay on the rug in front of the fire, making up reasons for the delay, testing them against the patterns and the progress of the sparks. Eventually, he went to bed, curled up beneath the blankets, ears primed to every sound. Is that them? Is that? And each time it wasn't, he felt not just dismay, but a stab of anger, as if they had deliberately let him down once again. And in time, satisfaction too, for each failure gave fuel to the anger and disappointment, and seemed to prove his emotions right.

At some point they had returned, full of apologies and an excuse – a broken-down car, out in the wilds, where no one came by to help – and he discovered that it was not so late as he had imagined. But he greeted them with hurt and surliness, rather than joy. Yet afterwards, he had reflected on it and thought that he could see a lesson in it all, and one he would remember and by which he could live. The worry and the imagining had achieved nothing. They had not brought relief or understanding, nor hastened his parents' return. They had just consumed him and stretched the time out. Better just to be patient, wait, let events take their course.

Could he do that now, he wondered; just sit, wait, let the world go its way? Addie would return, or she wouldn't. The gold would never come back. What would fretting achieve?

And yet he knew he could not. For he was part of the world, and in some small way might affect it, change it, bring it to a different end.

He had no choice. A woman was missing; his gold had gone. He had to tell the police.

He went to the truck, called Viva to jump in, climbed into the driver's seat and with a stamp of his foot, a scatter of gravel, sped off.

*

As he drove, he could not help searching. For still he believed that she must be out there somewhere, hiding, fleeing, lying injured, or just walking alone in the cocoon of her thoughts. He believed because each of those was better than any alternative he could summon: that she'd been killed, kidnapped; that she had taken the gold and run.

Yet how do you search when there are no signs nor trails to follow, and you do not know where to look?

Do you hurry in blind pursuit, rushing to reach her wherever she may be, or go slowly, scouring every nook and cranny on the way? He wanted to do both. He wanted to search everywhere – not just along the road, but out in the bush, on the hills, back the way he'd driven, all the way to the claim. In the places they'd walked, in the places she'd been before, when she was first lost. Around the cottage, in corners and shadows where he might already have missed her, every place he could or could not see.

He wanted to find her, hold her, make it all good again.

Instead, he drove steadily, scanning the roadside as he passed, slowing occasionally, alerted by some instinct to a possible hiding place, peering more intently; catching a glimpse of something – a flash of colour, a movement between the trees – and stopping, reversing, staring into the bush. At the bridges over the river, he got out, looked underneath, checked in either direction. Twice, where forest tracks led off, he followed them for a while, until hope or expectation gave out, and he found somewhere to turn, retraced his route.

In the mud beside a ford in the road, he stopped, got down from the truck, searched for footprints. There was the spoor of deer and birds, and the trails of worms, no human traces.

After an hour, he knew he wouldn't find her, but kept looking all the same.

He drove, searched. Tried to make sense of it all. Tried to put the world right.

But the world stared back, unmoved.

When the road at last levelled and the bush thinned, he took out his mobile, switched it on. It was the first time he'd done so since he went to Greymouth to buy Addie tampons, clothes. There was no signal. But over the next ten minutes, messages crept in from the queue that must have built up in the days since then, each one announced with a small burr of the phone. Each time, he picked it up, scrutinised the number, hoping that in some way it might be her. But the calls were just workmates, his dentist, the garage where he had his truck serviced, announcements from his service provider. Messages that meant nothing, just babble from some other world.

Outside Silverstone, he checked his phone again. There was a signal, now. He got out, leaned against the cab, wondering whether he should make the call, what else he could do instead.

He started to dial: one-one-one. Each digit an effort. Like a nail in the coffin of his hopes, his dreams, his love. But before he'd finished, he snapped the phone shut. Despite the scale of the theft, the hurt, was it really an emergency – was Addie really in any danger at all? And he knew what the conversation would be like. A call-centre somewhere, in Christchurch or Auckland, where no one would know the places he was talking about. The obvious assumption: gold gone, woman missing – she took it, case closed. Next.

He thought of driving into Hokitika, reporting to the police there. Yet the idea of sitting in front of some officer half his age, explaining himself, explaining about the gold and about Addie, facing the same deduction, felt too much like a condemnation, not just of her, but of him. The devious woman, the love-blind fool.

He opened up the phone again, called directory services, asked to be put through to the Greymouth police.

A woman answered, took details, transferred him to the crime reporting line. He went through a series of automatic questions, each with half a dozen options, circled round them, got lost, ended up back where he started. Eventually a human voice asked: 'And how may I help you?' A man, laconic, country-bluff.

'I want to report a theft – and someone, a friend who's missing.'

'I see. Well, you're in the right place for that: I'm the duty sergeant. But first, let me get some details. Name?'

'Evan Cadwallader,' he said, and spelled his surname, then spelled it again just to be sure.

'That sounds Welsh.'

'It is.'

'What's your home address, Mr Cadwallader?'

He gave it.

'Christchurch? You're a long way from home.' There was a pause. Evan could hear the click of a keyboard, each letter followed by a silence as if the sergeant had to search for the next key.

'Is that the address you're ringing from, Mr Cadwallader?'

'No.' He explained where he was.

'Silverstone? That's out of the way. So a theft, you say, and a missing friend. What sort of theft?'

Evan started to explain: a store of gold had been taken.

'Gold, you say?'

'Yes.'

'How much?'

'About forty ounces.'

'Four ounces.' The man said, typing.

'Forty,' Evan corrected. 'It's worth about 60 000 dollars. Maybe more.'

A silence. 'OK. That's a lot of money.' Then: 'Forgive me asking. Is this real?'

'Real? You mean did it happen? Yes of course it did.'

'OK. It's just – well. It's April the first today. You never know.'

'I didn't know. About the date I mean.' It seemed to add to the cruelness, made it absurd, and he sucked at his lip, fighting to keep his emotions under control. 'I've been in the bush, I've not been counting the days. But it's real. I can assure you of that.'

There was the sound of more typing. 'So how was it taken? Have you any idea?'

'I have a suspect.'

'This friend of yours, I assume.'

'No. Not her. But I think she might have been attacked, during the theft.'

'Attacked. Do you know that?'

'Not for sure. No. But she was there; she's gone now. I can't find her. I'm worried.'

'Have you looked?'

'Yes. For an hour, two.'

'And where was this? Where was the theft?'

Again, he tried to explain, telling it briefly, missing out as much as he could, yet discovering all the same how elusive the truth could be. All its subtleties and ambiguities, its false paths and seeming contradictions. The secrets it required to be revealed.

'Now forgive me asking,' the sergeant said. 'But are you sure it wasn't her – your friend Miss Watson – who's taken your gold? I mean, it sounds as if she had the chance.'

'I'm sure.'

'It does happen, you know. Surprisingly often. That it's someone you know, someone you trust.'

'It's not her.'

'OK. I understand.' There was another pause while the man typed. Then he said: 'So tell me about Miss Watson. When did you meet her? Where is she from?'

'She's from Dunedin, originally, but I don't know where she lives now. On the West Coast, somewhere, I think. We met out at my claim. We became friends, and she helped me with the dredging.'

'And when did you meet her exactly?'

'About two months ago. A bit more. Mid-January.'

The officer typed. 'Can you describe her?'

'She's twenty-five. Short – about one metre fifty-five or sixty. Slim. Black hair, thin face.' The words didn't describe her, he knew – not the Addie he'd found, loved, lost. She is a snake and an egg and a bird, he wanted to say, and she swims like a fish. She has large eyes that seem to engulf you when she looks at you, and lips that are firm and hungry and possess you when she kisses. She has small yet perfect breasts –

'Maori, you think?' The man's voice cut into his thoughts.

'Part. On her father's side.'

'You and she were – what shall I say, lovers?'

He hesitated. The word seemed so final, so enclosing, as if it fixed them in some small and locked-away world. Is that where she still was, trapped inside? Was it he who had slipped out, somehow escaped, fled? Or was it from that that she had run – from the prison of his love?

'Yes,' he said, and more firmly: 'Yes, we were.'

There was the click of typing again, a pause, more typing. Then the noise stopped.

'So is anything missing other than the gold?' the officer asked.

'No. Oh, yes – a gun.'

'A gun?'

'A hunting rifle. And some ammunition.'

Evan heard a small intake of breath, then silence. At last the sergeant asked: 'When did you say you met her?'

'Mid-January.'

'Can you be more specific?'

He tried to calculate: how many days had it been after he'd arrived on the claim? Ten, twelve? 'About the eighteenth,' he said.

Another silence, noises of papers being shuffled, or a message being scribbled, off-phone.

'Can you just hold the line, a moment? I need to talk to a colleague.' The sergeant's voice was replaced by clicks, a burr, a recorded message offering useful advice to the public: how to report crime, how to make your home safe, how to become a community officer.

'Good afternoon, Mr Cadwallader. This is Chief Inspector Hastings.' A new voice, brisk and officious. 'Your case has been referred to me. I just want to ask you some more questions, if you don't mind. And to make it as easy as possible for you, we'll record the call, if that's alright.'

And so it started again. This time, though, there were no pauses, no typing. Just questions, each one direct, yet strangely nuanced, as though there was more to it than the words implied. Questions about how he'd met Addie, about the state she was in, about what she'd done while she'd been living with him out in the bush.

'And she gave her name as Addie Watson, you say?'

'Yes.'

'And you found her, lost in the bush?'

'That's right.'

'And you were lovers? Is that right?'

'Yes, we were.'

'But you'd never met her until then? Didn't know her.'

'No.'

'Did she tell you anything about herself? Where she'd come from? Where she'd been before?'

'No. Only that she was lost. She seemed to be confused about the route she'd taken.'

'And before that? Did she say anything about earlier?'

'Just that she'd fallen out with her boyfriend. She'd run off.'

'Do you have a name?'

'Of the boyfriend? Yes. Mark something – Mark Brown.'

'I see. And no address. No mention of where she lived.'

'She said that she was between addresses. Something like that.'

'And did she suggest anything about where she might go next?'

'No. Nothing. We – I wanted her to stay with me. But she said she couldn't think about the future, only the present.' He gave a hard laugh. 'I didn't understand.'

'Yet you told her about the gold. Where you kept it.'

'No. She knew I had it. She'd helped me find it; she helped on my claim. But she urged me to hide the gold in the cottage, to keep it safe. I didn't tell her where.'

'So where was it?'

'Under the floorboards,' Evan said dully. 'I suppose that wasn't very original.'

'No. Not very. But you never suspected her until it had gone?'

'No. I still don't. I trust her. I –' He wanted to say 'love her' but could not make the words come out. Not because they weren't true, but because they were. Yet they were words he had not managed to say to her, could not divulge to someone else. 'I'm worried about her,' he said.

'Did anyone else know about the gold? Or anyone else visit you?'

He explained about the hunters.

'And might one of them have taken it?'

'Yes. Maybe one, a man called Todd.'

'And why do you suspect him?'

Why did he, he wondered; what reason could he give? Because he was young and louche and brazen? Because he had taunted him and Addie, flirted with her, tried to lure her away?

'He knew about the gold,' he said. 'He seemed especially interested.'

'No surname?'

'No.'

'OK. I'll make a note of it. But for now, let's go back to Miss Watson, shall we? I think that she is our most important concern.'

'Yes. She is for me.'

There were more questions, repeating the ones the duty sergeant had asked. About what she looked like, how she was dressed, what clothes she'd been wearing. About the gun. But at last the questions stopped.

'I want you to do something for us,' the Chief Inspector said. 'I want you to go back to your cottage. I'm sending a team out to you; they won't be far behind. When you get there, just wait. And please, don't touch anything. Can you do that for me?'

'Yes. Of course.'

He thanked the officer for his help, for the attention they'd given the case. Their sense of urgency. Then he asked: 'Do you think you'll find her?'

'I'm sure we will,' the Chief Inspector said. 'That's our job.'

*

He restarts the truck, turns it round, drives back towards the cottage. He feels empty, drained. His mind is a hollowed shell, scoured and raw.

He sits with his head forward, eyes fixed, hands gripped on the wheel. He drives steadily, letting the world slide past him of its own accord. Time and space seem as one, blank and without form. He tries to reach back into his memories, can find nothing; he tries to imagine the world ahead, the place he is driving to, what he will find there, and that it is the same.

He drives on.

The road seems to suck him into itself, eating him up. Field and forest, bluff and ravine flee by, eager to escape.

A bridge comes and goes in a rumble of wheels on wood.

A harrier stands by a road kill, watches him approach, languidly flaps aside.

Behind him, the dust hangs in the air, like a curtain across his past.

Now and then, small fragments of thought swill in his mind, then fade again. The Chief Inspector's voice: 'And you were lovers, is that right?' The silence of the empty house. The darkness of the water tank, when he'd peered in, searching – for what?

Another voice: 'Are you sure it wasn't her? It often is you know.'

A posy of wild flowers, scattered, crushed.

Addie, dancing.

He clutches at the image, clings to it.

With no intent, he changes down, brakes slightly, swings around a hairpin bend, thrusts his foot down for the long haul up the slope on the other side.

She seems to hover at the edge of his mind, at the furthest limits of his imagining.

Might it still be true?

His own words: 'I trust her.'

Might he believe it?

Past the side-road to the old Black Cap mine, just a tangle now of bush and rusting metalwork.

Another stream, another bridge.

Addie standing on the veranda, rabbit in hand. Its soft fur still warm with life.

Just believe, he thinks.

The corner, where once, years ago, a car had rolled; the place marked now by a small sad cross, the frond of dead flowers replenished at intervals by an unseen and unforgetting hand.

Just believe, and all will be well.

Into the gorge, where the road narrows and the crags crowd in, and ferns hang like spider-webs from the jutty rocks.

Only a few more kilometres, a few more minutes.

He is impatient now, eager to arrive, his will and belief weakening.

He reaches again into his memories for the sound of her, touch of her, the dark gloss of her hair as she rises from the water in a shower of silver spray, laughing.

Just believe. Just trust and believe and she will be there, waiting.

The ford where he had stopped as he drove out. The bridges where he had paused to look for her.

Another twist in the road, another bluff, another dip.

And then he has arrived. The gravel of the track turns to grass and silt. The forest retreats, becomes an open glade, and at its edge is the small, hunched cottage where Addie will be.

He brakes, stops, turns off the engine, sits, waiting for her to appear. To come to the door, stand on the veranda, wave. For everything that has happened to unhappen, for the world to be made kind again.

But no one comes. The clearing remains empty, Addie is nowhere to be seen. The cottage stands dull and dowdy, offering no shred of hope. Only the scornful buzz of the cicadas, the laughter of magpies mark any life in the place.

The memories fade.

And in that instant, the truth floods in, uncontestable. There is no other explanation. There is no salvation. She has taken the gold and gone.

He has been duped, deceived again.

Tears well and he tries to fight them back. He does not believe it, he trusts her, loves her; it cannot be right.

Yet the world refutes him, for it is what it is, and the people in it are just the way they are. Not evil, not even callous, neither bad nor good. If they sin, if they steal, if they cheat and hurt, it is only because that is what they have to do in the world they find themselves in.

Addie is simply no different from the rest.

The tears come. He beats his fist against the steering wheel. Viva nuzzles him, whimpering with canine concern.

He strokes her, then wipes at his tears.

He looks again at the cottage, and it returns his gaze, unpitying. He wonders again: what should he do?

How can he get out of the truck, go to the house, open the door, knowing that she is not there? Just broken memories, the tattered remnants of his dreams. All else, all other meaning, lost.

How can he face what is coming? The police, more questions, searches of the premises, looking for every sign and semblance of her. Digging over the entrails of their time together. Eating into those few precious days. Checking the cottage for fingerprints, swabbing it for DNA. The toothbrush she'd used, the clothes she'd worn. Even the sheets on the bed where they'd slept.

Who knows how far it will go, where it will lead: what they will discover, what they might take? Afterwards, how little might be left. Memories and meaning.

More destruction, more loss.

He thinks of the river, as he'd left it, all ravaged and despoiled, and the irony mocks him. The serial abuser, given a taste of his own medicine: isn't there justice in that? Yet he knows the difference. During the winter, the river will heal; will he ever do so?

He wants to turn round, be gone, perhaps never come back. To flee from the scene of the crime.

He sighs, opens the truck door, steps down. Viva rises to follow him, but he tells her to stay. The police might bring tracker dogs; better that she is shut up.

He goes up the steps, heavy on dragging feet, unlatches the door, pushes against it as it sticks. The familiarity of it is like a taunt: this is how life used to be. He stands in the doorway.

But the room that greets him is not the one he expected. It is a different room, disarranged. The same furniture, shifted, his belongings scattered, the same mess. Yet something else, too. A newer difference.

Not the room he left.

He stands there, puzzling.

*

'I warn you. I have a gun.' The voice startled him. It came from the right, behind the door. Thin and sharp as steel.

'I mean it,' she said.

'Addie?'

'I'm not joking. I'll use it.'

He stepped forward, cautiously, peered around the door. She was sitting on the sofa, her legs drawn up in the way she so often sat. She had the rifle in her arms. It was pointed at him.

'One more step,' she said.

'Addie,' he said. 'It's me.'

'Evan?' She looked past him. 'Are you alone?'

'Yes. It's just me.'

Still, she seemed unconvinced, craned her head.

'I'm alone,' he said.

She lowered the rifle.

'Addie. What's happened?'

Her head jerked, the smallest movement, as if the question were a shock.

'Addie,' he said again. 'It's me. I won't hurt you. It's alright.'

He moved towards her, hand out, inviting her to give him the gun.

'I'm sorry,' she said. 'I thought it was him.'

He reached for the gun, but she snatched it away, as if it were a child that he might take from a mother's breast. Then she smiled, clicked the safety catch, and released her grip. 'Just in case,' she said.

He propped it outside, against the doorframe, went back to the sofa, perched on the edge.

'What's happened?' he asked again.

'It was my fault,' she said. 'It was all my fault. I'm sorry.' She gave a wave, indicating the room. 'I'm sorry about all this.'

He wanted to reach out to her, take her in his arms, but her look stilled him. She seemed taut, confused, at the limits of any reason.

'I thought I'd lost you,' he said. 'I've been so worried.'

'I'm sorry.' Then she smiled, suddenly bright, almost mischievous. 'I've got your gold.'

He nodded. 'I know.'

'I took it,' she said. 'I took it with me.' She looked at him, her big brown eyes full of victory and pride.

'Why?' he asked.

And the pride faded. She bit at her lip, blinked back tears. 'Oh Evan. I was so scared.'

'Scared of what? What happened?'

'He tried to take it. He tried to make me give it to him. But I wouldn't. I ran off with it, into the bush. I could hear him following me, searching for me. I thought he'd kill me.'

'Who? Who are you talking about?'

'Todd,' she said. 'Who else?'

'Todd?' His mind felt dull, old – too old for this. She seemed to move too fast for him, change colours too easily, the chameleon again.

She reached out her hand, and he took it.

'He came after it,' she said. 'He came while you were away.'

'He tried to take it?'

She nodded, lips tight.

'I thought it was you,' he said. 'I thought I'd lost you.'

She shook her head. 'You should have known.'

'Yes, I should. I'm sorry.'

'You should have known,' she said again, more vehemently. 'You should have trusted me. I thought you did. I'd never have done this. Never, after all you've done for me.'

She started to cry. He drew her to him, held her against his chest. 'I won't. Never again. I promise.'

For a while, they sat there, clinging together, saying nothing. On the mantelpiece the clock still beat its lop-sided tick.

So far, he thought. Their minds seemed to have so far to travel: whole lands and oceans to cross, back to where they'd been. So much to unravel, put together again. Worlds and civilisations to remake.

He stroked her hand, felt a roughness on it, and turned it over to inspect the wound on her palm. It was red, still swollen, but the skin had drawn together, making a clean scar. He leaned down, kissed it gently. As he did so, he saw bruises on her arm. He touched them.

'That was him,' she said. 'Todd.'

'What happened?' he asked. 'I still don't understand.'

Slowly, she explained. She did so quietly, calmly, but with anger in her voice. And as she told him he let himself imagine the scene, filling in the details that she didn't recount – the words that she or Todd spoke, the looks they exchanged, the seething tensions – so that he seemed to know the event with a sharp intimacy, as though he were there.

Four days after he'd left, she'd been washing her hair, she told him, using the kitchen sink. She'd heard a vehicle, approaching from the direction of the saddle, assumed it was him. She ran out to greet him, still half-dressed, towelling her head. It was Todd.

'I thought he must be in trouble,' she said. 'I thought he'd come for help.'

She had asked what he wanted, invited him in.

'Evan's away,' she had said. 'He's on his claim.'

Only then did she see his eyes. They were hard, wild. He was on something, she guessed, meth probably. Or just wild with imagining. She could guess what, knew at once that it was she who was in trouble.

'Looks like you were expecting me,' he'd said, grinning.

'He's due back soon, though,' she had lied, thinking quickly. 'I'm expecting him any moment.'

'Better get on with it, then.' He'd made a grab for her, but she'd backed away.

He laughed. 'What's wrong? Aren't I good enough for you?'

She'd ignored him, turned to the bedroom. 'I'm getting dressed.'

He'd stood in the doorway behind her, watching.

'There's not much to you, is there?' he'd said. 'Skin and bones, mainly. Still, what there is looks good.'

'Why are you here?' she'd asked. 'Other than to ogle me, insult me.'

'I'll let you guess.'

'The gold?' she'd said. 'If so, you'll be disappointed. He reckons it's been a bad year.'

But Todd had persisted: 'How bad?' And when she'd shrugged the question away: 'Go on. You can show me. Show me what he's got.'

Again, she'd feigned ignorance. She didn't know where the gold was, she'd said, where he kept it. She thought he probably had it with him in the bush.

Todd hadn't believed her. He'd grabbed her arm. 'Don't give me that. You know well enough. Stop arsing around.'

She was angry by then. She'd sworn back at him, told him to leave.

'Or what?' he'd asked.

For a while, her account became more jumbled. Just the fear, still lingering, or the emotion churning? Evan couldn't tell. But it was as though there was something in what followed that she did not want to remember, could not reveal.

'Is that when he hurt you?' he asked.

She looked at the bruises on her arm, shrugged. 'That's not really hurt,' she said. 'Not with someone like Todd.'

Evan had to prod her with the question again: 'What did he do?'

'He threatened me,' she said. 'Unless I told him where the gold was.'

'How? What did he threaten?'

She shrugged. 'Every way he knew.'

'Violence? Rape?' he asked, imagining how it would have been the cruellest weapon of all. 'Did he threaten you like that?'

'He was raping me all the time,' she said. 'With his eyes.' Then she shrugged again. 'But the gold was more important. First, he wanted to get his hands on that.'

He could have threatened her how he liked, she went on; she wouldn't have told. She had just kept repeating: she didn't know.

By this time, Todd had been getting restless, was threatening to trash the place, burn it. She had tried to think of a plan – a way of getting rid of him, heading him off. Or if not that, getting the gold herself and running away.

'Anyway,' she'd said, 'Don't you think I haven't looked? If I could have found it myself, I'd have grabbed it and walked out of here long ago. I'm not that much of a mug.'

'That's not very daughterly,' he'd said.

'Well, he's not been much of a father, either. Not that I've ever seen.'

He'd laughed. 'That's true.'

'I'll help you look, if you like,' she'd said. 'But in that case, we share.'

'Why should I do that?'

She'd smiled, coquettishly. 'It's your choice.' And then, before he could waver again, she'd said: 'Fifty-fifty. And you take me with you. That way I won't tell, and no one will ever know.'

As she knew he would, he argued, but she had told him: 'You've no alternative, have you? Otherwise you have to kill me to stop me telling everyone who it was. This way, he'll just assume it's me.'

'Twenty per cent,' he said.

'A third,' she suggested at last – 33 per cent. That was as low as she'd go.

The reasonableness of her claim seemed to persuade him, and he'd agreed. He had no reason to, she knew; he could dump her and take the lot if he wanted – either here or out in the bush. Having raped her first, no doubt.

'He'd have regretted it if he tried, though,' she said.

She'd tricked him again, when they started to look. He was easy to trick, she said: he had no imagination. You just had to play on his suspicions, double-bluff.

They'd searched the living room together. Then, when it was nearly done, she'd headed for the bedroom. Todd had called after her: 'Where are you going?'

'To look in the bedroom,' she'd said. 'If it's not here, it's the obvious place. There or in the loft above the spare room.' Immediately he'd grabbed her, pulled her back. He'd search the bedroom, he'd told her, and in the loft. There was no point them both looking. She'd pretended to argue, then acquiesced. 'OK. I'll look in the kitchen.'

As soon as she was there, she'd found the screwdriver, lifted the floorboards, taken the box. She slipped out, ran off into the bush at the back of the house.

‘How did you know?’ Evan asked. ‘How did you know where it was?’

She laughed, laid her head against him. ‘I heard you, of course. I heard you when you were putting the last lot of your finds there, when we came back from the claim. And I checked as soon as you’d gone. I don’t like secrets. Not other people’s anyway. Mine are my own.’

He kissed her on the forehead. ‘You never cease to amaze me.’

‘That’s always been the plan,’ she said and laughed again. ‘Anyway, I wasn’t as clever as I thought. Todd must have seen me, or guessed, because I hadn’t got far when he came out, yelling and cursing.’

She’d tried to creep away. But whatever his other limitations, Todd’s hunting skills were good. Although she probably had a 200 metre start on him, he’d heard her, tracked her. For over half an hour they’d played a game of cat-and-mouse out in the bush. She had circled, doubled back, crossed the stream, then crossed it again. Each time, just when she thought she’d got away, she’d hear him again, still yelling, still cursing.

‘I was lucky he hadn’t thought to bring his rifle,’ she said. ‘Otherwise, I’d have had no chance. Without it, his only chance was to catch me with his bare hands, and he couldn’t do that. So he just tried to scare me, with his yelling and swearing, his threats.’

Then she said: ‘Mind you, he was lucky I hadn’t grabbed yours. I’d have got him otherwise, more than once. And enjoyed the experience.’

‘No,’ he said. ‘You wouldn’t. You wouldn’t have done that.’

‘Anyway, he couldn’t catch me.’ She grinned. ‘He might know about stalking deer and pigs, but he doesn’t know about people.’ She’d found a big rata, she told him; hanging with epiphytes.

She'd shinned up it, hid in the foliage where no one from the ground could have seen her, stayed there for hours, until long after dark. She could hear him blundering around. Still swearing, still shouting. Once, she had heard gunshots and imagined him back at the cottage, blasting off wildly into the shadows. But eventually, the sounds had ceased. Still she didn't come down. She stayed there all night, into the next morning. Then, at last, she crept back to the cottage, watched it from the edge of the bush. There was no sign of him, and his ute had gone, yet still she feared it might be a trick. Eventually, she crept up to the house, sneaked in, grabbed food, some clothes, the gun and the cartridges, then spent the rest of that day and the next night out in the bush. She'd gone back only that afternoon.

'He'd ransacked the place,' she said. 'He must have still believed there was something here. Or just out of spite.' She looked around the room. 'I'm sorry.'

'It doesn't matter.'

'It does. It was my fault, all of this. It was all my bragging in front of the hunters. Making you show them the gold. I was just – so upset with the way he taunted you. So proud of you. I just wanted to shut him up.'

'Proud?' he asked, in wonderment.

She nodded.

'And the gold?'

'It's here. Under the sofa. All thirty-seven ounces of it.'

He laughed. 'Thirty-seven. How do you know?'

'I weighed it,' she said. 'When you left for the claim.'

'You knew the combination?'

'Your birthday, of course. It didn't take much guessing.'

He shook his head, dumbfounded, admiring.

'Christ, I love you,' he said, but heard his words and froze.

'I know. You poor man.' She regarded him steadily for a moment, shook her head: 'What shall I do with you?'

But she knew the answer, of course. She took his hand, stood, said: 'Come with me.'

In the bedroom, she turned, began to unbutton his shirt, then undid his belt. When he started to help, she stopped him. 'No. This is for me.'

When he was naked, she pushed him down gently on to the bed, knelt beside him, pulled off her jumper, slipped off her bra. She was wriggling out of her jeans, clumsily, still kneeling, when he remembered.

'We can't,' he said.

'We can.'

'No. You don't understand. I came here this morning, saw everything. I thought it was you.'

She sat back on her heels, looked at him, puzzled.

'I know. But I forgive you – though you must never, never do that again.'

She bent to kiss him.

'I reported it to the police,' he said. 'They'll be here soon.'

He thought she'd laugh, tell him how silly he'd been – how much embarrassment he'd cause. Instead, she seemed to freeze, then shrink, her mouth slightly open, her brow furrowed in horror or shock. She tried to speak, seemed unable to find the words and looked away, her face contorted in what might have been confusion or pain.

'No,' she murmured. 'No, no.'

'Yes. I'm sorry.'

'No!' she cried.

'I didn't know,' he said. 'I'm sorry. I'll explain to them when they come.'

She shook her head, fiercely, as though to shake the whole world off.

He reached up for her, tried to turn her towards him, but she flapped his hand away.

'Addie,' he said. 'Please?'

Her head was back, eyes closed, her hands clenched. Then slowly she crumpled. Her face became a turmoil of sorrow and anguish and pain. 'Oh, Evan,' she said. 'You foolish, foolish man.'

And she started to laugh. Not in amusement or relief, but something deeper and almost primaeval. A madness, a wildness, as if she had uncovered some strange and unimaginable code to the way the world worked, making the whole thing a mockery, a farce. Something beyond gods and physics, an absurd truth that no one had ever imagined. A joke on life itself.

Then she stopped.

'What is it?' he asked.

'It's now,' she said. 'It's now. It has to be. Here and now and for evermore.'

And she moved on to him, leaned forward to brace herself with her hands against his chest, took him into herself and slowly, slowly, began what might have been a dance, and like her other dances might have been of journeying and searching and discovery, for it seemed to take him to places he had never been before.

Fifteen

He lay with her in his arms. It was the same as the first time. The same shape that she made against him, the same way her breast lay, cupped in his hand.

The same small pressure of her nipple against his palm. The lightness of her and the delicacy, like a flower that might so easily be crushed. A moment from the past, stolen, made live again. A precious time.

The police would be here soon, he knew. He should have got up by now, dressed, been ready to greet them with dignity and calm. Being found like this would only add complexities, cause tensions, make for ambiguity and disdain and doubt. He'd tried to persuade Addie, but she clung to him, refused to move.

'I can explain,' he assured her. 'It was just a silly mistake. You've nothing to worry about.'

'This isn't to do with you, or your gold,' she said. 'This is about me.'

So he stayed beside her, holding her in his arms.

And still they had not come. He wondered why? Confusion in the reporting room, some other emergency dragging them away, a blown tyre, a mix-up with the address? Who cared? She'd been restored to him. She was here beside him. Nothing could part them now. 'I love you,' he said.

'I don't deserve that,' she whispered in reply. 'I don't deserve you.'

'Stay with me,' he pleaded.

And her tears were wet against his skin.

*

The noise was small at first, distant. Was it them?

As he listened, it seemed unlikely. No police car or truck on the road. Further, more diffuse, less threatening. A throb, a bark, a soft puffing exhalation. Like thunder in the hills. Or the wind gathering, rippling the trees. Winter coming.

He dismissed it, but the noise stayed, grew.

He looked towards the window. It was open, but the curtain did not move.

The noise grew louder.

Beside him, Addie stirred. 'It's happening,' she said.

'What do you mean?'

'They're coming. Can't you hear?'

'No. It's not them. Not yet.'

'Soon,' she said. 'Soon.' And she turned her eyes on him.

Such tragedy, he thought. How could eyes speak of such pain?

'Tell me,' he said. 'What is it? What's wrong?'

'There's no time now. No time for words. Just for looking, remembering.'

'I don't understand.'

'You will. One day you will.'

*

The noise was devouring, irresistible. An insistent vibration, a pounding staccato that seemed to engulf their world. Like the horses of the apocalypse, he thought; like time itself, galloping to claim them.

Sky and mountains, the cottage itself, joining in the cacophony. Walls trembling, windows rattling. Viva howling in alarm.

Addie clung to him. Her limbs were taut, her fingers gripped him; her nails bit deep.

'I'm sorry,' he said. 'It shouldn't have been like this.'

'It's not your fault. Know that, Evan; know that, please.'

'I brought it upon us,' he said. 'I should have trusted you.'

'Yes. Yes, you should.' She kissed his chest. 'But it was me who brought them. It was always me. Me and Todd.'

The name racked him, making his stomach turn. Yet again, he wondered what Todd was to Addie, what he had done. Had they been lovers? In some strange way, did he have some claim on her, did she owe him something?

He didn't want it to matter, didn't want to know, but he asked nevertheless: 'What do you mean, Todd? What did he do?'

She was silent, curled against him, her face close to his. 'He recognised me,' she said at last. 'He knew about me. He threatened to tell.'

'Tell what? What do you mean?'

But outside, the noise had turned to movement, to a wild gale. It blew hungrily, showering grit and leaves at the walls. The curtain flapped, stretched tight.

She buried herself against him, and he locked her in his arms.

He would hold her, protect her from the memories and men who hurt her, from storms and armies, from the devil himself if that were needed. He'd hold her for ever, carry her away.

Then the noise subsided, the gale ceased.

She turned her head, looked up at him with her large brown eyes, and they were full of sadness and love and farewell.

'Will you forgive me?'

'Forgive you for what?'

'For not being the woman you wanted me to be.'

'You're everything I want,' he said.

*

There were voices as well now. Distant shouts, commands, queries. The distorted yammer and crackle of radio-talk. The sound of people moving around.

Then a face at the skylight, peering down. Framed in black.

Too late.

He drew her closer, counted the seconds; each one, he knew, one more stolen from whatever future approached. One more added to the small total of their togetherness. One instant longer in which to know her, feel her, mark himself with her presence.

The warmth of her groin beneath his thigh; the lingering stickiness of their love-making.

The valley that her hips made where his elbow lay. Her breast cupped in his hand.

The imprint of her. The first and the last.

How long could he retain that?

He kissed the nape of her neck, A hair caught in his lips, tugged as he withdrew.

Another second and another.

*

Addie flinched.

His grip on her tightened.

The crash of the door, the stamp of feet, the shouts spilled into the room. Noise smashed against them.

She screamed.

A jabbering command which he could not make out.

The sheet torn from them.

Addie shrank away, trying to pull it back.

More shouts, more commands.

That glimpse of her, from the corner of his eye, naked, defenceless, her smallness emphasised by the enormity of everything around. The armour-bloated men, the bristling weapons, the white expanse of the bed beyond her withdrawn feet.

Three men, in black flak jackets, standing at the foot of the bed, weapons – guns or tasers, in the confusion he could not tell which – trained upon them.

Addie cowering.

'Hands behind your head. Do not try to move or escape. Do not speak unless requested.'

A policewoman entered, looked quickly around, picked up one of the shirts from the floor, handed it to Addie. She pulled it on, clenched it around her, smaller still.

He was being led away. His nakedness embarrassed him and he tried to turn his back to the policewoman.

From behind him, he could hear a voice, barking a caution at Addie. Phrases came to him, jumbled and without sense. 'Josephine Lucinda Blake . . . I am arresting you on suspicion that on or about . . . you did wilfully escape from custody . . . Do you wish to say anything . . . You are not obliged to . . . may be given in evidence.'

The wrong woman, he thought, incredulously: they think she's someone else.

He stood in the living room. A policeman passed him his clothes. 'Please, get dressed. Then sit down.' He put on the clothes, clumsy in his movements, had to yank at the zip.

He sat on the chair, glanced out of the window. A helicopter was parked in the clearing, its rotor blades drooping like the limp bare branches of a winter tree. Nearby were two police cars, four-by-fours, made for the rough terrain. They were spattered with mud.

The officer opposite took out a notebook, drew up a chair.

'I can explain,' Evan said. 'This is all a mistake.'

'Are you the householder?'

'Yes. And I'm the one who reported the theft. It was a mistake.'

'Your name?'

'Evan Thomas Cadwallader.'

'Address?'

He gave it.

'And this is your property, also.'

'Yes. I inherited it from my father.'

'You understand why we're here?'

'Yes. Because I reported a theft of my gold. But I've told you. It was a mistake.'

'No. Not that. We're here to arrest an escaped prisoner. Josephine Blake. The woman in the next room.' The officer regarded him stonily. 'The woman you were in bed with when we arrived.'

'No. You've got it wrong. That's not her.'

'We have a warrant to search the property. Would you like to see it?'

'I suppose so.'

He was shown a document. He glanced at it, but did not take anything in. He nodded. 'Thank you.'

The officer took it back, refolded it, lay it on the table. 'You are not under arrest. You understand that. But as an accomplice to a crime, it's possible that we might want to charge you. If so, you'll be cautioned. Understand?'

'Yes. But no – I don't understand what you're doing, why you're here. You've got the wrong woman. She's Addie. Addie Watson. She's been living here with me. You've come to the wrong place.'

The officer leaned forward, spoke slowly, as if to a child. Josephine Blake had absconded while on remand, he said. She was now here in the adjacent room. She had already identified herself, and submitted herself to re-arrest.

Evan shook his head. The information made no sense.

Again, he was asked: how long had he known her? This woman he knew as Addie Watson.

'Ten or eleven weeks,' he said.

'The date you met, exactly?'

He tried to calculate once more. 'I'm not sure. January the eighteenth, I think.'

'How did you meet?'

He explained: he'd found her lost and injured on his claim.

Then the question he'd been expecting: what was the nature of their relationship?

'We became lovers,' he said. 'We fell in love.'

'And it was you that reported that she'd stolen a quantity of gold from you? Forty ounces, I understand.'

'Yes. That was me. But she hadn't.'

The officer smiled, thinly. 'No, I assume not, given the way we found you together. Would you like to explain?'

'It wasn't her. Well, she'd taken it because someone else had tried to steal it. But she brought it back.' It sounded confused, far-fetched. He tried again, explaining more carefully.

'You should talk to the man, Todd,' he said. 'He's the villain in all this. Not Addie. I tried to tell the Chief Inspector that.'

'We're more interested in your Addie at this moment – in Miss Blake.'

But he insisted, and the officer sighed, as if going along with a foolish pretence. 'Alright then, tell me about this man, Todd.'

He tried, yet as they had when he tried to explain to the Chief Inspector, the words seemed to fall apart. He could give no details, produce no evidence, not even a surname. He mentioned Klas, suggested that the officer trace Todd through him, immediately regretted the suggestion. The ripples were spreading, he thought; more innocent people being drawn in. Where would it stop?

'Addie could tell you more,' he said, refusing to play their game by calling her 'Miss Blake'. 'He was here with her. He threatened her. She ran away.'

It was badly said, he knew, and the officer gave a small twist of his mouth, as if it confirmed his suspicions: an escapee.

'So you've only her word for what happened?' he asked.

'Yes. But I trust her.'

The contradiction – trust and accusation, his ability to switch from one to the other then back again with barely a pause – belied any claim to credibility. Instead, it spoke of prejudice and whim and easy offence.

It disturbed him, too; made him recall his doubts. His torment as he sat in his truck, denouncing her. Had he ever really believed in her, he wondered, or had he always been ready to doubt? If he'd trusted her, wouldn't he have resisted it, denied it, railed against it with all his strength, never yielded? Defended her to the end.

'Now, let me try to get some of the chronology clear,' the officer said. 'How long have you been living out here, out in the wilds?'

Evan told him: about thirteen weeks.

'So where were you before that?'

'At home, and working.' He explained: he worked for a lines company, did other work contracting, moved around from project to project.

'January the fifteenth. Where were you then?'

'Here. Well, on my claim probably.'

The officer tried earlier dates, some going back to the previous October. Days that he could not remember, were just a blur in the past. Part of a different world, a different time. A time before Addie. He answered as best he could, sometimes got confused, wondered if he should correct himself, decided not to.

More lies, weaving themselves into the story, he thought, for no reason other than that sometimes a fiction was easier to sustain.

'And before you met her?' the officer asked. 'Before, as you say, you found her lost on your claim – you'd never heard of Miss Blake? Neither under that name, nor Addie Watson?'

'No.'

'And while she's been with you, she never told you anything about the charge against her? About being on remand?'

'No. And I don't believe it. I can't.'

'Did she explain where she'd come from? Why she was in the hills alone?'

'She said she'd had an argument with her boyfriend, had run off to be alone.'

'And his name?'

'Mark. Mark Brown, I think. That's all I know about him. I think he lived near Fox Glacier.'

'Nothing else?'

'No.'

'You were never suspicious? You never wondered about her?'

'No.' Another untruth, he thought – or something less than the truth. He'd wondered about her constantly, tried to fit the pieces together, never succeeded. But as he got to know her, love her, his focus had simply shifted: from who she was, what she had been, to what she might be to him. The rest had ceased to matter.

'And you hadn't heard about her absconding, or our search for her, even though it was covered in the news.'

'No. But I've told you: I've been out here since early January. I've heard no news, had no contact with the outside world.'

'None at all?'

He remembered his trip to Greymouth, once more wondered whether he should correct the lie. 'No,' he said.

'Except when the world came to you,' the officer said wryly.

Then he smiled, closed his notebook, thanked him. He walked over to the bedroom, spoke to the policeman who stood at the door, knocked and slipped inside.

For a while, Evan sat there, wondering what he was meant to do, what would happen next. From the bedroom he could hear the continuing murmur of voices, tried to make out Addie's.

But if she was talking it was quietly, in the gaps where nothing seemed to be said.

He looked at the guard on the door. He was armed, held his gun slant-wise across his chest. The man's eyes lay on him heavily, giving warning. He got to his feet, and the man at the door stiffened slightly, a hand went to the gun.

Evan turned, went outside. The action felt like the ultimate betrayal, as if he were leaving her to her fate.

He walked slowly down the steps, crossed to the truck, let Viva out and took her to his chair on the veranda. He sat there, stroking her, calming her, trying to calm himself. She crawled on to his lap, curled there, crouched low.

'Poor girl,' he said. 'Poor girl.' Viva and Addie both.

He tried to make sense of it all, to see the pattern it made, see where it was leading. All he could see was turmoil. Confusion and mistake, a world gone mad.

Could they be right?

He wanted to deny it, but knew that he could not. At some point, Addie might have been arrested for a dozen different reasons. Speeding, dangerous driving, even petty theft. In the state she'd been in, almost anything was possible.

Would she have run away?

Perhaps, he thought. There was wildness in her. Impulsiveness. Even something worse – self-harm.

But all this? This invasion of armed men. This assault. Could she have done anything to merit that?

He could not believe it. Not in any sane and ordered version of the world.

Yet not Addie at all? A different woman, a different name. How could that be true?

'A nice dog you have there.'

He looked up. The policewoman who had handed Addie her clothes was standing in the doorway.

'Yes.'

'What's her name?'

'Viva,' he said.

The woman stepped forward, reached for the dog, ruffed her neck. 'Viva l'Español. I like it.'

The words felt like a touch of friendship, almost understanding, and he looked up, gave a small smile of gratitude. 'You know, you're almost the only person who's ever seen that. Normally I have to explain, and even then they don't get it.'

'It's all that training they give us, I guess. Section four, bullet point three: look for intended insults and puns.' She pulled up the second chair, asked, 'May I?' and sat down. 'This can't be easy for you,' she said. 'I'm sorry. I hope it'll be over soon.'

He nodded. He wanted it finished; he wanted them to leave, yet he dreaded it, too. What then? Would they take Addie? Lock her up? What would happen to him?

'I've a couple of questions I need to ask,' the policewoman said.

'More?' he said.

'Just a few things I've been asked to clarify. Do you mind?'

'I suppose not.'

'About the rifle. Is it yours?'

'Yes. It was my father's. I inherited it.'

'Do you have a licence for it?'

'No. I didn't even know it was here until Addie – until we found it in the shed a few weeks ago.'

'But it's in good order; it was loaded. Had you been using it?'

'We'd used it to shoot rabbits. Todd – one of the hunters – helped clean it up and gave us some ammunition.'

'The man you said stole the gold?'

'Tried to, yes.'

She gave him a wry glance. 'It's complicated, isn't it?

'Not really. It just sounds that way. So – will you charge me for that? Not having a gun licence?'

The policewoman shook her head. 'I suppose if they want to get you for something, they might use that. But just now that's not the main thing on their minds, so I shouldn't worry about it too much.' She looked away, towards the door, where the rifle had been. 'Is that what you'd been doing? Rabbit shooting?'

'No. Addie had it when I got back. She had it for protection. She thought that Todd might come back.'

The woman was silent, as though digesting the significance of his words, then she smiled. 'You're not the usual sort of witness I deal with, you know. Most of them wouldn't have told me that, in case it looked bad.'

'There's nothing bad in it,' he said, primness in his voice. 'But yes, I try to be honest. Sometimes, though, it seems to me all this questioning – the way it's done – makes that hard.'

'Yes. I feel that, too. So what happened?'

'I took it off her. She gave it to me. I put it there.'

She smiled. 'That was your bigger mistake, you know. That's what earned you the barn-storming entrance: the helicopter and the boys with their toys. We saw it when we arrived in the first car, and thought the place might be bristling with arms. That's when we called the professionals in the helicopter. I'm sorry about that.'

He was relieved, tried not to show it. If that was all that provoked this invasion, then the reason was not Addie. Whatever she'd done, whatever she was on remand for, would be sorted out. She'd be released. They'd be together again.

'It wasn't, of course,' the policewoman said. 'Bristling with arms, I mean. Just you and her, together in bed. That didn't really merit Stallone and his buddies, did it?'

She was silent, and Evan looked away, wanting her to leave. Her irony unsettled him. It didn't fit the occasion, nor his own anger and bewilderment. It eroded the difference between them – oppressor and victim – and made him doubt his own sense of hurt.

'I've another question,' the policewoman said. 'It's about the gold that was stolen. You've got it all back now, is that right?'

'Yes. Well – yes, I think so. I've not checked.'

'Shouldn't you?'

'I don't need to,' he said. 'Addie told me. I trust her.'

She glanced at him, nodded. 'Well, I'm glad of that. But for my sake, can you do so? We need to know whether a theft of any sort has been committed.'

He resisted, but she asked again: 'Please. It's part of our investigation, and it may save us having to take it away as evidence.'

'If you insist,' he said. He got up, went inside to the sofa, where he'd sat with Addie, felt beneath it. The box-safe was there.

As he straightened up, the door from the bedroom opened. Addie was led out. She didn't look at him, kept her eyes down. She walked in small, reluctant steps. She was handcuffed to a policewoman. He watched as they went to the bathroom. The door closed.

Was it another ploy, he wondered? Another of her tricks? Would she find a way to escape? It seemed impossible, but for a few moments, the notion burned bright. She must have done it before – when she'd first absconded – had done it a second time when Todd had pursued her. She was nothing if not elusive; she could do it again.

He willed her to try, to succeed.

Then the door opened again, and she was led out, back to the bedroom. He tried to catch her eye, send her a signal of hope, trust, love. She did not look.

He picked up the box-safe, went out on to the veranda.

'Have you opened it?' the policewoman asked.

'Not yet.'

'Are you worried after all?'

'No.' But as he keyed in the lock-code, he wondered: was he? Why should he trust her, given all the lies she seemed to have told?

He opened the lid. A sheet of paper faced him. He unfolded it to reveal a childish drawing of a woman, dancing. Beneath it was written: 'What is dance? Dance is a journey to where you want to go.'

'Can I see?' the policewoman asked.

He showed it to her.

'A private joke? Not some cunning code, I hope.'

'A joke,' he said. He folded it up, slipped it into his pocket.

'And is it all there? The gold?'

He looked at the row of bottles, phials; took a few out, shook them, held them up to the light.

'Well?'

'I wouldn't tell you if it wasn't,' he said. 'But yes, it's all here.'

He closed the box. He felt suddenly relieved, almost triumphant, as if his belief in Addie had been vindicated after all.

'I'm glad,' the policewoman said. 'And because of the sort of man you seem to be, I'm sure that you're telling the truth.' She raised her eyebrows slightly, as if inviting a challenge. 'So where does that leave us, now? What about this charge of theft? Not against Addie, but against the man, Todd. It can't be that any more – theft; attempted perhaps. Do you want to pursue that?'

He frowned, uncertainty flooding back, leaving him deflated. In his mind, Todd was responsible for all this mess and confusion. Without him, Addie's presence would still be unknown. They'd still be together. The glade would be quiet. Perhaps she'd have told him everything; perhaps they'd have found a way.

'It will be difficult to prove,' the policewoman said. 'Just be aware of that.'

'I know. But it was still wrong. The man is still a menace.'

Yet what did it matter, now? And could he face it? More questions. More accusations. And what would Addie want; what was best for her?

'I don't know,' he said. 'It depends on Addie.'

'I understand. Just think about it. If you want to follow it up, talk to Chief Inspector Hastings again.'

She closed her notebook, and he asked: 'Is that it?'

'As far as I'm concerned, yes.'

'In which case, can I ask you something?'

'Of course.'

'What was Addie being held for? Why was she on remand?'

The policewoman shot him a glance, as if he were testing her, playing a joke. 'You really don't know? Didn't they tell you? Didn't you hear about it?'

'No. They didn't tell me anything.'

She frowned. 'I don't see why not. You of all people deserve to know, I'd have thought.' She regarded him quizzically, her brow furrowed. Then, quietly, she said: 'She killed someone.'

The words rocked him, scattered his thoughts in tatters. He gave a shake of his head, as if to flick them away. 'No. No, I don't believe that.'

'It's true I'm afraid. She killed her daughter.'

'No,' he said again. 'She couldn't.'

'I'm afraid she did.'

'How do you know? She might be innocent. She's not even had a trial.'

'She thinks she did,' the policewoman said. 'She confessed when she was first arrested.'

Evan beat his fist on the arm of the chair. 'No! I still don't believe it. She wouldn't. There must have been a reason. It must have been an accident. She wouldn't do something like that.'

The policewoman spoke quietly, exuding reason. 'Are you sure? Do you really know her, know what she'd do? Do you know her well enough to know what she's capable of?' But then she seemed to see the way he flinched, and apologised. 'That was unkind, unfair. But – but we have to accept, Miss Blake, Addie, isn't all we might believe her to be.'

'Well, maybe that's it. Maybe she's just a fantasist. Maybe she has a mental problem. I don't know. But she wouldn't do that.'

The woman shrugged. 'You might be right. I don't know the full story. I only know what's on the file. But I'm sure the tests will have shown it one way or another. And she will have the opportunity of a trial.'

'What tests?'

'She'd been having psychiatric tests when she absconded. She was on the way back from Christchurch.'

They talked on; he asked the woman what else the files said about Addie, listened stonily to her replies, told himself that he wanted no more of these unkind truths, but asked again.

At last, she stood up. 'That really is all I know,' she said. 'I've not met her or talked to her before. As I've said, I only know what the records show. And you're right, of course, they might not all be true. Right now, though, I have to admit that I feel sorry for her. I'm sorry for you both.'

*

When she'd gone, he sat there in the silence. Viva sat beside him, her head on his lap.

So much change, he thought, so much upheaval. As if all logic had been overturned, all physics banished. What kept the world together any more, held it in place?

He groped for some fixed point to which he might cling. One truth, one fact. Yet everything he found seemed false. Her name, her age, where she'd grown up, been to school, her time at university, her story of her step-father and what he'd done. Each one, had been denied. Josephine Lucinda Blake, aged twenty-two. Born and brought up as the daughter of a farm-labourer in Taranaki. Ran away from home at age fifteen. Lived on a commune of some sort in the East Cape for three years, during which time she developed alcohol and drug problems; spent a year in psychiatric care and rehab; gave birth to a daughter, Becky, when she was nineteen; father unknown but suspected to be the commune leader. Arrested for Becky's murder five and a half months ago. Absconded from custody while returning from psychiatric assessment ten weeks later; subject of a police hunt ever since.

The information he'd gleaned from the policewoman had been cold, heartless – a profile of a life that took all humanity from it, reduced it to the bureaucratic essentials. She'd apologised as she told him, tried in the telling to give it some kindness and grace, yet failed, for the facts of life that such records were interested in were largely those that showed people's inhuman face.

How could he love such a thing?

Pity, yes. Regret for whatever it was in the world that had given her such a life. But love?

Yet the enchantment she'd woven still snared him, and seemed to tell him of some other person that must lie inside. The inventiveness, the resilience. The quickness of wit. The way she danced, the way she moved, the way she made love.

Where had they been in her life? Why had they not borne her and brought her to happiness?

Could circumstance suppress so much?

He tried again to picture her as he'd been told that she was, imagine himself with her, nursing her, talking to her, laughing with her, working beside her on the roof and in the stream. Lying beside her on the mountain-top. Holding her, kissing her, making love. Could it have been done? With that other Addie?

He knew her less now, he told himself, than the moment he found her on that bare rock.

He'd fallen in love with an illusion. And behind an illusion there is nothing but mirrors and smoke. How could he hope to know that?

The door of the cottage opened. Two policemen came out, clumped down the steps.

In that same moment, the engine of the helicopter whirred, barked, growled into life. Viva flattened against his legs.

The policewoman appeared beside him, touched him gently on the shoulder. 'Stay here,' she said.

On the helicopter, the rotors spun lazily, prostrating the grass.

Another policewoman emerged from the house, treading slowly, one shoulder twisted awkwardly back.

Half a step behind, a dark and limp shape. Like a malformed Siamese twin, lugged by its more favoured sister. Head down, feet dragging. Clothed for some reason in a black police cape.

Then she turned, and he saw that it was Addie.

Addie. Not Josephine Lucinda Blake. Not some stranger he'd never met, or who had lived some other life about which he'd never known.

Had killed her child.

Just Addie.

And she smiled. Grim, tight-lipped, but with bright, fierce eyes.

And her lips moved, and though she said nothing, or nothing he could hear, he read her words. 'I love you.'

'I love you,' he mouthed back.

Then she stumbled as she reached the steps, almost fell, and instinctively he leapt up, went towards her.

The policewoman caught him, gently pulled him back.

Down the steps. Across the grass. Her shape diminishing now, becoming a shadow, a phantom, a shroud.

She was helped into the helicopter. A last glimpse of her, face pale from the darkness of the cabin. The door closed.

Noise and wind filled the world. Grit seethed and spat. The trees cowered.

Then the helicopter rose, dipped its nose towards him, rose again, became a strange insect, black against the darkening sky, twisted, hovered, and head-down, as if grazing the land below, skimmed across the forest, disappeared.

He listened as the sound faded, one hand on Viva's head, the other still gripping the box-safe.

Then he turned away and wept.

Sixteen

She rings the bell, waits. She doesn't hear it, and wonders whether it works. Out on the street, the air is cold, the wind personal. She pulls the coat around her, rings again.

From inside comes a bark, the scrabble of feet; panting, whining from behind the door. Viva is home, at least.

It's a Sunday, and she has come without warning, on what might be a whim, except that she has planned it and rehearsed it half a dozen times in her mind. What she's doing, as the hacks and bureaucrats would say, is 'beyond the call of duty', but she's learned that that is where a lot of the good deeds happen – where she can do the things that make a difference. And with this case, with this man, she'd like to do that.

Viva jumps up at the door. A voice commands her to get down. The door opens.

'Hello. I hope I'm not disturbing you.' She holds out a hand. 'You probably don't remember me.'

There's the smallest hesitation, then: 'Yes, I do. You were there at the cottage.'

She nods. 'D I Saunders. Kathryn Saunders. But Kate, since I'm off duty. I wondered if I could talk to you.'

They shake hands. As they do so she is looking at him, trying to compare him with the man she'd interviewed at the cottage that day, three months before. Has he changed? Does he look older, more indrawn, more burdened by life?

She can't tell. Instead, another comparison comes to her mind. That glimpse of him naked in the bedroom, as she followed the advance squad in. Disturbingly, it allows her to imagine the man inside, the man beneath his shabby Sunday clothes – the body strong, limbs taut. She pushes the thought away.

He releases her hand, steps back and invites her in. Viva is nuzzling at her like a lost friend. She crouches and fondles her ears.

In the living room, he stands for a moment, looking awkward as though he doesn't know what to do. Then he asks: 'Would you like a coffee, tea? I was about to make some.'

She accepts coffee, and he goes into the kitchen, shouts back: 'How do you like it?'

She has not yet been invited to sit, so she prowls around the room, reading the messages it gives. A man living alone – though she knew that, of course. A reader: books on New Zealand and the land, history, exploration, many of them old and in the plain, hard covers of books from half a century ago, culled perhaps from second-hand shops. Paperbacks by Grisham and King and Harris, but a few authors she reads as well. Softer, more allegorical writers: de Bernières, Niall Williams. Some poetry, too. They are not what she would have expected, but they make a point of convergence between them; somewhere their lives meet.

She imagines him, sitting there alone at night, reading. Another similarity, she thinks.

The room is simply furnished. A large table in heavily varnished wood, an assortment of chairs, one armchair that is obviously his favourite and another, with a blanket on it, that is presumably the dog's. The only new item is the TV, a large LED screen that sits on an old sideboard, looking out-of-place. His one luxury, bought with the money from his gold? The few pictures on the wall are landscape photographs, artistic but, in their way, clichéd. The land in half-focus, made into a mystery. The main ornaments are pieces of rock: crystals, minerals of various colours and textures, fossils. She recognises one – an ammonite – and picks it up. She found one once, as a child in England, on the beach at Lyme Regis, where the classic specimens were found. For years she cherished it, took it with her to university, then lost it in one of her many moves from one flat, one boyfriend, to another. She returns it to its place.

He enters with the coffee, a tray bearing two blue mugs, a plate of ginger biscuits, sugar in a bowl, the milk in its carton. He's forgotten spoons, so sets it down and goes back for them.

She thanks him, picks up a mug, stands there, cradling it in her hand. But then he offers to take her coat, so she has to put the mug down again, and he apologises for the complication he has caused. It is all confusion and embarrassment, and she laughs.

'I'm sorry,' he says again, as he stands, holding the coat. 'I'm assuming that you have time for all this – time to stay.'

He wants her to, she realises. He's disturbed by her, by the unexpectedness of her visit, but he welcomes the company. Perhaps he welcomes hers especially – as a woman, and as someone who was there at the cottage, and has a connection to it all. That's a good sign, she thinks. It makes her task easier. He folds the coat over the back of a dining chair.

'I came to talk to you about Mr Skelton,' she says, 'Todd Skelton. I hope you don't mind.'

'Of course not.' He indicates the sofa. 'Please. Sit down.'

She does so, perching delicately on the front, her legs at an angle from him, her knees close, her mug on her lap. He sits in his armchair opposite, regards her questioningly. 'I didn't know that you were involved.'

'I wasn't. But I was recently appointed the case officer. It's a new idea. It means they have someone to blame if things go wrong.' It's a weak joke, and she tries to strengthen it with a smile, but receives no response of any kind. 'In which role,' she continues, 'I've been checking up to see where we've got to – which isn't very far I'm afraid. Mr Skelton was interviewed about your complaint, but he denies any wrongdoing, says he just called in at the cottage to thank you for your hospitality, and wish you well. That everything was in order when he left. Without corroboration from Miss Blake, it's your word against his – and of course, you never actually saw it happen. On that basis, we can't do much, not even give him a warning.'

He nods. 'It's what I expected. If Addie – if Miss Blake had made a charge, I suppose it would have been different.'

'It might have been,' she says. Then she smiles again. 'But shall we call her Addie – just between the two of us? I know she still is to you, and to be honest, that's what I've come to call her in my own mind.'

He gives another nod, a small grimace. 'Are we going to talk about her, then?'

'In a moment, if you like. But there are other developments about your Mr Skelton to mention first. I can't go into details because the matter is still before the courts, but shall we say that there were additional misdemeanours that he appears to have committed. Related to his hunting activities. We have charged him with those.'

'Poaching you mean?'

'Maybe. That and other things. Assuming he's convicted, it won't mean prison or anything, just a fine, but he'll probably lose his firearms licence. It will clip his wings for a while. I thought you'd like to know.'

'Yes. Thank you.'

She sips at her coffee, regards him steadily, trying to decipher his thoughts. He's not really interested in Todd Skelton, she thinks. He filed a complaint against him more out of the need to assuage the wrong to Addie than any injury to himself, and he's wise enough to know it was never going to succeed. He's more interested in what she has to say about Addie – or perhaps, just in the excuse to hear and use her name.

'Did you come all this way to tell me that?' he asks. 'I'm very grateful.'

She shakes her head. 'I was coming this way anyway – I'm visiting my daughter.' She indicates her clothes. 'That's why I'm dressed up like this.' None of it is strictly true. She will make use of the trip to catch up with her daughter, whom she's not seen for several months, but the real motive is to see him. The choice of clothes likewise; her daughter will mock her for them, and claim that promotion has gone to her head. She's wearing high-heeled shoes, a blue skirt, tight-fitting, cut above the knee, a pale pullover that falls slightly off the shoulder and is shaped to her bust. She wants him to relax with her – to see her as a woman, not as the police officer he'd encountered before: all flak jacket and bum, as one of her colleagues had once remarked. But a different allusion comes to her, now: heading out to a Manchester club, in what one of her student friends used to call her hunting gear, hoping for a pick-up. Is that how she looks to him?

'Anyway,' she says. 'How are you?'

He shrugs. 'Busy. Very busy. Working all the days I can. You're lucky to catch me in.'

He tells her about his work. Winter came early this year, and already the storms have been doing their worst. There's no shortage of opportunity, he says.

She asks him about the gold. 'Did you get a good price for it?'

'I've not cashed it in yet. Most of it anyway. I've just banked it. I won't spend it on things I don't need that way.'

She can't avoid a smile. It's what Addie had told her he'd do. 'He's not miserly,' she'd said, 'though I think he worries that he is – he worries about everything. But he just sees no point in extravagance.'

'What about you?' he asks.

'Oh, much the same. I got promotion – hence the grand announcement when I arrived: D I Saunders. It still sounds presumptuous. I keep thinking that someone will catch me out and show that I'm a fake.'

The words carry too much of a double meaning, and to cover up, she says: 'Actually, compared to what I was before, in England, I've just about caught up with myself. I had to drop a grade when I came here.'

'So why did you move?'

'Oh – life.' His face doesn't alter and he probably isn't interested in the details, but she gives them anyway. 'A failed marriage. I wanted to put it behind me. It seemed better to get as far away as I could.'

He nods.

She wonders whether to say more, to explain: that she'd blown it – ruined it all for nothing other than the brief thrill of sex. And afterwards had tried to turn the blame not on herself, for her foolish infidelity, but her husband – for not being everything she'd wanted, for not being forgiving enough. For simply being the man she'd married.

For a moment, she considers telling him something of the remorse she feels, but says instead: 'My daughter was here. She married a New Zealander. It seemed a good place to be.'

They are both silent, and she wonders if even what she's told him is too much. Does he want confidences like that, or does he want her just to be what she was: a police officer, doing her duty?

'Have you seen her?' she asks at last. 'Addie?'

'No.' He swirls the coffee in his mug, looks out of the window. She follows his gaze. Outside the world is grey. A blanket of cloud, drizzle in the air, the street drab and lifeless. Not a day for hope or new beginnings, she thinks. Those will have to wait.

'No,' he says again. 'I tried, but she didn't want to see me.'

'I have,' she says, and notices the way he winces. Why should she have that privilege, he's thinking, when he is denied it? 'I made an official visit, to ask her about Todd Skelton.'

'How is she?'

'Prison's not nice. Not even the women's prison.'

It's not the answer he wants to hear. He gives a small shrug, says nothing.

'Have you come to terms with it all now?' she asks. She means not just the outcome of the trial – a formality, since Addie had pleaded guilty as she always said she would do – but the sentence. Twelve years, ten before the opportunity of parole. And for him, the reality of life without her.

She's not the first woman to have deceived him, he tells her. Nor probably the last.

She nods, reading past the words, the lie they carry. With Addie, it wasn't that; not in his eyes.

So she asks: 'How do you feel?'

'I'll survive.' He looks down, as if denying his own indifference, admitting its pretence. 'There's so much I still don't understand, though.'

'What sort of things?'

'Everything. How it happened. How I never guessed. All the things she told me about herself, the lies I believed. Who she was, her age, everything.'

'She was hiding, trying not to be recognised. You weren't to know.'

'Perhaps not. But I still feel – well, stupid. Blind. As if I got taken in by a cheap trick.'

'It wasn't that,' she says. 'It wasn't planned. You realise that, don't you? None of what she told you was meant as a deliberate lie. She was just trying to protect herself. From the moment she ran away, she was just improvising, living off her wits.' She sees him frown, pauses, then continues: 'She told me some of the things she said, the things she invented. Her name, for example. Didn't you ever wonder about that?'

'Addie, you mean?' He looks surprised. 'No. I just assumed it was short for Adelene, or something like that.'

'You didn't notice the coincidence? Addie, Evan. Adam and Eve. She said that it was her first moment of panic. You told her your name, asked her what she was called, and she simply gave the first name that came into her head. She was surprised you didn't realise even then. The same with the surname. Like the old knock-knock joke. "What's your name?" you asked. "Yes, Watson."'

He gives a laugh, short and bitter. Again, she thinks, it's not what he wants to hear; it seems to diminish Addie further, or what he thought their relationship was. Just a piece of silly repartee, a game of consequences.

'What else did she tell you?' he asks.

'She told me she felt guilty for misleading you. All the stories she made up. About losing her pack. She hadn't, of course. She'd just run off with what she had. Yet you'd gone looking for it: she felt really bad about that. About her boyfriend, too. But she had no choice. At first, she was afraid that you'd guess who she was; later that you wouldn't, and you'd hate her for all the deceits when you found out. Is she right? Do you?'

He frowns, as if wondering what his true feelings are, then says inconsequentially: 'Yes, there were lots of things I didn't really understand at the time, but I do now. She even asked me to buy her hair dye. It was for disguise, I suppose; if anyone came.' He shrugs, rueful, regretful. 'Still, it didn't work, did it? Todd recognised her anyway. That's what he threatened her with.' Then he shakes his head. 'No. I don't hate her. I couldn't – I can't.'

'So what? You did love her, didn't you? Do you still?'

He glances at her, surprised perhaps by her directness, by the insistence, but slowly his expression falters and uncertainty takes over. 'I don't know,' he says. 'I don't really know what I feel, what I felt then. Was it love? Or just infatuation? She was young. She'd come to me from nowhere, like a gift, as if brought by – by fate.' He gives a small, hard laugh. 'Does that sound silly?'

'It doesn't sound like you, not the person Addie told me about,' she says. 'I don't see you as the spiritual type.'

'No. No you're right.' He sighs. 'And you're right about what I felt. I loved her. Foolishly, perhaps, insanely. But, yes, it was love. Now – I don't know. I feel bruised. Rather lost. I feel sorry for her.'

It's more than pity for Addie, she knows. It's pain and sorrow for himself. It's that state that comes when love is thwarted – when it's left loose, untied. She's heard people call it emptiness, yet it's anything but that, for you are full of unspent love and yearning, sadness, flickering hope.

'It's just that I don't know who she is. What I really fell in love with. It was all an invention, a fiction. It makes no sense to love that.'

'She loved you, still does. She told me that. And maybe it wasn't all lies. Maybe there were truths in it as well.'

'Truths?' he asks. 'Like about her step-father? Like about being raped? There was no step-father. There was no rape. They were both lies.'

She shrugs. 'You're right. There weren't. But it wasn't necessarily all false. In the life she lived, I'm sure there were plenty of chances to be abused. Other men who would have taken them. The guy who ran the commune she joined for a start. From what I understand, he seemed to regard the female members as one of the perks of his role.'

'Is that meant to console me, or make me feel worse?' he asks, with a flash of irony.

'The truth is often uncomfortable,' she says. 'We both know that. And I thought you wanted the truth.'

He nods. 'Yes. I do.' But she sees the turmoil in him all the same, a turmoil that seems to grip him, churn him, make him reach for more pain.

'It's the same with all the other things,' he says, his voice bitter again. 'Going to university, dancing, playing in a rock band, being a nurse. They were all fictions.'

'Were they?' she asks. 'You tell me. You lived with her.'

He is silent, remembering perhaps, trying to make sense of his memories. Then he says: 'I suppose you're right. Some of the childhood stuff was true – about growing up on a farm. That much at least. And she could do the things she said: catch trout, rabbits; shoot. She could play the guitar. She could dance, as well. She must have learned them all somewhere, I suppose. I just don't know how, where.'

She smiles. 'Yes, she did. And that's proof of something. That shows she's intelligent, that she learns quickly, probably knows more than either of us give her credit for. In her life, I expect that's how she survived. What she didn't learn on the farm as a child, I suspect, she learned when she was living in the commune. It was out in the wilds, supposedly self-sufficient. In drugs, it seems, it certainly was. I imagine poaching and mushroom picking and health care of one sort or another were all on the curriculum, too.'

'She told me she didn't do drugs,' he says, reflectively. 'She said they were evil. That was a lie.'

'She doesn't use them any more, hasn't for years. It was something else she learned. She learned it the really hard way.' She pauses, then adds: 'More than anything, I think that's what she was ashamed of, didn't want to tell.'

'And the way she danced?' he asks. 'What about that? Did she learn that in that commune?'

'Again, you're right. She does dance. She dances in her cell. It keeps her fit, she said. And from what I've been told she was reading books about dancing while she was on remand. Where she learned, I don't know. Maybe she had lessons as a child. Or maybe she learned to pole dance in some awful club. But – I wonder: was she so good? Or did you just want her to be? Is that what you saw?'

He looks at her sharply, as though her words are an affront.

'I'm sorry,' she says. 'I'm not trying to belittle her, or you, or what you felt. But I think that the woman she was creating – the person she was trying to be – was more or less the woman she wanted to be, and she was creating her for you. And without meaning to, you helped, because it was the woman you wanted her to be, as well.'

Again, he is silent, and his gaze turns to the window, to the world outside. Her eyes follow him, share the view. It looks so drab, so humdrum, she thinks – the world out there; compared to the torment he is grappling with, so lacking in drama. And yet, out there, similar tragedies must be playing out; other people must be struggling just the same, unseen.

'I still don't understand why?' he says.

'Why she killed her daughter – Becky?'

'Why she pleaded like she did. Did she tell you that?'

'But you know about Becky, don't you? That she was ill.'

He hadn't attended the trial, she's aware of that. Addie had asked him not to go, and he had, of course, complied. There seems to be nothing he wouldn't do for her, she muses; nothing he wouldn't give up. But she assumes that he followed the case in the newspapers, or on the web, and there would have been much to follow. For a case like this always attracts the press and its more lurid headlines.

'I know – that she had a disability of some sort,' he says. 'Something congenital. I know that's why she killed her. But I don't see why she pleaded guilty the way she did. It was a mercy killing – she did it for the girl's sake. She could have gone for infanticide – two or three years instead of twelve. Why didn't she?'

'I don't know – not for sure. I asked, but she wouldn't tell me. Though I have an idea.' She studies her hands, searching again for the right words, the gentle way of telling him. A way that won't hurt too much.

'I looked at Becky's medical records,' she says at last. 'It was progressive cerebellar hypoplasia. Do you know what that is?'

He shakes his head.

'It's an abnormality of the nervous system. It causes blindness, kidney malfunction, brain defects. It's not curable; it gets steadily worse. Average life expectancy is less than twenty years – much less in many cases. Becky had been given nine or ten years at best, and most of those would have been in a state of serious impairment.'

'So she killed her instead.'

'Yes. But there's more to it than that. One of the common causes of Becky's condition is exposure to toxins in the womb. Alcohol or drugs. I think that that is what Addie believed happened. She was heavily into drink and drugs by then. Cocaine, heroin. I think she believes that she killed Becky from the start. All she did later was finish the job, as painlessly as she could – for Becky's sake. So in her own eyes she was guilty before Becky was even born. She wants to be punished. She thinks she deserves it.'

Evan groans, a long, low moan of misery and pain. Viva hears and goes to him, lays her head on his knee.

'She shouldn't do that,' he says. 'Be so self-destructive.'

'It's in her, though, isn't it? Self-harm. She did it in the past. Did you know that?'

He nods, grimaces. 'So that was true. Amongst all the lies, that was true.'

'I've told you,' she says. 'I think there was probably more truth in what she said than you admit. Not in the details, perhaps; the places and events. But what they told you about her, what she is inside. I say it again, because I think you need to believe it. The Addie you saw wasn't really a lie at all. I think it was the real Addie, the one she always could have been, if someone had loved her like you did.'

'Did? Do?'

'I can prove it, you know. That what you saw was the real thing.'

He regards her suspiciously.

'When Becky was born, Addie changed. She was a good mother, a true mother. For three years, she looked after Becky alone, did everything possible to make her life good. She changed her own life completely. But she knew that she couldn't stop the condition – the condition she thinks she created. In the end, that's why she did it – why she made the choice she did. If someone had to suffer, she thought it should be her, not Becky.'

He sits, slumped. He might be carrying the weight of the world. His head is cupped in his hand, his elbow on the armrest. His brow is creased, his lips screwed taut. There is so much he seems to be searching for, reaching for, trying to hold on to. Pity wells within her, and she wishes she could go to him, give him comfort of some sort. She has to hold herself back. Poor man, she thinks.

'So why did she abscond then?' he asks. 'If she wanted to be punished. It makes no sense.'

'Doesn't it? Do you really not understand why?'

He is silent again, and she watches him, seeing the anguish in his eyes. It's not self-pity, she realises, that prevents him from answering all the questions in his mind, from seeing what is there to be found, but the fear of somehow losing even more of Addie. Explaining her away.

'Panic?' he asks. 'Doubt? Second thoughts? I would have had all of those if I'd have been in her shoes. I'd have tried to run away.'

'Probably,' she says. 'But another reason, too. It was for the memory. That's what she told me. So that she'd have something to cling to while she was inside. Initially, she ran away just to grab some time, a last week or two on her own – the memory of freedom, fresh air and hills. When she got lost, she said, she was almost relieved. It seemed to offer a different way of ending it all, an even more fitting punishment: death rather than prison. But you found her – or Viva did. And it all changed. She remembers you carrying her – like a child, was the way she described it, safe in your arms. She remembers waking in the night and finding you beside her, with your arm around her, protectively. She knew then that she still wanted to live, wanted to see it all through.'

He gives a small, flickering smile, as though something in her words touches a memory of his own – carrying her, perhaps, or lying beside her.

She is silent, letting him cherish the moment, then continues: 'But it didn't end there. You kept on giving, she told me. You refused to send her away or even doubt her. And it was all so unconditional – you asked for nothing in return. You nursed her, helped her, fed her. Respected her, too. Didn't force yourself on her, or take advantage of her because she was a woman. Just offered her your affection and love. I don't think she'd ever been treated like that before, not since a young child, at least.' She pauses, letting her words sink in. 'She told me how precious that was to her. It would carry her, she said; she'll remember it and live off those weeks with you for all the time that she's there. Afterwards, too. She told me to thank you.'

'Then why won't she see me?'

His voice comes like a cry, plaintive and shrill, too long held back.

'For the same reason,' she says. 'Because of what I've already told you – what you've done for her. Because she has your memory, and for now that's enough. And because if she knew you were waiting for her, then she'd be waiting, too. And every day would be a day that she's being kept from you and that future; and every day would be a day subtracted from what she might have had. She couldn't stand that, she said – the waiting, the constant and repeated loss.'

He nods slowly. 'Yes. She told me that once. She can't cope with futures, she said; she just lives with the now.'

'And the past, I think. The past you gave her.'

Again, they sit in silence, while she weighs her next words. She wants to drive home her message, score it into his mind – yet she doesn't want to hurt him. Already the hurt she's given him seems too much.

'You understand, don't you? It would kill her if she thought you were waiting. If you made her wait, too.'

Pain creases his face. He gives the smallest of nods.

'You can go on loving her,' she says. 'There's no reason why not. But you mustn't wait for her. You mustn't imprison her more than she's imprisoned already. She doesn't want that. She wants you to move on. She asked me to tell you that – to make it absolutely clear. She knows that you won't, not easily. But she hopes that she might have made it easier for you, not worse – that perhaps she's shown you how good you are, how easy to love, and that you're capable of love yourself. She begs you to try. She doesn't want that guilt on her as well – of having ruined your life. She wants you to promise.'

He says nothing, and she asks: 'Will you?'

Once more, he tilts his head in the tiniest of nods. 'Yes. Though I don't know how. Do you?'

She smiles, grimly, shakes her head. 'I wish I did. But I'm no expert, believe me. Though I think you just have to be ready, be prepared. And be – accepting. Someone will come along, I'm sure, and see the man you are. Your qualities. Your strength, your honesty. Reach out to you. When she does, you shouldn't expect her to be perfect, the girl of your dreams. Just good enough to be worth the benefit of your doubt.'

He gives a short, bitter laugh. 'Yes. I've a lot of that. Doubt.'

'But you can still give her the benefit,' she says, seriously. 'Just as you did to Addie.'

They are silent. His head has sunk again. He seems lost in thought. It all seems too difficult, too much. Then he says: 'I could have taken her away. With all that gold, we could have gone overseas and had a new life, if you hadn't turned up when you did. If I hadn't told on her.'

She shakes her head. 'She wouldn't have gone.'

'I know.'

He sits, staring at his hands, as if seeking a solution there, some sort of redemption. 'A daughter would have been better,' he says at last, almost to himself.

His words surprise her, catches her off-guard. 'What do you mean?'

'If she'd been my daughter. I thought she was once. She pretended to be.' He waves a hand as if batting at a fly. 'I could wait for her then, be something to her when she got out.'

Again, he is silent, and she regards him, and thinks that she glimpses the dilemma that confronts him. Too old to be Addie's lover when she is released – when she'll have life to catch up with. But no father, either, whatever fancies they might have entertained, because of what they have been.

'I'll give her the gold, though,' he says, with sudden determination. 'That's why I've saved it. I want her to have it when she gets out. It will give her a chance, a new start.'

She nods, and a small smile forms on her lips, slowly spreads. 'Yes, you should do that. It's a good thing to do.'

'You think so?'

'Yes. Really good.' It's not just for Addie that she is pleased, but for him as well. She has been worrying about the gold all along. With it, every woman that he meets will be framed in his eyes as a gold-digger, someone interested only in his money. This way, there is just him.

'Do it,' she says. 'Put it in a bank for her, and just leave it there for her to find. It's the best thing in the world that you could do.'

She stands up, walks across to him, lays a hand on his shoulder.

'I need to go now,' she says. 'Will you be alright?'

He nods, and reaches up, touches her hand, though whether in acknowledgement or to push it away she cannot tell.

She goes to the chair, picks up her coat, then pauses, hesitant. She has another message she wants to give. It's for him, but maybe it will be for herself as well one day. Who knows? She likes this man. She liked him when she interviewed him at his cottage. She likes his old-fashioned honesty, and the way he struggles with life, even though it brings doubt and pain. She said so to Addie. 'Then help him,' Addie had said. 'Please. For his sake, for mine. Do what you can. Help him to move on.'

At the time, it had seemed like a chalice, passed to her in desperation, and probably poisoned, one she should refuse. Now she is less sure. She wants to do that, she's come to realise. She wants to help him, keep in touch, perhaps see him again.

She feels in the pocket of her coat, extracts her business card, hands it to him. 'Just in case you want to talk,' she says.

He takes the card, puts it on the table without a glance.

'Thank you,' he says.

She starts to pull on her coat, and dutifully he stands up to help her, then precedes her to the door, opens it to let her out.

She offers a hand. He shakes it stiffly, steps back, thanks her again for coming.

Yet she does not turn; instead, regards him intently.

'Evan,' she says. 'Listen to me. You're a good man. And what you do is good. You think, you analyse, you doubt. I don't see people do enough of that in my business. People prefer certainties, opinions, crude belief. I like it when people think for themselves, work things out. But – but it seems to me that love's different. It's not something that you can deduce, dissect. It's just something that happens, something we create. And like most things we make, it's not perfect. It has flaws and contradictions, gaps. Things that make no sense. Love's – like a story, like a good book. You just have to let it carry you along. What is it they say? The willing suspension of disbelief? That's what love needs to make it work. Life, too, perhaps. Isn't that what happened with Addie? Isn't that what she taught you?'

She pauses, searches his face for evidence that he understands, or at least is taking her words in.

'Remember that,' she says. 'Remember it for the next time. Be ready for it, and remember.'

Slowly, she walks down the path, holding her collar to her throat against the coldness of the day. But at the gate she glances back. To her surprise, he is still standing there, watching, Viva at his side. She offers him a smile – a quick, tightening of the lips, in both enquiry and encouragement.

For a moment he does not respond but then, eyes half closed, answers with a nod.

Acknowledgements

This book owes its inspiration to two things. The first is the landscape of New Zealand. It is difficult to live in this country and not be inspired by the scenery, and the Southern Alps, where this story is set, are especially inspirational. That said, for those who do not know them, a word of caution is perhaps required, for they are very different from their European counterpart. They do contain dramatic, snowy peaks and expanses of open summit land, but for the most part they comprise precipitous and heavily wooded valleys and hills. They are also very remote. There are few roads, very few towns or villages, and the main means of access are via trails cut through the bush for mining or logging, many years ago. Crucially for this story, radio coverage is also limited, and you are lucky to get a mobile phone signal unless you run a high-spec satellite phone.

Where exactly within the Southern Alps this story is set, however, is more difficult to tell. In my own mind, it should rightly be in the headwaters of the Arahura River, somewhere west of Arthur's Pass. But in order to make the story work I've had to shift the geography around. The presence of goodletite – a beautiful and rare mineral – would fix it in a narrow area east of Hokitika. The discovery of jade would broadly match this. But the presence of gold probably moves it rather nearer Reefton, fifty kilometres north, while the descriptions of the landscape might place it further south. And the claim itself is loosely modelled on the upper reaches of Baton River, more than one hundred kilometres to the north-east. If you went to look for the location, therefore, you wouldn't quite find it. It is there, though, in its various guises, scattered across this beautiful part of New Zealand.

My second source of inspiration is a book: George Eliot's *Silas Marner*, initially published in 1861. I first read this, at the suggestion of my wife, in my twenties and was lucky enough to hear it soon afterwards as a BBC radio *A Book at Bedtime*, read by the incomparable David Davis. I felt then that it was one of the most perfectly crafted novels I had had the fortune to encounter, and in the years since I have not changed that opinion. So when this story began to emerge in my mind I inevitably found myself thinking of it, and seeking to recapture not so much its storyline as its simple structure and some essence of the character of Silas in my portrayal of Evan. Deliberately, however, I did not reread, or even refer to, *Silas Marner* during the course of my writing, so any apparent plagiarism is accidental and the product of latent memories from many years ago. In any event, I encourage you to (re-)read it.

Of course, I also have personal acknowledgements to make. For matters geological, I have made use of *The Field Guide to New Zealand Geology* and *Gemstones* (both by Jocelyn Thornton) and *Explore West Coast of New Zealand Minerals* (published by Development West Coast), along with the generously shared expertise and experience of fellow members of the Nelson Rock and Mineral Club. For background information and technical details on gold prospecting I have mined (apologies) the many websites that are now available, including *Detector Prospector, Gold Prospecting Online, Keene Engineering, Mine for Gold* and

The New 49ers. I owe particular thanks to Dave Mack from the last of these for answering practical questions on gold dredging. For information on theories of dance, I started with Aila Breshnahan's *The Philosophy of Dance (Stanford Encyclopaedia of Philosophy)* and continued, out of unexpected interest, much further than I needed to go.

I also owe huge thanks to Clare Christian, Heather Boisseau, Anna Burtt and the rest of the team at RedDoor – a publishing team that has been truly delightful to work with, from start until finish. Equally – and as ever – I need to thank my wife, Ann, for her unstinting encouragement, tolerance, support and advice, as well as her immaculate proofreading and editorial skills. Not much in my life would have been achieved without her. My dog, Merlin, also merits a mention: he is in many ways the inspiration and model for the canine hero here, and there are few writer's blockages that a walk with him will not solve. Likewise, I am indebted to the various friends – notably Richard Cullingworth, Anna Hansell, Monika Kron, Jean-Francois Robert, Elaine Singleton, Michael Smith (BMS Books Ltd), and fellow writers in the Nelson branch of the New Zealand Society of Authors – whose interest, encouragement and critical opinion have helped me sustain and hone my writing over recent years. But I dedicate the book to my son who – to my envy – spends so much of his time exploring the sorts of wild places where this story is set, and whose own stories and photographs are always an inspiration for my writing. Keep tramping, Matt.

Book Club Notes

The story is built around Addie's deceits. Did you guess any of them before they were revealed, and if so, what was your reaction? Did they change the way you felt about her?

Could Evan have realised that Addie was deceiving him? What stopped his disbelief?

Why does Addie dance?

Why do you think there is such detail about the nature of gold and the process of gold dredging in the story? What function does this serve?

Evan unknowingly betrays Addie. Should he have told the police? How might the story have ended if he had waited longer and not gone to the police?

The New Zealand landscape figures strongly in the story. Other than as context, what role does this play in the story-telling? Would the story have worked in a totally different landscape?

The theme of 'the girl versus the gold' is an old one. Is there anything new in this telling?

It can be argued that every book needs at least three endings: the one you think will happen, the one that you'd like to happen (or are afraid will happen), and the one that it actually has. In this book, what were the different endings that it might have had? And, for you, did it have the right one?

At the end, Evan is told that love – like a good book – requires the willing suspension of disbelief. Do you think that this is true? How was it illustrated in the story?

What does the final chapter offer? Why is the focus on Kate, not on Evan?

What do you think happens next for Evan?

Find out more about RedDoor Publishing and sign up to our newsletter to hear about our **latest releases, author events,** exciting **competitions** and more at

reddoorpublishing.com

YOU CAN ALSO FOLLOW US:

 @RedDoorBooks

 RedDoorPublishing

 @RedDoorBooks